THE
DATING
DARE

ALSO BY JAYCI LEE

A Sweet Mess

THE DATING DARE

A Novel

Jayci Lee

ST. MARTIN'S GRIFFIN
NEW YORK

First published in the United States by St. Martin's Griffin, an imprint of St. Martin's Publishing Group

THE DATING DARE. Copyright © 2021 by Judith J. Yi. All rights reserved. Printed in the United States of America. For information, address St. Martin's Publishing Group, 120 Broadway, New York, NY 10271.

www.stmartins.com

Designed by Gabriel Guma

Library of Congress Cataloging-in-Publication Data

Names: Lee, Jayci, author.
Title: The dating dare : a novel / Jayci Lee.
Description: First edition. | New York : St. Martin's Griffin, 2021. |
Identifiers: LCCN 2021008143 | ISBN 9781250621122 (trade paperback) |
    ISBN 9781250621139 (ebook)
Classification: LCC PS3612.E2239 D38 2021 | DDC 813/.6—dc23
LC record available at https://lccn.loc.gov/2021008143

Our books may be purchased in bulk for promotional, educational, or business use. Please contact your local bookseller or the Macmillan Corporate and Premium Sales Department at 1-800-221-7945, extension 5442, or by email at MacmillanSpecialMarkets@macmillan.com.

First Edition: 2021

10 9 8 7 6 5 4 3 2

To Lulu: it all began with you.

THE DATING DARE

CHAPTER ONE

The wedding was picture-perfect. The spring garden outside the groom's restaurant overlooked the Kern River, and was drenched with the soft hues of sunset. Just being there made Tara Park sigh dreamily. She couldn't imagine a more romantic venue. Celebrity chef Aria Santini, the couple's close friend, had prepared the locally sourced gourmet dinner. It was exquisitely presented, and tasted even more delicious than it looked. Add to that the abundantly flowing California wines. The reception rocked the night.

Tara scanned the warm, happy scene from a quiet corner in the bustling garden and smiled, briefly ignoring the distraction that marred the glorious evening. Aubrey and Landon—the bride and groom—existed only for each other, every look and whispered word a declaration of their love. The guests chatted and laughed, basking in the happily-ever-after glow of the beautiful couple.

Myriad contradicting emotions threatened to overwhelm Tara. She scattered them with a resolute shake of her head, reminding herself that Aubrey would always be her best friend. But it was more than that. *Stop it, Tara. You have no time to sulk.* It was time to deal with the gorgeous man who'd been staring at her all night. His undivided attention made her want to fidget or maybe preen a little.

She couldn't decide which. Either way, ignoring him had taken some major willpower.

Well, her dear friend's new brother-in-law or not, enough was enough. She'd been irritatingly aware of his whereabouts the entire evening, so it wasn't difficult to locate him now. Seth Kim stood by a bar on the other side of the garden, sipping from a clear glass beaded with condensation. He looked enticingly elegant in his classic tuxedo, and her eyes eagerly perused his body until she caught herself. *Cut it out.* She hiked up her floor-length dress, marched over, and stopped in front of him. It was time to put the best man in his place.

"You need to stop staring at my ass," she said with her fists planted on her hips.

He smiled and turned to face her squarely, sliding a hand into his pants pocket. "On the contrary, I was studying all of you. Not just your stunning backside."

"Studying me?" Did he say stunning? *Huh.* She was tempted to swivel her head for a peek at her ass.

"I'm a photographer. It's hard for me to ignore things of beauty," he said smoothly, his dark eyes holding her gaze. An involuntary trill shot down her spine.

"Oh, please." Tara snorted, masking her reaction to him. If she angled her head to her best side, it wasn't for his benefit.

Besides, it had to be a practiced line, coming from a player like him. Seth Kim wasn't just any photographer, but a sought-after fashion photographer. Gossip sites loved to post pictures of him with an ever-changing parade of gorgeous models on his arm. Of course, one shouldn't believe everything on the Internet. But even if just a small percentage of the gossip had a grain of truth in it, his playboy status still held firm.

"You don't think you're beautiful?" He arched an eyebrow with mastery that almost matched her own.

"No one actually looks at themselves in the mirror and thinks, 'Wow. I'm beautiful.'" *Geez. Why do I always do that? I am beautiful, dammit. Inside and out.* She needed practice owning it.

"Is that a no?" The surprise on his face morphed into a sultry, hooded glance that traveled her body. "Because I'm prepared to convince you otherwise."

Her heart tripped on a beat and tangled itself up. *Gah.* Her body begged for a detailed demonstration of how he planned to convince her of her beauty, but she couldn't let her libido distract her from her mission.

"Look, I know I clean up nicely." There. She owned it. Sort of. "And this dress doesn't exactly hurt me in the looks department."

It was true. The crimson mermaid dress hugged her curves like a long-lost lover and made her boobs look like full, round globes of glorious flesh. As though reading her thoughts, Seth's eyes dropped to her chest.

"But you've had enough anatomy lessons for tonight," she said, waving her hand in front of his face. "Quit ogling my breasts."

"For the record, I wasn't ogling you." His eyes flew back to her face, and she was gratified to see a little color suffuse his cheeks. "I was gawking at you."

"And the difference is?" She crossed her arms in an impatient gesture, and waited for more playboy bullshit from him.

"Ogling requires lewd intent, which I definitely did not have. Gawking is more like staring at something in a trance because they can't help it." He paused to give her a lazy half smile, which probably gave countless women pudding knees. "If I was gawking, it's because I find you captivating."

What. The. Dickens? The way his voice dipped low and turned rumbly on "captivating" was ... *yowza*. Tara willed her pulse to slow the hell down. He was a player, all right. Quite an accomplished one. Regency-rake level accomplished. She needed a damn fan to flutter on her face.

"Will it help if I hide my captivating self behind some shrubs over there?" She narrowed her eyes to hide his effect on her.

"That'll be tragic." He chuckled, his face transforming with boyish charm, and it was her turn to gawk at him. *Come on. Be honest. You're* ogling *him.* "You're the only thing helping me get through this wedding."

"This is your brother's wedding. You're his best man." She stopped ogling and switched to glaring. "Do you seriously need to drool over my body for hours on end to 'get through' it?"

"Yes," he said, using his smoldering voice again.

Shit. She was disconcerted and majorly turned on at the same time, her cheeks pulsing with heat.

"Look at them." She threw an arm out toward the newlyweds, and missed a server by a nose. Tara nodded her apology then pinched a bacon-wrapped date off the platter. "They're deliriously in love. Aren't you even a little happy for them?"

"Who said I wasn't happy for them?" He drew his head back in surprise. "Landon's a lucky bastard for landing someone like Aubrey."

"Then why are you moping around like a wet blanket, soaking up the open bar?" Her mouth was full of the delicious hors d'oeuvre—the date was stuffed with blue cheese—but she managed to put some disdain into her question.

"I don't like weddings," he said, a dark shadow flitting across his face. There was a finality to his words that glued her lips together.

Tara peeked at him from under her lashes, wondering what his story was. A broken heart? Warning bells rang in her head, telling her to run like the wind in the opposite direction of the man. She was in no position to *fix* him . . . she had enough baggage of her own. One nightmarish relationship had been enough for her to swear off any emotional entanglements. Still, she was helplessly drawn to him.

Seth Kim was devastatingly handsome, and any woman who didn't tingle in their undies when near him was a dead one. He wasn't built like a tank but had a sinewy, well-proportioned body, radiating with restless energy. With light-brown skin, dark hair, and eyes the color of black coffee, he screamed beast-in-the-sheets. But it wasn't only his looks that caught her attention. The flash of vulnerability he revealed tugged at her heart and wobbled her iron self-control.

If she didn't rein in her hormones and empathy and all that, she was going to end up naked tonight. She refused to jump into bed with a virtual stranger—no matter how attractive he was—with her feelings in a jumble over her best friend's wedding.

Watching Aubrey marry Landon, her true love, reminded Tara that she'd chosen to keep her heart safe rather than to seek her own happily ever after. She'd never regretted her decision before, nor was she questioning it now, but a deep hollowness settled inside her.

"Fine. Stare, if you must. You won't be difficult to ignore," she said haughtily even though it was a blatant lie. "But understand one thing. There will be no hookup between the best man and the maid of honor at this wedding. Do I make myself clear?"

"Crystal," he said without a hint of mockery.

Tara spun on her heels, whipping her long hair over her shoulder. *Shit.* The hair whip? It must've been an accident. She wouldn't flirt with a man she was trying *not* to sleep with. And she definitely was not sashaying her hips for his benefit. Walking like a lingerie model was second nature to her. *That's my story and I'm sticking to it.*

It took all her willpower not to glance over her shoulder to see if Seth was watching her. She couldn't decide whether she was hoping to find his eyes on her or off her. She swore under her breath. Hadn't she just confronted the man so he would *stop* staring at her?

Resisting her attraction to Seth Kim must've thoroughly sapped her strength. She suddenly felt light-headed and out of breath. She needed to either take the damn dress off—she ate way too much to be contained in a corset-tight dress—or maybe throw up a little. Both scenarios required privacy, so she made like a penguin and waddled to the bathroom as fast as she could, shoving the door open with her shoulder.

"Ahhh!" Tara and Aubrey screamed in unison.

"Holy roadkill." She'd nearly bulldozed her best friend and bride onto the monochromatic tiles of the ladies' bathroom. "Are you okay?"

"Yeah. I'm fine." Aubrey lowered the arms she'd flung out in front of her and trained her eyes on Tara. "What's going on?"

"Nothing." She eased herself into the restroom, making sure her friend was a safe distance away, and closed the door behind her.

"Purple isn't your color."

"What? I can rock purple just fine. Besides, this dress is a deep red."

"I know, but your face is purple and you aren't rocking it, babe."

Tara caught her reflection in the mirror and snorted. "You're right. I can't breathe in this damn thing."

"God, me neither." Aubrey walked behind Tara and unzipped her partway, and Tara returned the favor. Lusty sighs echoed on the bathroom tiles. "Let's just hide in here for five minutes."

"Are you sure Landon won't come charging in here to claim his bride?" Tara quirked an eyebrow at her.

Her friend rolled her eyes, but a rosy blush blossomed on her cheeks. She looked so beautiful Tara's breath hitched. She was so happy for Aubrey. The ache in her heart meant nothing.

"He's putting Morgan to sleep, and he'll use that as an excuse to hold her for way too long. Our baby girl is barely a hundred days old, but she has her old man wrapped around her teeny tiny pinky." Aubrey wiggled her pinky with a dreamy smile. "I'm safe from any charging husbands for now. But seriously. What's going on?"

Tara had thought she'd dodged the question. *Damn.* Aubrey wasn't going to settle for another evasive maneuver. "I'm sorry, but your brother-in-law's an ass."

"Seth?"

"Does Landon have another obnoxious younger brother?"

"What did he do? It can't be that bad. He's so sweet."

"So sweet he's been gawking at me for the last two hours?" She adopted his more benign word for ogling for no particular reason.

"Is that all?" Aubrey crinkled her nose. "All the single men, as well as some married ones, have been doing the same thing. Men stare at you all the time. Aren't you used to it by now?"

"They do not."

"You just never notice." A sly grin spread across her face. "So why would you notice Seth's attention?"

Curse you, hyperintuitive, recently married woman.

"I have to pee. See you outside, Mrs. Kim." Tara spun Aubrey around, zipped her back up, and pushed her toward the door. She had no desire to find out where the conversation would lead.

"Seth is a really good guy. You should talk to him. Just tell him to quit doing whatever it is that's bugging you." Aubrey ignored Tara's not-so-subtle shoving to help zip up her dress, and pecked her on the cheek. Only then did her best friend turn to leave. "You know where to find me if you need me."

When the door closed behind Aubrey, Tara sagged against the sink. The good thing was she didn't feel light-headed anymore. The bad thing was she didn't know what it was about Seth that annoyed her so much. There was no harm in some light flirting. So why did it bother her in this case? Maybe it was because of her heart-stuttering reaction to him . . . *No.* Her heart was not to be trusted. Ever. She blinked rapidly and pulled herself back from the darkness she was tiptoeing around. *None of that tonight.*

Where the hell was she going with this anyway? All she knew was that she was very bothered. And hot. She just needed to have a firm word with herself. *There will be no hookup between the maid of honor and the best man tonight.* There.

Tara liked men. She enjoyed sex with men. But she kept her love life completely separate from the rest of her life. The men in her life have never, ever crossed paths with her family. Serious relationships went against the very fiber of her being. There was no point in having her family meet men she had no intention of keeping. It would make her life unnecessarily complicated and messy. And she was so done with complicated and messy.

She liked things light and simple. Like with her traveling lover, Roger Stephens. He used to be Weldon High's revered quarterback. He was a couple years ahead of Tara, and she'd had a giant crush on him. Then his family moved out of town, and she was heartbroken. *Young, unrequited love.* But until college, all she knew was love of the unrequited sort.

When he returned for a short stay at Weldon as a salesperson for a pharmaceutical company, he came into the brewery and they hit it off. He'd never noticed her in high school as a lowly freshman, but he seemed to appreciate the woman she'd become. Since then, they would get together a few times a year whenever he was in town. She liked and respected Roger and enjoyed their convenient, no strings attached arrangement. Even after three years, no one, other than Aubrey, knew of their dalliance, and that was how it was going to stay.

But with Seth, he'd already met everyone. Her parents, her older brothers, and of course Aubrey. And Tara had met his mom and Landon. Everyone knew everyone. It was much too cozy. It would be risky to get involved with him. It could bring her love life crashing into her real life, causing dimensional imbalance. It might mean the annihilation of her deliberately compartmentalized life, and create complete and utter chaos.

Was she being overly dramatic? Yes.

Did she want to risk annihilation and chaos? *No, thank you.*

Seth watched Tara walk away and disappear into the restaurant with hurried steps. Maybe she'd decided to hide from him after all. He chuckled under his breath. Had he really been that obvious? His playboy persona was usually much smoother than that. But maybe his persona had nothing to do with his interest in Tara. Maybe it was the real him. *Ridiculous.* He'd cultivated his playboy persona so the real him would never come into the picture. That was what he decided when he locked his broken heart away.

But Tara was a stunning woman, graceful and strong, and she captivated him beyond the physical. The hint of vulnerability she hid behind her prickly exterior called to him. It was as though something inside him recognized her as a kindred spirit. His chest constricted at the alarming thought. He gulped down the rest of his club soda and walked away from the bar. He wasn't on the market for a kindred spirit.

He followed the throng of guests migrating indoors and settled beside another bar near one end of the room. It gave him the best view in the house, so he could watch the wedding festivities from afar. People fascinated Seth. When he photographed his clients, he chatted with them throughout the shoot, not only to help them relax but also because learning about them allowed him to breathe life into their pictures. Everyone had their little flaws to make them perfectly imperfect. Thus, beautiful.

He spotted Tara almost immediately, laughing with a group of women, and willed himself to look away. But as champagne flowed and laughter imbued the air inside the dimly lit restaurant, her eyes met his and flitted away with increasing frequency.

This was a lighthearted, carefree wedding reception, where everyone was hell-bent on having a good time. There was no reason to overanalyze his feelings. He should just go and ask the beautiful woman to dance with him. Simple.

"Tara." He tapped lightly on her shoulder. She'd declared herself off-limits, and he intended to respect that, but one dance was far from a hookup.

When she turned toward him, her gaze remained suspicious. "Seth."

"If I stop being an asshole, will you dance with me?"

"Oh, is there an asshole switch you can turn on and off? I thought it was congenital."

"Okay. I deserved that." Seth laughed, rubbing the back of his neck. "Look, I didn't realize my gawking was so obvious. You caught me off guard, and I covered my embarrassment with some defensive cockiness. I'm truly sorry."

"I accept your apology." A soft blush washed across her cheeks, but her expression remained resolute. "But still no hookup. Is that clear?"

"Yes, ma'am. No hookup. Just a dance."

Tara smiled at last, and he wanted to puff out his chest and maybe pound on it a little. But he restrained himself and led her to the dance floor. They had seen the bride and groom off to their wedding night, and the crowd was dwindling. The band was playing a lazy jazz piece, but the band leader winked at Seth and transitioned to a sensuous, old-time ballad. He nodded his thanks to him.

When Seth pulled Tara close, his body reacted as though he'd touched a live wire. His smile faltered and was replaced by slack-jawed shock. Every hair on his arms and the back of his neck stood at attention, and the shiver running through his body felt hot and cold at once. He'd never felt desire so instantaneous and powerful before. What the hell was happening?

Tara stared back at him with eyes filled with alarm. She must've felt it, too, and was as startled as he was by the electricity humming through them. He wanted to reassure her . . . let her know this was something new for him, too.

"Wow," he said, taking a small step back. "I . . . will you catch me if I swoon? My knees feel like Jell-O."

Tara huffed a husky laugh, her chest rising and falling rapidly. "Each person to their own."

He returned her smile and waited a moment before he pulled her close again. He shivered and she nestled her cheek in the crook of his neck, tightening her hold on him. *Probably just in case I swoon.* Her scent intoxicated him—citrus, cream, and aged oak. It was an unexpected but sexy-as-hell combination, and he couldn't get enough of it. He couldn't get enough of *her*. But he intended to respect the line she drew. For tonight.

Seth was moving to Paris in a little over a month. He was rearing to start the next chapter of his life as an esteemed photographer in the world's fashion capital. It was the opportunity of a lifetime that he had every intention of exploiting. He already had most of his belongings packed and a lease on a condo in Paris.

But he couldn't leave their wild attraction unexplored. He and Tara wouldn't have much time, but there was enough for a bit of fun. He just needed to come up with a plan to win Tara over for a sweet spring fling.

The music came to an end much too soon, and he held her for an extra beat. Then Seth cleared his throat and asked, "Do you want to get a drink?"

She hesitated, staring hard in the vicinity of his bow tie. After a moment, she met his eyes. "Sure. I could use some company."

"I make great company," he assured her.

Tara hid a small smile. He was surprised by her change of heart, but she seemed more comfortable around him. And less suspicious about his intentions. Whatever the cause, he was glad he could spend more time with her. But when he searched for the closest bar, the bartender was busily closing shop. Seth's dismayed eyes sought out the other bars, but they were already closed.

"It looks like the bartenders are wrapping up for the night," she murmured with something akin to disappointment. She worried her bottom lip for a second then asked, "Do you . . . want to take a field trip?"

"I'm game," he said with a bit too much enthusiasm. He didn't want the night to end, yet. "Where to?"

"I want to drown my sorrows in my beer barrels." She didn't quite succeed in making it sound like a joke.

"What sorrows?" His eyebrows drew together in concern.

"A corner of my heart feels hollow," she whispered after a brief hesitation.

"Is it because of the wedding?" Instinct told him it was.

"More or less. I'm happy for Aubrey and Landon. More than words can say. But Aubrey is my best friend and her life is changing . . . she's moving on. I can't help but feel left behind. Stuck in the present."

He wasn't sure what to say. Landon was his older brother, and he always seemed to walk a few steps ahead of him. This was just another instance where Landon stepped forward first. But Seth was about to take his own step forward—not toward marriage, but toward professional success and personal growth—by moving to Paris. But if he weren't, would he feel left behind? Yes. Like a lone tree trunk rooted to the floor of a river.

"She might be moving on, but that doesn't mean you're stuck," he said hesitantly. "It just means that you'll have to figure out your own way forward."

"You're probably right." She paused as though searching for the right words. "But my best friend grew a mini-human in her stomach, and got married to her soul mate. I'm going to miss daydreaming about the future with Aubrey, because her future is already here." She tilted her head and met his eyes, seeking reassurance. "It's normal to feel a little melancholy, right?"

"Without a doubt. And you know what helps with a bout of melancholy?" Seth smiled, wanting to chase away the sadness in her eyes. "Drowning it in copious amounts of beer."

"Right. Let's get out of here."

"Lead the way," he said, holding out his arm toward the main entrance.

"I'm afraid you need to be my chauffeur," she said as they walked to the parking lot. "I drove here with my family, and they're long gone."

"With pleasure," he said happily. "You can be my navigator."

"Actually, are you okay to drive?"

"Don't worry. I've been drinking club soda for most of the night."

"How very responsible of you," she teased.

The short drive to Weldon Brewery would've been scenic, but it was pitch-black and they couldn't see beyond the patch of road in front of them. But when they approached downtown Weldon, soft muted streetlights lit the way into the charming town, lined with a potpourri of mom-and-pop stores.

Seth pulled into the brewery's parking lot and followed Tara inside through the back entrance. When the dim corridor opened up into the dining hall, he let out a long, low whistle. The vaulted ceiling and dark wooden beams bearing its weight made him feel as though he'd walked into a lofty ski lodge. The elegant simplicity and strength of the design alluded to a sense of freedom and steadfastness.

"So this is the famous Weldon Brewery," he said, still surveying the place. The floor-to-ceiling windows lining the back opened up the space even more and highlighted its rustic appeal. "This place is impressive."

"Thank you." A proud grin spread across her face. Motioning for him to follow, she walked across the floor and rounded the bar. "What would you like?"

"I'll leave that up to the expert."

"Oh, my gosh." Mischief lit up her face and laughter tumbled out of her. "Do you want to hear something funny?"

"Sure." He smiled at her infectious laughter, curious about what brought it on. "It must be a good one."

"When your brother had the nerve to show his face here after writing that horrible review about Aubrey's bakery, I told him he should drink Witch's Brew, which gave heartless jerks permanent impotence."

"You did not." Seth laughed, incredulous. She was so awesome.

"Oh, yes, I did." She cocked her hip to one side and planted a hand on her waist in an unmistakable badass pose.

"Well done. Landon definitely deserved that dig. As for me, I'll stay far away from Witch's Brew. I'm not a heartless jerk, but better safe than sorry," he said with an exaggerated shiver. "So which brew would you recommend for me?"

"Let me think about that one." Tara pinched her chin between her thumb and index finger, seeming to give it some serious thought. "Back at the wedding, I would've recommended Buzz Off for sure. But you've grown on me over the course of the evening. Don't get smug. It just means I'm not quite ready to kick you to the curb."

"Very kind of you," Seth murmured wryly. "On the bright side, that means you're not immune to my charms."

"You know what? I'll create a special brew for you, and call it Inflated Ego."

"Ouch. Even if I did have an inflated ego, spending time with you is sure to bring it down a few notches."

"It'll be good for you. You know, it builds character," she smirked. "But I'll give you a break. Why don't you have Buckle Down, our barrel-aged stout. I'm pretty proud of that one. It's not perfect, yet, but it's getting there."

"I can't wait to try some," he said with genuine enthusiasm.

She filled a heavy snifter with dark, rich stout, finishing it with a thick, creamy head. It was the perfect pour. As she handed him the beer, his fingers skimmed across hers, and desire enflamed his entire body. Her quick, indrawn breath told him she'd felt it, too. They stared at each other, unnerved by their reaction to each other. Their breathing became shallow as sexual tension wrapped around them.

Tara broke eye contact first, and poured herself a light golden brew in a chalice. She cleared her throat and held her cup toward him with a too-bright smile that belied what just happened between them. "Gun bae."

The moment had passed, but his blood still pumped loudly in his ears. But following her cue to dismiss the flare of attraction, Seth clinked his glass against hers with an answering smile. "Cheers."

His eyes widened after the first sip, then he took a slower sip with his eyes closed. It was full-bodied, rich, and just the right amount of bitter. One of the best damn beers he'd ever had.

"This is amazing. How is this not perfect?" His face scrunched up in confusion.

"The judges don't think so. Weldon Brewery came in silver to Mountain Brewery's gold in the wood-aged stout category for the last three competitions. I think I know why. Their finish is a smidgeon smoother," she admitted grudgingly. "But I don't want to sacrifice the bite of bitter coffee in my stout for the smoother finish. I'm getting there, though. I just need to fine-tune the malt and caramel ratio with the hops."

"I hope you're planning on beating them."

"Hell, yeah. The next competition is at the San Diego Beer Festival, which is a good-sized event. That'll be a good start," she said. Seth leaned forward with his elbows on the counter and waited for her to continue. "But what I really want is to brew the best beers out there and have Weldon Brewery sweep gold medals for the top beer categories at the World Beer Cup. It's the biggest beer competition out there, and we're entering in the next couple years. If we establish a name for ourselves, we can start bottling our beer for retail sales. I want to put Weldon Brewery firmly on the map."

"That's fantastic." Her talent, her strength, and her spirit blew him away. "You certainly have the drive to make it happen."

"Maybe I overshot it a bit, but I definitely want to win the gold medal for the barrel-aged stout at this year's San Diego Beer Festival. My IPAs have been doing great, so it's time to let my stout shine."

Seth raised his glass in salute and downed half of the beer. Tara lifted her own beer and finished it to the last drop.

"Whoa. What's the rush? We're not having a drinking contest." He thought she was in a better mood, but her melancholy seemed to have stayed with her.

"Hmm." She tapped her finger on her lips. "I like that idea."

"What idea?" he asked, distracted by the soft give of her lips under her finger.

"Why, having a drinking contest, of course," she said with a cheeky grin. "Why don't we bet a hundred bucks to keep it interesting?"

"A hundred bucks? You're not messing around." Seth chuckled, enjoying her boldness. Then a brilliant idea lit up his mind. *Dude, you're a fucking genius.* If it worked, he might get his spring fling with Tara after all. Reining in his excitement, he said casually, "Why don't I suggest the game? Do you think you can handle some truth or dare?"

"Bring. It. On."

CHAPTER TWO

Here, let me switch out the glasses to something more civilized," Tara said, reaching for his snifter. They were going to pass out before the game got interesting if they chugged from their full-sized glasses. "And we'll both drink the white ale to keep the alcohol level even."

"Sounds like a plan. Should I start?" He rubbed his hands together like he was relishing the thought of annihilating her. *How precious.* "Truth or dare?"

"Truth." She crossed her arms in the universal bring-it-on gesture.

"When was your first kiss and with whom?" he asked with a friendly smile.

"Seriously? You just went there?" Her arms dropped limply to her sides.

Tara felt warmth seeping up from her neck and spreading to her cheeks. She was a late bloomer, and her first kiss hadn't been until college with her first boyfriend. She never spoke about Jason. He had been her first everything, including her first heartbreak. He'd done such a thorough job of it that she'd buried her heart deep inside so no one could touch it again. It took her a year of friendship and a lot of beer before she'd even told Aubrey about the abusive bastard. Tara shook her head. Despite her notorious competitiveness, she picked up her cup and drained it.

"Really?" Seth's eyebrows rose. "*That* was a question you couldn't answer? I thought I was going easy on you."

"Shove it." She resisted the urge to pout. She couldn't believe she had to admit defeat in the first round. "Your turn. Truth or dare?"

"Dare," he shot back.

"Ooh, fun." She looked around for the perfect feat, and smiled. "I dare you to carry six full steins to that corner table, and walk back without spilling."

"Come on. I bet even you can't carry that many at once, and you're a professional."

"*I* can carry eight at a time, kiddo. Do you accept the dare, or are you drinking more free beer?"

"Hang on. *Kiddo*?" Outrage deepened the groove between his eyebrows. "I'm only a year younger than Aubrey."

"And I'm a year older than her. So that means I'm two whole years older than you. In fact, you should be calling me noona."

"Older sister? No way. Not happening."

"We'll discuss that later," she said, laughing at his stormy expression. Annoying him was far safer than fawning over him. "For now, are you accepting the dare or not?"

In response, he unbuttoned his shirtsleeves and rolled them past his elbows.

Her jaws went slack at the sight of his manly forearms, and lust flared in her stomach. She tore her eyes away before she reached out and trailed her finger down his arm. *Chaos and annihilation lie that way.* Taking a fortifying breath, she proceeded to fill six steins with water. She refused to waste a drop of one of her beers.

"Here you go," she said, placing them on the counter. "Three in each hand."

Seth confidently picked up the steins and promptly sloshed water onto the counter. "Shit."

"Be careful." The veins and muscles in his forearms strained against the weight of the steins and she bit her cheek not to moan out loud. "If you bring back half-empty steins, you lose."

With intense concentration, he walked toward the corner table, cursing every so often. But he soon returned with a decent amount of water left in the steins. He carefully placed the six steins on the counter and flexed both his hands repeatedly. They probably felt pretty cramped up. In truth, Tara could only carry four at a time herself. Maybe she should massage his strong, masculine hands for him.

"Dare accomplished." She clapped her hands loudly enough to make herself snap out of her lust-filled thoughts. "Impressive for a first try. Let me know if you need a part-time job."

"Don't try to distract me with your pretty words." Seth jerked his chin at her. "Truth or dare?"

"Dare." After the last round, dare seemed to be the safer choice. She'd had her reservations about her rash decision to invite Seth to the brewery, but it was turning out to be a good one, despite her brief lapses into hornyville. She didn't want to risk making things awkward again.

"Okay. Give me a sec." Seth thought for a moment with his mouth scrunched to the side. She reveled in all his different expressions—all much too attractive—and this one was just adorable. Then he snapped his fingers, and said, "Mirror me."

"Let's go."

The first one was easy. With his arms outstretched, he touched the tip of his nose with one hand then the other, like the sobriety test. She had to concentrate a bit to land her fingertip on her nose. She must be getting tipsy. All the more reason she had to succeed in this dare. Chugging one more glass might tip her right over to drunk.

"Is that all you've got?" she said.

Crap. Why did she goad him? It seemed trash talking was second nature to her. Last year at a beer competition, she yelled out to a competitor that their beer looked a bit flat and offered to lend them some of her carbonation. They were worthy opponents and good friends, so she didn't get beaten up or anything, but she really needed to mouth off a little less.

"Oh, no. I have loads of fun up my sleeves." Keeping his arms outstretched, Seth slowly drew his knee up and assumed the Karate Kid pose.

Tara snorted and mirrored his move. "You're such a dork."

"That I am." With a roguish tilt of his lips, he put his foot and arms down and stood tall. Then he proceeded to do the weirdest, most fascinating thing. With his tongue.

His red, wet tongue slid up his upper lip as though he was about to lick it, but his tongue kept moving upward. Up and up until his tongue hit the tip of his nose.

Holy Mother Teresa. How was he doing that?

She stuck her tongue out. Maybe it wasn't that hard. She'd just never tried it. Tara valiantly contorted her face and craned her neck, trying to copy the maneuver. It wasn't easy. It was impossible. Her tongue just wasn't long enough. *Wait a minute.* That meant Seth's tongue was long, and . . . full of potential.

When she started drooling—from keeping her mouth open too long or from daydreaming about Seth's potential, she didn't know—she knew she'd lost the dare. She closed her mouth and dragged her sleeve across her slobbering mouth.

As soon as Tara gave up, Seth ceased his weirdly erotic tongue magic, and burst into laughter. "Oh, my God. You should've seen the faces you were making. Dammit. I should've recorded it."

With a glare that threw a thousand daggers, Tara tilted back her beer and slammed down the empty glass.

"Your turn." She wore her game face, but she was having a fantastic time. Seth had somehow chased away her restlessness to the far corner of her mind, and she felt happy and relaxed.

"Truth," he said without hesitation.

"When was *your* first kiss?" He probably started his playboy ways early. Maybe at the tender age of six. But she should rule out the innocuous pecks. "With tongue."

He pulled at an earlobe that was turning an interesting shade of red. "When I was eighteen."

"Eighteen?" she practically yelled, eyes bulging. She clamped her mouth shut before she repeated herself. *Eighteen?* She'd assumed that he'd lost his virginity before then.

"Yeah, I was a late bloomer," he said, shrugging sheepishly.

It was endearing, and she wanted to hug him and plant kisses all over his face. She liked him. She really liked him, and it wasn't because she was drunk. Then again that was exactly what a drunk person would say.

Besides, she couldn't forget that liking him was a bad idea. *Chaos and annihilation. Remember?* She should focus on why she agreed to have a drink with him in the first place. Because she didn't want to be alone. She didn't want to be sucked into the hollowness left by

Aubrey's wedding. And like Seth had said, he made great company. That was all this was.

"Cool, cool. I'm down with that." That was probably the least cool thing she could've said.

"Okay. Moving on. Truth or dare?" he asked, putting an extra dose of challenge into his words.

"Dare." She could handle dares. They were harmless.

"I was hoping you'd say that." A warm, seductive smile spread across his face.

"Stop playing mind games with me." Her stomach fluttered at his smile, but Tara crossed her arms and narrowed her eyes. "Do your worst. I can take you."

"I want you to go out on four dates with me—"

"What?"

"I wasn't finished. I want you to go out on four dates with me, and not fall for me."

She stared at him slack-jawed for three seconds before busting out laughing. "You've got to be kidding me."

"Not at all."

"Aren't you leaving for a new job in Paris soon? And how do we fit in four dates when you're in Santa Monica and I'm here?"

"I volunteered to house-sit for Landon and Aubrey while they and the baby are off on their extended honeymoon. I'll be your neighbor for a month, so meeting up should be easy enough."

Go on four dates with him. *Pfft.* It was a ridiculous proposition. She should just drink the beer and be done with it. Then why wasn't she reaching for her glass? *Why? Because you're seriously tempted. That's why.*

"Why do you want to date me anyway?" she asked on a spurt of annoyance.

"Are you fishing for compliments?" he teased with a charming grin. "Because I'll gladly oblige."

"Oh, quiet, you." She glared at him for being so annoying yet so good-looking. "Were you planning on doing this the entire time we were playing truth or dare?"

"Yup. That's why I suggested the game. It was a stroke of genius," he said excitedly, so proud of himself. He needed to quit being so adorable.

How did his eyes twinkle when he smiled? It shouldn't be possible. Maybe it was the lighting at the bar. She tested out a smile to see if she could do it, too.

"Um . . . you okay?" Seth asked, his gaze skimming her face with concern. "Your eyes are twitching."

"Of course, I'm okay." She whipped away her smile, abandoning her failed experiment.

"I think you're stalling."

"I don't need to stall." She was stalling.

Temptation sang its siren's call to her. It would be for a short duration with a hard end time, so it couldn't become anything serious. And there was no chance her love life and real life would collide into each other if they were discreet. They would keep their dates completely under wraps for a month. No one needed to know. *There. Chaos and annihilation avoided.*

She was obviously oversimplifying things, but she wanted this. Besides, Seth Kim was a player. He was just looking for a fun fling while he house-sat in a sleepy little town. That was exactly what she wanted, too. There was no doubt she was attracted to him, and he was fun to be with. And she really wanted to be not-alone for a while. Of course, she wasn't going to jump into bed with him right away, but she wasn't adverse to considering it. Her vagina cheered.

She briefly thought about Roger, but their arrangement was flexible and nonexclusive. They had paused their arrangement while he was in a relationship for a few months a couple years ago. This would be something like that but even shorter. There was no deterrent there.

As for the last bit about not falling for him? That was laughable. Tara hadn't made the mistake of giving her heart away since college. She was a quick learner. Love warped some people into jealous, possessive, and manipulative assholes, while it turned others into simpering putty who desperately molded themselves to fit the person they loved. Soon the relationship felt like a cage without light. She valued her autonomy too much to risk falling in love. And she never wanted to become the one to stifle another person's spirit.

Plus, Seth was Landon's younger brother and Aubrey's brother-in-law. Hell, he was practically *her* little brother by default. A sexy-as-hell, mama-would-like-some stud of a little brother, but there was no way she would fall for him.

Are you done convincing yourself? Yes.

His sobriety test assured him that Tara was the one making the decision and not the alcohol. No matter how much he wanted to date her, he wanted her to choose him because she wanted to, not on a drunken whim.

"So what will it be?" he prodded. Her prolonged silence was fraying his nerves. "I understand it'll be challenging not to fall in love with me."

"Honey, please." Tara snorted. "You're pretty to look at, and I might be a smidgeon attracted to you, but love is definitely not on the horizon."

A smidgeon attracted to me? I'll take that. He liked having room to grow.

"That's perfect. I'll be moving out of the country in a month. What's the harm in going out on a few dates with me?" It would be short and oh so sweet. A perfect pastime to keep his stay in Weldon interesting. "At the very least, I'll make certain we have fun."

"What's up with the absurd condition anyway? The chances of me falling in love with you is a big fat zero." She stared at him as though he was an alien species. Then her expression turned wily. "Maybe you're *afraid* of someone falling in love with you. Have you sworn off love and happily ever after? Is that why you hate weddings?"

Seth blinked rapidly as her words triggered unwanted memories. He'd been burned. Very badly. And love wasn't something he intended to give another try. But in this instance, he'd placed the condition mainly to coax Tara into accepting. With her competitive edge, she would no doubt love the chance to prove him wrong. But maybe he'd inadvertently revealed too much of himself as well.

"Not believing in love and being afraid of it are completely different things," he said lightly. "I just wanted to ensure that no one's feelings got hurt in our little month of fun."

"So does the condition apply to you as well? Can you go on four whole dates with yours truly and not fall for me?" Tara fluttered her eyelashes at him. "I don't know. I think your chances are pretty slim."

"I'm willing to take the risk." His stomach did a funny little dance. Was he underestimating the risk? *No.* He'd vowed to never fall in love again after Jessica, and his heart hadn't been in the remotest danger since. And it wouldn't be now. "Okay. Let's stop playing around and get to the point. Do you accept the dare or not? There's no shame in chickening out, Tara. All you have to do is say uncle and drink that lovely glass of beer in front of you."

She worried her bottom lip, drawing his attention there. *Damn.* She had the most kissable lips he'd ever seen, and he'd seen many beautiful women in his line of work. There was just something about them. He wet his lips, imagining how they would feel against his own. They were the perfect shade of deep pink, and the bottom lip was just a little fuller than her top one with a light split down the middle, plumping up the two halves. Heat spread through his body, and the need to kiss her became almost unbearable.

"I accept your dare," she said, slapping her hand on the counter as though she was calling his bet at a poker table.

Seth stared blankly at her, struggling to disperse the fog of desire clouding his mind. More than anything, he was shocked by her acquiescence. He didn't think he had a real chance with her. Even though he was the one who'd suggested the dare, a flash of nervousness hit him. He had no idea what he was getting into, did he? She wasn't just any other woman. She was Tara. He was already well on his way to being infatuated with her. Taking his eyes off of her when she was nearby was a study in discipline.

Could he say with confidence that he wouldn't feel more for her as the month passed? It was a solid maybe. *Well, fuck it.* He was moving to Paris in a month. He intended to make it a month to remember with this incredible woman who made him dizzy with desire. *Call it a farewell gift to myself.*

"Good choice," he said, unable to hold back his wolfish grin. "You won't regret it."

A soft blush climbed to her cheeks, but her words were as dry as the Mohave Desert. "There's that inflated ego again."

"Come sit down," Seth said, patting the seat beside him. He still could hardly believe that she'd agreed to his dare. He wanted her close by to assure him that it was really happening. "You've been standing behind the bar this whole time. Don't your legs get tired?"

"Nah. I'm used to it. But I'll join you to celebrate our ridiculous arrangement."

She filled up a pitcher and set out some beer nuts before coming to sit beside him.

"To the dating dare." He raised his glass with a happy grin, and forced aside his unease. He would have Tara to himself for four whole dates. How could that be anything but fun? "It's going to be a wild ride."

"You're so corny. Is this what I have to look forward to in the next month?"

"This and so much more awesomeness," he said, hamming it up.

Tara rolled her eyes, but her smile was blinding. "You certainly won't be boring."

Since their drinking game had come to a very satisfactory conclusion, Seth switched to water, being mindful that he had to drive back to his hotel later. While Tara appeared to be in a lighter mood than before, she continued to drown her lingering sorrows in her beer.

Her alcohol tolerance was impressive. Her gaze was focused and she enunciated each word perfectly even after drinking all the penalty beer, as well as from the pitcher in front of them. The woman could probably drink him under the table. But with a suddenness that startled him, Tara's eyes went from sparkling with humor to clouded with alcohol.

"Are you feeling okay?" Seth asked. "We should call it a night."

She seemed to be trying to focus on his face, but ended up staring at the tip of his nose, making herself cross-eyed.

"Don't be such a . . . um . . . party pooper," she slurred, drawing her brows down. Then she burst into a fit of giggles. "Party pooper. It's funny because . . . poop. Quit pooping on the party, Seth."

"All right then." He chuckled under his breath. Potty humor was a clear indication that sobriety was far gone. "Let's get you home."

He stood from his seat, and tidied up the best he could, rinsing the cups and pitcher in the bar sink. Seth worked quickly, but Tara began slumping on the stool.

"Whoa." He got to her side just in time to prop her up. "You need to tell me where you live."

"I live over yonder with my faithful parents and overprotective big brothers."

Overprotective? God, he had to get her home if he didn't want his ass kicked by Jack and Alex. He'd had no idea she was this drunk. She literally went from sober to hammered in a hot second.

"And where might yonder be?" he asked.

"The street where the houses are," she whispered as though she was telling him a closely held secret.

Oh, boy. Seth wiped a hand down his face. "Okay, let's get you to my car."

"Onward ho," she hollered, pointing toward the ceiling.

"No, not that way. This way." He redirected her arm toward the back entrance, and led them out through it. "We need to lock up. Where are your keys?"

She waved vaguely at his arm where her purse hung. With a heavy sigh, Seth rummaged through it, trying not to notice what was in there. When his hand wrapped around a jingling set of keys, he pulled it out and held it up to Tara.

"Which one?" he asked. She laughed in his face, and leaned her forehead against his shoulder, shunning the keys he held in front of her. He huffed a defeated sigh. "I guess I'll have to try them all."

After several failed attempts, Seth finally found the right key, and locked up the brewery. *Why does the woman have so many keys anyway?*

"Here." He wrapped his arm around her waist and drew her arm over his shoulder. She was practically dead weight in his arms, bogged down by a vast amount of beer. "I need you to help me walk you to my car. Otherwise, I'm going to throw you over my shoulder like a sack of potatoes."

"French fries. Mashed potatoes. Tater tots. Mmm . . . I love tater tots."

"We'll get some tater tots on one of our dates." Seth laughed despite his frustration. How could he not have known how drunk she was? Regardless, she was adorable.

Turning his attention back to the task at hand, they stumbled slowly to his car. When they arrived at last, Tara whispered with awe, "Look. A car."

"Yup. It's a car all right," he agreed, opening the passenger-side door. "Please get in."

"Okie dokie." She made an awkward dive for the seat.

"No, no, no. Don't climb in that way. Your bottom goes there not your knees. Here, let me help you. Wait. Watch your head." He inserted his hand between her head and the roof of the car just in time to stop her from banging her head against it, and crushed his hand instead. "Ow."

He grunted and cursed as he maneuvered her onto the passenger seat, but finally had her safely ensconced in her seat. When he came around to the driver's side and reached over to buckle her in, her eyes were drooping.

"Tara, you can't fall asleep now." He gave her shoulder a gentle shake. "You need to focus and tell me where you live."

She snored softly in response.

"Wait a minute," he said to himself. "Her driver's license."

He reached for her purse and searched through it with a mumbled apology. He saw her giant set of keys, her phone, a tube of lipstick, and some crumpled up cash in there, but no license. Then he remembered her telling him that she had driven to the wedding with her family. She must've left her driver's license at home.

Seth grabbed fistfuls of his hair and groaned. He had no idea where she lived, and taking her to his hotel wasn't the best idea for his sanity. She was so breathtaking, especially when she'd relaxed and laughed with him. He'd been tempted to kiss her all night until she went from zero to drunk in the blink of an eye. Sleeping next to her soft warm body was going to be torture.

But what choice did he have? He wasn't going to leave her alone at the brewery. Nor was he going to spend a night in the car with her when he had a warm bed waiting for him. Well, for them.

"Shit," he said, which helped marginally with his frustration.

He pulled out of the brewery's parking lot and drove the few blocks to his hotel. Lola's Inn and Trattoria was a charming Italian restaurant with a few welcoming, thoughtfully appointed rooms on the second and third floors. He loved everything about it. The warm, dark wood of the décor in the restaurant to the cozy, farmhouse-style rooms. This was his go-to spot to stay when he visited Landon. His brother let him get away with staying at a hotel since Seth wouldn't get a good night's sleep with Morgan waking up several times during the night.

It was past two o'clock in the morning, so there was no one watching the front counter, which made sneaking into the hotel with Tara a bit less nerve-wracking. Even so, he scanned the parking lot to check that there was no one around. She was a local, and he didn't want her subjected to prying eyes while she stumbled out of his car dead drunk.

"Tara. *Tara*," Seth said, unbuckling her. She mumbled something and opened one eye.

"Wassit? Who's you? Seth?" Then she closed her eye again.

"I don't know where you live so I brought you to Lola's. I need you to walk up with me to my room. Okay?" Seth shook her lightly by her arm. "I'll make you a cup of coffee, and take you home once you sober up."

"Mar-ma-lade. *Orange* marmalade," she said with gravitas as though her words were of great importance.

"Yes. Marmalade. Sure," he said agreeably. He just needed to work quickly while she was conscious. "I'm going to help you out of the car, and we're going to walk a few small steps at a time. Easy peasy, right?"

"No, peas. Hate. Much hate."

Despite the predicament he found himself in, Seth couldn't help but laugh. She was so fucking cute. There wasn't a hint of her signature sarcasm in sight. Not that he didn't enjoy her prickly side, too.

Even though her eyes were open, she was far from alert. When he rounded his car and hefted her out of the passenger seat, she sagged against him. He wrapped her waist tightly with his arm, and held her hand over his shoulder so she wouldn't slide down. He took a careful step forward. Her foot moved a step as well. *Thank God*. One step at a time, they reached the entrance to Lola's. He dug around his pockets, holding Tara up with one arm.

Once they got through the front entrance, Seth quickly looked left and right. A vise wrapped around his lungs and squeezed, nerves jangling through his veins. He wasn't doing anything wrong, but to anyone watching, he *was* sneaking around with an alcohol-drenched woman in his arms. This had to be the most ludicrous situation he'd ever found himself in.

He adjusted Tara so he could bear more of her weight, and resolutely walked down the hall to his room. He grabbed the key card he'd been holding in his mouth and waved it against the sensor, all the while balancing her against his hip. Opening the unlocked door, he backed into the room, half dragging Tara with him. When the door shut behind them, Seth sighed with relief. They were finally safe in his room.

"That wasn't so bad," he said, winded from the exertion. He righted Tara in his arms, wondering where to settle her, when she raised her head and looked straight at him.

"Seth," she said with surprising clarity.

Her eyes were focused on him, burning with intensity. For a moment, he thought she was going to kiss him, and his blood sizzled. But it wouldn't be right to kiss her. While he thought of gentle ways to refuse her—to remind her that they had time—Tara bent at her waist and hurled on his shoes. He quickly moved to her side and held her hair back in one hand and thumped her back with the other.

"You okay?" he asked as dry heaves wracked through her body. He rolled his eyes at himself. It was highly unlikely that she felt okay.

"Stop. No more." She weakly waved her hand behind her, trying to grab his arm to stop the thumping. "Bathroom."

When her knees buckled, Seth caught her by her arms and led her to the sink, where she rinsed her mouth swaying left and right. He hovered near her to catch her in case she fell, but she managed to stay upright.

"Better?" Maybe she was awake enough to tell him her address. "Do you want me to take you home? Can you tell me your address?"

Instead of answering, she sank down to the floor with a miserable moan.

"Oh, for God's sake," he muttered.

After propping her up against a wall, he grabbed a towel and held it under running water. He returned to her side with the wet towel, and cleaned her clammy face and neck. Tara had fallen asleep again and didn't stir at his ministrations. He was about to lift her off the floor to carry her to bed when he noticed that the front hem of her skirt was soiled. He couldn't let her sleep wearing her own vomit, so Seth took a steadying breath and got to work.

He pulled her into his arms, her head resting on his shoulder, and unzipped the back of her dress. After he leaned her back against the wall, he maneuvered her floppy arms free and dragged the dress down, making a heroic effort not to stare as her lacy black bra revealed itself to him. God, she was so fucking sexy. He took a deep breath and doggedly tugged her dress down further, preparing himself to be slammed with a matching pair of black panties. But she surprised him with her choice of . . . What exactly was she wearing? It covered her up from right under her breasts, down to her mid-thighs. Ah, it must be one of those body contouring things. He shook his head, working the dress down past her legs and off of her. She was perfect. She didn't need shapewear.

"I can't stand wearing this thing," she mumbled as though she'd read his mind.

Then she promptly tugged and squirmed until she pushed her undergarment down to the top of her hips. *Yeah, baby. Take it off.* What? Where the hell did that come from? But, of course, he knew exactly where it came from, so he told his dick to shut up. He refused to take advantage of her in even the smallest way while she was drunk. And to prove that his head still ruled him, he averted his eyes before she exposed more of her glorious body.

"Oh, God," he groaned when her underwear flew past him. He squeezed his eyes shut when her bra followed in its wake. The woman he'd been hungering after all night was naked in his bathroom, but he couldn't do anything about it because his mother raised him right. Even so, the temptation to peek at her was too powerful. "Stay right here. Let me bring you a T-shirt."

He went to his luggage and fished out his one and only T-shirt, the one he'd been planning to wear tomorrow. He brought it back to the bathroom, keeping his eyes focused on a spot over Tara's half-prone form. Seth pulled the T-shirt over her wobbling head and pushed her limp, uncooperative arms through, all the while making a valiant effort not to notice how soft her skin felt.

While his shirt was huge on her, she was undeniably naked underneath it. And his continued effort to keep his eyes averted was about to burst some blood vessels. He needed to get her under the covers. Seth hugged Tara tightly against his chest, and heaved to a stand. He carried her to the bed, and laid her down on it. She was sleeping peacefully, her features soft and relaxed. A rush of affection flowed through him as he arranged the duvet around her. He stepped away before he acted on his impulse to drop a kiss on her forehead.

Next up was the puke pile. Without overthinking it, he grabbed a lined trash can and a whole roll of toilet paper, and got to work. He cleaned up everything he could, but he couldn't do anything about the stain on the carpet. He would leave the maid a big tip for the rest of the cleanup.

After a long, hot shower, Seth put on a pair of boxers. It was as decent as he could get with his unexpected guest wearing his only spare T-shirt. Being careful not to disturb Tara, he slipped under the covers, and turned his back to her. The only way he could fall asleep was to pretend she wasn't there. *Fat chance.* Every hair on his body stood at attention, acutely conscious of the beautiful woman next to him. He might as well give up on sleep and read a book on his phone. But as the minutes ticked by, Tara's warm presence settled his restlessness and he drifted off to sleep.

CHAPTER THREE

Tara lifted her arms high above her head and stretched down to her pointed toes. When she released her taught muscles, her body relaxed into a gelatinous blob, and a satisfied sigh escaped her lips. She loved this part of waking up. The first stretch of the day, where you surrender every muscle in your body. It was one of life's simplest but greatest pleasures.

She turned to her side, keeping her eyes closed, like a lazy cat sitting on a patch of sunlight. It took her a couple seconds to realize she wasn't alone. With a chill of alarm slithering down her spine, she forced her eyes open. Her heart took a flying leap into her throat as she stared into Seth's beautiful sleeping face.

"No," she choked, holding herself very still.

She stomped down on the panic that was rising inside her, and forced herself to rewind her mind to last night. She remembered playing truth or dare with him at the brewery, and her impulsively agreeing to date him. It had seemed a perfectly sane idea at the time. She was lonely; he was hot. A no-strings-attached month of dating sounded like exactly what the doctor ordered.

But her memory turned hazy after the part where they toasted to the dating dare. *Oh, God. Did I sleep with him?* Well, it was obvious she slept with him. She was in bed beside him, and the sky was softening with the colors of approaching dawn. But did she *sleep* with him?

She carefully lifted the duvet covering her body, and saw that she was naked underneath an oversized T-shirt, which presumably belonged to Seth. Tara briefly considered lifting the blanket further to see what Seth was wearing on the bottom, because from what she could see, he wasn't wearing anything on the top. But she promptly chickened out. What if he was naked? The thought made her blood rush south even as she freaked out about the implications.

She wanted him—last night and this morning. That much was certain. Her body was apparently a wild thing with a mind of its own. Even now, it begged her to touch him. To slip a hand underneath the sheets and feel up his broad chest and tight abs. *Simmer down.* If she felt this out of control, sober and wide awake, how would she have behaved last night? She might've acted on her desire without restraint.

Why did Seth bring her to his hotel room? He wasn't the kind of man who would take advantage of a drunk person. *But look at the evidence.* She was in his hotel room, lying next to him in nothing but a T-shirt. Why would she be half-naked if they didn't do the deed? No, she didn't buy it. There had to be a different explanation—probably a hugely humiliating one for her.

But if they *had* slept together last night, she'd probably participated wholeheartedly. She was ridiculously attracted to the man. She wouldn't call it the best decision of her life, but she could own it. The thing that bothered her the most was that if they really had had sex, she didn't remember any of it. Even the orgasm. She was certain he would've made her come. The mere sight of him made lust pump through her veins. Besides, weren't playboys supposed to know their way around a woman's body? Tara wanted to groan out loud, but she couldn't risk waking up Seth.

She had to get out of here before he woke up. Whatever happened last night, it would be humiliating to face him with no memory of it. She shifted gingerly toward the edge of the bed, wincing as her brain rattled in her head, and removed her weight from the mattress with excruciating care. Wouldn't it be funny if she accidentally jostled him awake? Yeah . . . no.

Her dress hung neatly behind a high-backed chair with her bra and Spanx next to it. With a grimace of distaste, she put on her uncomfortable push-up bra and Spanx and quickly stepped into the dress. The hem felt cold against her bare feet for some reason. She paused to sniff the damp skirt, but it smelled clean. *Whatever.* She had to find the rest of her stuff. Once she found her shoes and her purse, Tara made her escape. She would've sprinted down the empty hallway if her brain wasn't attempting to shove her eyeballs through their sockets.

Once she made it out the main entrance, the gentle light of the rising sun pierced into her pounding head. It was just past six o'clock, and the streets were still empty. Which was good and bad. It was good since there was no one to witness her walk of shame. The bad was that her chances of catching an Uber in her tiny town at sunrise were slim to nothing. Besides, taking an Uber would create a witness to her unplanned sleepover, which she didn't need. Waddling home in her mermaid dress and high heels was her only option. It felt like her comeuppance for drinking without restraint when she was feeling so off—with a gorgeous man she had a hard time keeping her hands off of.

When Tara got safely home with sore feet and a guilty conscience, she pushed everything out of her mind so she could get more sleep to do away with her hangover. She didn't want her brothers giving her a hard time for staying out late and getting so drunk. They had a cowbell they loved to ring around her head when she overdid it with the adult beverages.

She stripped out of her tight dress and the wretched undergarments, put on an oversized T-shirt—which reminded her of the feel of Seth's shirt against her naked skin—and slid into bed. She closed her eyes with a sigh, and dreamt of the peaceful face of the sleeping man she'd left behind in a cozy hotel room.

Tara woke up for the second time that morning, the sun shining brightly into her room. To her great relief, the pain stabbing at her head didn't feel like medieval torture anymore. Unfortunately, her mortification had only grown like one of those magic sponge animals that quadrupled in size in water. Her remorse at her reckless actions didn't fit inside her mind, and her scalp felt stretched tightly around her head. She screamed into her pillow. It helped a little, so she did it again. Feeling marginally less likely to burst, she slowly swung her legs to the floor and stood.

No shooting pain in her temples. No dizziness. *Yup.* Her hangover was practically gone. Putting on her slippers, she dragged herself out to the kitchen to hydrate. Her mom had a giant jug of boricha—roasted barley tea—prepared in the fridge, and she gratefully poured out a tall glass and chugged it down.

"Hey, kiddo," Jack said, strolling into the kitchen. "How late did you stay out last night? I didn't hear you come in."

"Late," she said vaguely, hoping her brother wouldn't push it. Because *oh, I came home a couple hours ago after having a sleepover with Seth* was a conversation neither of them needed to have.

As sad as it sounded, she was a twenty-eight-year-old woman with an unspoken two A.M. curfew. She knew her parents only wanted to protect their little girl, but it was absurd to have a curfew at her age, especially since her brothers hadn't had a curfew since they were in high school. She loved her parents dearly, but some of their old-fashioned views were getting . . . old.

Thankfully, Jack just shrugged and poured himself a glass of boricha, too. "I can't believe Aubrey is really married. I mean, she's been living with Landon for a few months now, and they have Morgan, but that wedding ceremony made everything feel so official."

"I know," Tara sighed, feeling the hollow ache in her heart again. *Cut it out already.* To cheer herself up, she decided to tease Jack. He was such an easy target. He blushed and fumbled so wonderfully. He really was a sweetheart. "You know Mom and Dad secretly hoped for you and Aubrey to get together for the longest time."

"What? That's . . . ugh. What are you talking about?" he stuttered, turning a blotchy pink.

"Nothing," she said, all innocence.

"Aubrey's like a little sister to me. She's like you. How could Mom and Dad . . . ? I feel nauseous."

"Geez, bro. Calm down. I'm just messing with you." Tara released the laughter she was holding back, clutching her stomach.

"You're a little brat. When are you going to grow up?" Jack tried to glare at her, but he was holding back a grin. He was also a really good sport. "You know what you deserve?"

"No." Her laughter abruptly ceased. "Please not that. Mom told you guys not to do that anymore."

"She did? I have no recollection of that," her sweet oppa said as he lunged for her. He grabbed her around her midriff and used his other hand to tickle her belly.

"Ahhh. Stop. Please," she wheezed as she giggled like a kindergartener high on cotton candy.

Alex walked in on them and stopped in his tracks. After studying the scene for a few seconds, he dashed all her hopes for help from him. "It looks like you have the situation handled, Jack. I'll be in the garage if you need reinforcement."

Figures. Jack and Alex were fraternal twins and they always, without fail, sided with each other. Even so, it still stung. Shrieking with tortured laughter, she yelled, "You are heartless, Alex Park. Heartless."

"Good morning to you, too, baby sister." With an annoyingly jaunty wave, he went on his merry way.

"Assholes, the both of you." The insult gave her no satisfaction when it wheezed out of her in a breathless pant.

"Tara, you know better than to use such language toward your big brothers," her mom chided as she walked into the kitchen. But she wore a wide smile, as though she found the situation hilarious but felt it was her duty as a good mom to teach her youngest how to respect her elders. Just as Tara was about to howl in frustration, her mom continued, "And Jack. Stop that. You're thirty years old, not seven."

He promptly released Tara and walked over to Mom to peck her on the cheek. "Sorry. I'll do my best to remember that I'm old."

Her mom affectionately slapped her son on the shoulder and turned him toward the hallway. "Be on your way. I want to chat with my daughter."

"Yes, Mother." Jack winked at Tara and grabbed a Fuji apple from the fruit basket before he sauntered out of the kitchen, throwing and catching the apple in the air.

"You slept in today," she said, switching fluidly to Korean. "Are you feeling okay?"

"Of course, I am." *Oh, no. Mom knows. She always knows every-thing.* "It was a long day, and I just needed some extra sleep."

"Are you sure that's all?" Her mom peered at her with her X-ray vision. Tara's heart threatened to tear through her chest like the Kool-Aid man. "It's okay to feel a little down. Aubrey just got married. You could feel sad for all those girls' nights in and out you used to have, and worry about your friendship changing."

Tara should've been relieved that she hadn't been sniffed out by her mom for her late-night adventures. But talking about this wasn't a huge improvement, especially since her mom zeroed in on her inner workings.

"I know, Mom. I just need to let it all settle in. Aubrey will always be my best friend. Just because her life has changed doesn't mean that our friendship will change. We'll always be there for each other."

"That was my line. When has my puppy gotten so wise?" Mom cupped her cheek with a warm hand and smiled. "You're right. Just give yourself time."

"Thank you." Tara couldn't believe her luck that her mom wasn't bringing up her lack of a husband.

"And . . . maybe it's time you started thinking about your future. I married your dad when I was only twenty-three—"

"I can't hear you." She'd been too quick to be relieved. To avoid listening to her mom's story for the 378th time, Tara plugged her ears with her fingers. "I already told you I don't have time for marriage. The brewery is more important to me."

She probably said this a bit louder than necessary, thanks to the fingers muffling her voice, because her mom drew back with a cringe. With an exasperated eye roll, she drew Tara close, gave her a kiss on the forehead, and walked out of the kitchen.

Tara blew out a long breath. If she wanted a minute of peace, she was either going to have to hide out in her room or go into the brewery early. Her brothers wouldn't be coming in until around two, so Tara decided to head out to her happy place. She loved her family, but privacy was a rare commodity.

After a quick shower, she threw on her work uniform—jeans and a loose, lightweight shirt—and headed out. Tara rode her bike everywhere in town. She claimed that it was for the environment and her physical well-being, but the fact of the matter was that it was so much fun. It reminded her of being a kid. She even rang the bell occasionally when no one was around.

It was a brisk, sunny spring morning, and she hummed under her breath as she whizzed down the road. She reached Weldon Brewery before she knew it and let herself inside. It was her home away from home. The place where she felt most herself, but this morning it was all wrong.

As soon as she'd agreed to Seth's dating dare, Tara had been filled with a bubbling excitement. It wasn't a big deal. Just four dates. But it had felt like the promise of an adventure. Now she'd gone and ruined it by getting sloppy drunk. How was she going to salvage her tattered pride?

Besides, there would be nothing to salvage if they'd slept together. She'd told Seth repeatedly *no hookup* last night. Even if she'd thrown herself at him as she imagined, he should have resisted. But what if he couldn't? She could be very persuasive. Tara snorted out loud. Did she think she was irresistible? Talk about having an inflated ego. No matter how hard she came on to him, he shouldn't have given in. After all, they had their dating dare. He should've waited to be seduced properly when she was sober and horny.

Her thought train came to a screeching stop. Why was she getting worked up over an unlikely hypothesis? Even if he was a playboy, Seth was a decent man. She shouldn't assume the worst of him. But then why was she naked? *Grrr.*

When she walked up to the bar, she found something that reinforced her assessment of Seth as a good guy. She'd expected there to be a pitcher, peanuts, and glasses strewn across the counter, but there wasn't a speck of peanut crumble. When she went around the counter to inspect further, she discovered the neatly rinsed glassware in the sink. He'd cleaned everything up before taking her to the hotel.

Despite her urge to blame someone else for her guilt and frustration, blaming Seth didn't sit right in her gut. She couldn't assume the worst of him. And she had to resolve this if she wanted to go forward with the dating dare. It was a much-needed distraction that she couldn't give up easily. *Just call him, silly woman.* But what would she say? *Hey, Seth. This is Tara. I don't remember shit from last night. Did we fuck?*

"What the hell am I supposed to do?" she asked the sturdy, reclaimed-wood columns in the pub. They stood silent. "Some help you are."

If Seth had something to say, or explain, he was going to have to call her himself. There was no way she was calling first.

Seth woke up the next day with morning wood that felt more like iron, but the woman responsible was nowhere in sight. Disappointment slapped him in the face, but understanding soon eased the sting. She was probably too embarrassed to see him after throwing up and passing out on him, so she'd made an early-morning escape.

He would give her some time and wait for her to call him. Once she got over it, she would probably want to apologize or thank him or whatever. Not that he wanted any of that. He just couldn't wait for their first date. His heart took off on a gallop at the thought of spending more time with Tara.

But he had to tie up some loose ends before he treated himself to a date with her. He had to get back to Santa Monica to finish packing up his condo, and finalize the leasing arrangements with his real estate agent. He didn't plan on coming back to the States anytime soon, but his condo was the first home he'd bought, and he felt too attached to it to sell it outright.

Seth flipped back the bedsheets and heaved himself out of bed. Yawning long and loud, he trudged to the bathroom. After his shower, he needed some strong coffee to make up for his late night.

His mom had stayed with Landon and Aubrey last night, and was planning to stay for the rest of the week to help them prepare for their monthlong honeymoon. Well, he wasn't sure how much of a honeymoon it would be with a three-month-old baby with them, but his brother was an industrious man.

Landon's restaurant was opening in about eight weeks, and he wouldn't get a chance to take long vacations until the place was established, so this was their last chance to get away for a while. Aubrey's bakery, Comfort Zone, was a well-oiled machine with her sous-chef, apprentice, and other employees holding down the fort. As for Landon's restaurant, there was still cosmetic construction to finish and other minor utility work to be done, so Seth had agreed to oversee the final touches. He also solved the problem of their empty house by staying there while he was around.

And as a wedding present, he'd offered to create the restaurant's website. Landon could've hired anyone to build the website, but Seth wanted it to be centered on photographs of the restaurant—around Landon's dream. His brother should share what the restaurant means to him with his future patrons.

He was looking forward to all of it, especially now that it included spending time with Tara. Seth felt as giddy and excited as a schoolkid the night before a field trip. He whistled while he shampooed his hair, and stepped out of the shower feeling refreshed and motivated. With a promise to visit again soon, Seth checked out of Lola's and headed to Landon's before his long drive home.

Springtime in Southern California was ridiculous. With temperatures in the high sixties and low seventies, it was as though they were living in an ecosphere set to perfect weather. Seth pulled into Landon's driveway and parked in front of the house. He jogged up the steps and rang the bell, humming under his breath.

"Good morning, love," his mom said in a singsongy voice, opening the front door with Morgan carefully cradled against her chest. Holding up one of her little hands, she waved it at him. "Good morning, Uncle Seth."

"Morning, Mom." He bent to peck his mom's cheek, and planted a kiss on Morgan's forehead with a loud smack. "Morning, gorgeous."

"Come in and close the door. The wind isn't good for the baby."

"It's close to seventy degrees out there," he said mildly as his mom fussed over the cheerful baby girl, who did not seem the least bit bothered by the wind. But he obediently shut the door behind him before he removed his shoes in the foyer.

"The wind might get into her lungs." His mom shot him a warning look.

"Come on, Mom. You're the coolest, most forward-thinking person I know until it comes to Morgan. Then you start spewing superstitions about wind getting into her lungs. We *want* air in her lungs."

She relented with a smile and slapped him on the arm. "We have to heed our ancestors' wisdom sometimes. When she turns one, I'll relax on the mumbo jumbo, but until then you have to humor me."

"Of course," he said, giving her a one-armed hug. "Actually, I'm surprised you're okay with Landon and Aubrey taking her to Asia for a month. They'll be out and about with *people* and everything."

"Who said I was okay? But I'm not going to meddle in their parenting just because I get unreasonably overprotective around my baby girl sometimes. That's my problem."

"Ah, there's the amazing woman who raised me."

"Stop with your teasing and go find your hyung. See if he needs any help."

"Yes, ma'am." He rubbed his nose against Morgan's tiny nub of one and was rewarded with a happy gurgle before he walked off in search of his older brother.

He poked his head into the nursery, the study, and the master bedroom but couldn't find Landon anywhere. "Bro, where are you?"

"I'm over here."

Seth followed his muffled reply toward the back of the master bedroom, and found Landon standing inside the en suite bathroom, holding two bottles of toiletry in his hands with frustration stamped across his face.

"Are you having a stare off with your bubble bath?" Seth asked, grinning at the domestic scene. His brother had changed so much since he met Aubrey—for the better, of course—and fatherhood looked pretty great on him, too.

"Shut up," Landon said halfheartedly. "Aubrey bought these new washes for Morgan, and I can't figure out the difference between the two. Which one am I supposed to use?"

"Where is Aubrey anyway?" he said, looking around as though she was hiding behind the dresser.

"She's at Comfort Zone. You do remember that your sister-in-law owns a business, don't you?"

"You guys got married last night. I figured she'd take this week off to unwind and get ready for your honeymoon."

Landon's face took on a goofy, dreamy expression. "She just loves it there. She's so amazing at what she does, you know? She missed going in during her maternity leave, so she's making up for lost time before she takes more time off."

"Sounds like Aubrey." Seth sat down on the edge of the bathtub. "Do you need help with anything?"

"Nah. We still have plenty of time to pack. I'm just trying to put my other businesses in order before we leave, which you can't help with. Besides, don't you have way more packing to do than us?"

"It's mostly done. I just have to get the furniture and boxes into storage, and pack the portable part of my life into a couple of over-sized bags."

His brother studied him quietly for a second. "This move to Paris . . . is it what you really want?"

"What do you mean?" Seth removed imaginary lint off his T-shirt.

"Mom and I didn't think your fashion-photography stint would last as long as it has. But now you're making this huge commitment to root yourself in the industry."

"It *is* my profession," he said stiffly.

"But your art is your *dream*. It has been since you were a little kid. The way you brought your painting and photography together was beautiful beyond words. I *saw* you in each and every one of your works. You put your heart into them. How are you holding all of that in? More importantly, why?" Landon's gaze seemed to pierce into his soul. Older-brother superpower. "I know what it means to turn my back on my dream, Seth. Whatever happened to derail you from your path, don't you think it's time to make your way back?"

"Look, hyung. I know you mean well, but fashion photography is my calling, and the Paris job is a huge opportunity for me." *My calling?* That was laying it on a bit thick. "I'm not going to lose out on the chance to chase a childhood dream."

Landon looked unconvinced but gave a resigned shrug. "If that's what you want, then I'm happy for you. But remember, I'm always here if you need to talk."

"I know. I know. Don't get all sappy on me," Seth said, swallowing the thick swell of emotion in his throat. His older brother's wedding must've gotten to him more than he'd thought. His feelings were too close to the surface. Well, he couldn't have that. Slapping on a carefree grin, he said, "If you don't need any help, then I should hit the road."

"Yeah, you have quite a drive ahead of you." Landon pulled him into a hug. "Thanks for taking over for me while I'm gone."

"It's nothing," Seth said, hugging him back. "I'll see you next month."

After sneaking in a snuggle session with Morgan, he said his goodbyes and headed home to Santa Monica. *Home.* He wouldn't be calling it home much longer. Paris would be home to him soon. Excitement filled him, and his face morphed into a giant smile. He couldn't wait to start his new life there.

The wide, open road and the endless blue sky called to him, but he was tempted to stop by the brewery. Tara might be there early preparing for the day or working on a new brew, but he'd promised himself to give her time, so he drove on. He would hear from her soon. His heart jumped at the thought, making Seth grin even wider. He relished the anticipation coursing through him. The dating dare was promising to be something special.

CHAPTER FOUR

As soon as she was on break, Tara pulled her phone out of her back pocket. No missed calls. No texts. *Grrr.* Seth had mentioned he was going to Santa Monica to take care of his condo and the last bit of packing. But Aubrey had left for Asia with her family the day before. He should be back by now, housesitting as he'd promised. Why hadn't he contacted her? Was a guilty conscience keeping him at bay? Why else wouldn't he have at least texted her?

Maybe he didn't care about the silly dare anymore after whatever happened that night. She didn't want to care either. Nevertheless, she was still irritated that he'd ignored her for a week. She'd done the same thing, but that wasn't the frigging point. Then, as though her irrationally angry thoughts were venomous voodoo needles pricking at his mind, her phone chimed to announce a text from him.

SETH: Hey, Tara.

After a week of radio silence, this is what he texts me? Why was he texting her anyway? What did he even want? *Hang on.* Wasn't she just bitching about him not texting her a minute ago? *Oh, shut up.*

With her heart pounding and her hands trembling ever so slightly, she texted him a witty response.

TARA: Hey.

SETH: Are you working late tonight?

TARA: Do you consider nine o'clock late?

A simple *yes* would've sufficed, but why be accommodating when she could be passive aggressive?

She stared fixedly at the ellipses that scrolled and scrolled. Was he writing her a sonnet? Why was he taking so long to respond? Then she almost dropped her phone from shock when it rang. As soon as she answered, Seth's sexy, teasing voice nibbled at her ear.

"Since I'm not a seven-year-old with an eight thirty bedtime, nine sounds great."

"Sounds great for what?" Tara couldn't believe what she was hearing. He suddenly wanted to see her on such short notice? Like she had nothing better to do? She was obviously overreacting, but she was nervous and confused, which made her so mad at herself.

"I'm back in town, and I thought we'd meet up to talk about that night. I expected to hear from you during the week, but . . . that's fine," he said magnanimously.

"*You* expected to hear from *me*? To say what?" To fess up that she didn't remember a thing? No way. She couldn't.

"I don't know. To apologize or thank . . . wait a minute. Why do you sound angry?"

"I'm not angry," she said through gritted teeth. "I'm . . . curious."

"We obviously can't do this over the phone. Can you come over to Landon's place after work?"

"You want me to come over there?" She was repeating everything he said, but she couldn't help it.

Was he hoping for a repeat of whatever had happened that night? *You don't know what happened. Why are you freaking out so badly?* From Seth's casual tone, he didn't sound like a man ridden with guilt, but that could be good or bad.

"Look. I would love to meet you somewhere in Weldon, but it's such a small town," Seth explained calmly. "Do you really want to have this conversation in public?"

She wanted to tell him they could talk about whatever he wanted to right at the brewery, but Jack and Alex would watch them like a hawk and eavesdrop shamelessly. She didn't want her humiliation, whatever it was, revealed in public.

"Fine. But no funny business," she added in a rush of nerves.

"What? What funny business?" He sounded genuinely perplexed. Then silence stretched on, weighing down on her as heavy as a boulder. "God, if you're thinking what I think you're thinking, I'm going to be very pissed off."

"We'll talk later." Tara's stomach dropped. He already sounded pissed. "Bye."

She hung up the phone before he could say anything else, and went back out to the hall. It was a relatively quiet weeknight, so she had plenty of time to dissect her conversation with Seth. As she was in the dark about what went down that night, she'd been at a distinct disadvantage. Since Jason, not being in complete control of a situation terrified her—things could spin out of control in the blink of an eye—so she'd taken the offensive with Seth to hide her insecurities. She couldn't do that when she saw him later tonight. She had to be calm and reasonable.

"Hey, Alex." She put a hand on his arm to get his attention. She'd been wiping at the same spot on the bar for half an hour, and it was already a quarter till nine. "It's pretty slow tonight. Do you mind if I take off a few minutes early?"

"Nope. Go right ahead."

"Thank you." As she turned away to grab her purse, she remembered that she had to drive to Aubrey and Landon's house. *Dammit.* She'd rode her bike into work. "Did you drive in with Jack?"

"No, he had to run some errands, so we drove in separately. Why?"

"It's just . . . can I borrow your car?"

"Sure," he said without hesitation. He dug into his jeans pocket and threw her a set of keys, and she snatched it out of the air. "Don't do anything too wild with it."

"What do you take me for?" She scoffed at him. "I'm only taking it for a little drag racing."

She left Alex chuckling behind the bar and hit the road. Even though she was an excellent driver, the windy, narrow roads weren't easy to maneuver in the dark. At least, it kept her mind from drifting to what she was going to say to Seth. More importantly, what *he* was going to say to her. She couldn't think about it, or else she would freak out like she had during their phone call.

Tara drove up to Aubrey's brightly lit house and parked next to Seth's fancy electric car. After taking a long breath to calm her nerves, she walked up the short steps and rapped her knuckles hard against the front door. Now that she was here, she wanted to get the whole thing over with.

Seth opened the door as though he'd been standing on the other side waiting for her. His gaze met hers for a heated second before his eyes traveled over her body. He swallowed hard. "It's good to see you, Tara."

She struggled to breathe properly. Her memory of how attractive he was and how she reacted to his proximity was nothing compared to the combustible lust that hit her like a blast from a furnace.

"Seth." She sounded undeniably breathless. "Are you going to invite me in or are we having our conversation on the doorstep?"

"Shit. I'm sorry. Come in." He hurriedly stepped aside then led her to the living room.

It was Tara's favorite room in the house, cream colored and filled with overstuffed sofas and lounge-worthy chaises. Some of her anxiety eased as the cozy warmth of the room soothed her. Seth motioned for her to take a seat and chose an armchair for himself near her but not within touching distance.

Once they were settled, he just sat drumming nervously at his knees. After a while, he inhaled and opened his mouth to say something, then stopped, ridges appearing between his eyebrows. She couldn't take it anymore. She had to break the silence.

"So . . . what did you want to talk about?" Tara said with forced nonchalance. Maybe he would reveal what happened that night without her having to admit that she remembered nothing about how she ended up near naked in his bed.

"I wanted to talk to you before tonight, but I thought you needed time to get over your embarrassment," he said softly. "But you don't have to be embarrassed. It's not a big deal."

"Here's the thing. I *am* embarrassed. Mortified. Humiliated. *To death*. But not for the reason you think." She squinted at her nails, studying them with intense focus. "All I know is that I woke up next to you wearing nothing but a T-shirt."

"What do you mean?" he asked warily.

"I don't remember anything that happened after our toast to the dating dare." She couldn't look straight at him, so she peered at him through the corner of one eye. "Please don't be offended, but I have to ask . . . did we have sex?"

"God, no." His eyes widened and the corners of his mouth drooped in the most heart-wrenching, crestfallen expression. She felt like a complete jerk. "Of course, we didn't have sex. How could you even think . . ."

"I'm so sorry. I knew there had to be another explanation for why I woke up naked in your bed."

"There is," he said stoically.

"I know, but doubt kept butting in to tell me I was grasping at straws to deny what really happened. You must understand why I needed to hear you say nothing happened?"

"I do understand," he sighed, tilting back his head and squeezing the back of his neck. "But I wouldn't say *nothing* happened."

"Oh, no. What did I do?" She buried her face in her hands and groaned. "I kissed you. Didn't I?"

"No, no. Nothing like *that* happened." Tara peeked through her fingers at him. Seth nearly smiled. "You seriously don't remember anything?"

"Nope." She shook her head, letting her hands fall on her lap. "Nada."

"Jesus. Okay. Let me start from after the toast then." He leaned forward in his seat with his elbows on his knees. "I didn't know how drunk you were until you started sliding off the stool at the brewery."

"Which is irrelevant," she said pertly. He wasn't taking responsibility for how drunk she got. "I made the decision to drink however much I did. It was my choice and my responsibility."

"It is relevant, because if you got incrementally inebriated like most people, I could've asked you for your address before you got completely wasted." Seth ran a hand down his face as though just recounting the story was exhausting. "When I asked you where you lived, you said something about over yonder and onward ho. Do you have some kind of a pirate fetish or were you one in your past life?"

"I . . . uh . . ."

"And orange marmalade."

"Orange marmalade?" Coffee and toast with orange marmalade was her idea of fancy teatime. But why would she bring up orange marmalade out of the blue?

"Never mind. That bit really isn't relevant. The point is I couldn't get your address out of you. Since I didn't think it would do to leave you sleeping on the brewery floor, I had to improvise." Seth dragged his fingers through his thick, wavy hair. His hair really was fantastic. *Hello?* Maybe she should focus on this nightmarish conversation, not his freaking hair. She had to rein in her attraction to him if she wanted to be in control. "I brought you to my hotel room, and that's when you threw up on me."

"I what on you?" she sputtered. Maybe he already wrote off the dating dare. Nothing like some puke to snuff out a spark of attraction.

"You spewed vomit like a woman possessed. Mostly on my shoes, but you managed to get some on your dress as well."

"Oh, for the love of elves." Tara pressed her hands against her flushed cheeks. This might be one of the most humiliating moments in the history of her whole entire life.

"All I did was help you get out of your soiled dress. The rest you did on your own."

"The rest?"

"You insisted on stripping down to your birthday suit, bouncing and wiggling." Seth stopped to clear his throat.

"So I stripped naked in front of you? You saw me naked?" *Lightning, strike me now.*

"Don't worry. I didn't *ogle* you. I put my T-shirt on you as quickly as possible."

"But you still saw . . . everything."

The corner of his mouth twitched suspiciously. "Only for a few seconds."

She glared at him hoping to burn away his memory of that night.

"Once you were happily snoring," he continued, "I rinsed the vomit out of your dress so you'd have something to wear back home. Then went to sleep next to you. That's it. Nothing else happened. Not even a kiss."

"I was wondering why the hem of my dress was damp," Tara said under her breath. After all the kindness he'd shown her, he must've been shocked by her almost-accusation. "I can't believe I just panicked like that and ran out on you. I should've waited for you to wake up and asked you what happened. I'm sorry, Seth."

"I can understand how you could've reacted that way when you woke up with no memory of the night before. But you should've at least called me. I could've spared you the weeklong torture."

"Right? Panic is not conducive to thinking." And it had taken her this long to discover his kindness. He hadn't taken advantage of her. He'd taken care of her. Warmth spooled in her heart. "Thank you."

"You're welcome." His gaze softened as it roamed her face. He'd seen her at her worst. Truly, nothing was worse than vomit. How could he still look at her like that? But his expression turned serious once more. "Tell me one thing. I'm not questioning why you had to ask me whether we had sex. It's heinous, but it is something that happens to people in this messed up world. But do you really think I'm capable of taking advantage of a drunk woman?"

"No, Seth. I don't," she said, scooting on the couch to get closer to him. "I've seen how you are with your family and friends. You're . . . all right."

"You think I'm 'all right'? Wow, that's high praise coming from you," he teased with a genuine smile.

"Yes, it is. And if you don't behave, I'm taking it back." Her smile widened in response. "But you *are* kind of one of the good guys, I guess."

"That wasn't so hard, was it? But do you mean it?"

"Yes, I do."

"That's good." His expression turned tender again. "Because I wouldn't have held you to the dating dare if that was how you saw me."

He was giving her a chance to back out of the dare. She hadn't expected such consideration from a player. Wasn't his game to seduce and leave? But that just didn't sound like him anymore. Well, the dating dare was still on.

"I may have grossed you out by spewing vomit on you, but you aren't getting out of those dates," Tara said.

With everything cleared up, she knew Seth was someone she could trust, and she wanted to spend more time with him. Was it wise? Most definitely not. Especially since he kept diverging from the playboy she had him pegged for. But she needed to distract herself from the hollowness that followed her since the wedding, and Seth provided the perfect solution.

"You promised me four interesting dates, and I'm holding you to it." She narrowed her eyes at him so he knew she meant business.

"Is that so?" A cocky grin lit his face, wreaking havoc on her libido.

"That is so," she confirmed with as much hauteur as she could muster.

"I can't wait," he said in a low, panty-zinging voice.

The air between them sang with electricity, reminding her of their dance at the wedding. She really wanted to touch him again, and from the look in Seth's eyes, he wanted to touch her back. It was time for her to get out of there so she didn't jump him even before their first date.

"Great." She shot to her feet. "I guess I'll be on my way."

"Right." He stood up and walked her to the door.

A sudden thought occurred to her when they were almost at the door. "Does tonight count as one of our dates?"

"Oh, hell no." He shook his head emphatically.

"Even if I kissed you good night?" she asked huskily.

"No." Seth swallowed with some difficulty and croaked, "Not even with a good-night kiss."

"Okay. Just making sure." She rose to her tiptoes and placed a feather-light kiss on his lips. It was impulsive, but it felt right. Like marking the beginning of a new adventure. "Good night."

He stood at the doorway looking dazed even as she drove away.

Seth sat at one corner of Landon's restaurant, where it was only slightly dusty—they were putting in the hexagonal cement tile and wood flooring for the dining hall—and scrolled aimlessly through his Google search. He had vague ideas of a French restaurant in a neighboring city and a bar with live music, but it didn't seem right for Tara. He could imagine her yawning halfway through the night. He'd promised that their dates would be fun and interesting, but he was stuck. Before he got worked up about his sudden lack of creativity, his phone rang.

"Hey." He answered on the first ring, his heart beating like a deep bass drum.

"Oh, hey," Tara said, her voice infused with surprise. He was confused for a second as to who had called whom. "This is Tara."

"Yes, I know." Seth chuckled.

"Just making sure," she said, sounding downright nervous.

"So what is it?" he pushed. The urge to tease her was irresistible.

"What is what?" she said.

"I don't mean to be rude, but you called me." He grinned broadly, enjoying himself way too much. "I'm guessing you had a reason for doing that."

"I was getting to that. Quit being so rude."

"My apologies." He bit his cheek to stifle his laugh. "Go right ahead."

"Right. So . . . uh . . . what are you doing tomorrow?" She made a valiant effort to sound casual.

"Oh, this and that. You know, the usual," he said vaguely.

"How am I supposed to know what your usual is?" Frustration rose in her voice. "Are you *usually* this annoying?"

"I'm free." He'd better not push his luck. She might hang up on him, and it would be his loss. "I need to check on the restaurant in the morning, but other than that, my calendar is empty and sad."

"Okay then." There was a short pause before she said in measured tones, "I'm off tomorrow. Do you want to hang out?"

"Hang out?" he said slowly, as though the words were foreign to him.

"Yes, as in our first date?" She sounded mildly incredulous that he was being so obtuse.

"Ahh, now I understand," he said gleefully. "You're asking me out on a date."

"Oh, shove it." She was fully recovered from her brief bout of nervousness. "You already did the asking for all four dates. I'm merely choosing the time and the place."

"By all means," he said, leaning back in his chair. He'd gotten a good amount of work done at the restaurant with the subcontractors, and Tara's call was a welcome break. "So what's the plan?"

"I thought we could keep it simple. Maybe a picnic at the park and a walk along the river if tomorrow is as nice out as today."

"That sounds great." A quiet, easy day with her sounded like the perfect date. He wanted to get to know the real Tara, including the vulnerability he'd sensed in her at the wedding. "Since you came up with the idea, can I prepare the picnic basket?"

"Are you sure?"

"Yes, I'm sure. It won't be any trouble. Is there anything you absolutely won't eat?"

"I'll eat anything as long as peas and cooked carrots aren't involved."

He recalled what she'd said about peas the night of the wedding. *No, peas. Hate. Much hate.* But the carrots were new. "Do you eat raw carrots?"

"Yes, I love them."

"But no cooked carrots? Huh. Okay." Every quirk he found out about her felt like a hidden gem he'd unearthed. "What time should I pick you up?"

"I don't know. Around eleven thirty? Whatever works best for you. Let me give you my address."

"I know where you live," he said. "Over yonder where the houses are."

"Oh, prickly pears. Why would I even say that?"

"Oh, I don't know. Maybe because you're someone who says things like 'oh, prickly pears'?"

Laughter floated over the line. "We're not allowed to *say the Lord's name in vain* in our house, so I had to get creative. 'Gosh' got old after a while."

"Say no more. A lot of my Korean-American friends come from devout Christian families."

"I don't know about devout. My parents stopped going to church years ago because they got so much crap about promoting Satan's way with the brewery. But they still have their faith."

"Isn't judging others just about the most un-Christian thing they could do? Your parents didn't deserve that."

"Right? It's quite messed up," she said with quiet indignation. "Anyways, I think we were just setting up a date. Didn't you need something from me?"

"Yes, your address please." He grabbed a pen from his messenger bag and scribbled down the address on the back of a receipt.

"Okay, then," she said before he could find something interesting to say. "I'll see you tomorrow."

"See you tomorrow," he said quietly, reluctant to let her go.

If he didn't want to spend all day staring at the clock, willing the hands to move faster, he'd better keep himself busy. He pushed himself off the chair and scanned the dining hall with his hands clasped behind his head.

The afternoon light filled the restaurant, giving it a sleepy, dreamlike ambiance—like sunlight streaming through the window of a neglected attic room. What was clutter and mess suddenly became something magical and surreal. It made a familiar tingling run down his arms to his fingertips. Taking photographs just for the sake of capturing beauty gave him an instant high. He might even be able to use some of the shots for the website.

He rushed to grab his equipment from his car, hoping he'd brought the right lenses. Rummaging through his bag and case, he found one that would probably work. With a camera bag on one shoulder and a tripod on the other, Seth rushed back inside. Thankfully, everyone was gone for the day, and he was able to concentrate on his inspiration.

The light transformed the wood dust floating in the air into tiny birds coasting the sky, their movements sinuous and graceful. He wanted to take pictures of his birds until the sun dipped out of sight. But he grudgingly moved on to the other parts of the interior because he only had about ten more minutes with the light. Then he became captivated by what he saw in the nooks and crannies of the unfinished French-country interior—the brass rooster pan left lying on the mantel, waiting to be hung, and the crystals peeping out from under the covered chandeliers, creating psychedelic rainbows against the wall. There was beauty everywhere.

When the ethereal overlay dissipated with the light, Seth felt a familiar weight press against his chest. This was just the beginning, or at least it used to be. In his past life, the photographs he took would be transformed with another layer of enchantment—his paint work. In his mind, he saw a secret beauty in the world that he could only communicate through his art. It allowed him to make real what he saw through his soul. But that time was long gone.

He used to put his heart into his work, and held out his art to the world like exposed nerves. It pulsed with life and hope. Every encouragement brought him life, and every criticism felt like little deaths. But his love of art had always revived him. Until it hadn't. The thing that brought forth his creative death was when his first love rejected his art, the very core of him, at his debut exhibit in the most public and humiliating way.

He pushed away thoughts of his past. What had happened

happened. There was no point in lingering on it. Never again would he make himself so vulnerable that another person could destroy him. When he locked away his heart from love, his art couldn't survive, because art demanded the same raw vulnerability as love. The dreamer in him that had burned so bright now only existed as a glimmer.

But Seth was happy the way he was. Not pouring too much of himself into anything or anyone kept him safe. He would never go back to living with his heart on his sleeve. It would be foolish to take such a risk. He wasn't a masochist. Life was fun when he just skimmed the surface. He didn't need the intense joy that his dream and love had brought. Pretty happy was enough for him.

And his arrangement with Tara was going to fit perfectly into his lifestyle. His lips tipped into a smile. She was such a dynamic woman. He had nothing but respect for her ambitions and single-mindedness. He appreciated her honesty, intelligence, and loyalty. A conversation with her was an adventure—always interesting and often hilarious.

And, God, she was so beautiful that she literally took his breath away. Seth wanted Tara to the point of distraction, but that wasn't the driving force behind his proposition. It was about the fun and excitement of getting to know her better. He was moving to Paris next month, so he had to make the most of his time with her. And if their dates led to sex, he'd be fucking grateful. Getting to know her body would be another fascinating adventure.

He blew out a calming breath to slow down his suddenly pounding heart and dragged his hands through his hair. He felt a deeper connection with her than any other woman he'd dated, but that didn't mean this was going to be different from any of his other relationships. She knew he was leaving in a month, and all they'd promised each other were four dates. They had no expectations of this leading anywhere, and knew exactly when it would end. Clear and uncomplicated. It was going to be a fun spring fling for both of them.

Seth packed up his equipment and locked up the restaurant. Since he volunteered to bring a picnic basket, he had to figure out what went in one. His family used to have picnic lunches in the backyard or the park when he and Landon were small. He should've paid more attention to what his mom packed for their excursions. He was almost certain his mom packed their favorite sandwiches and a fruit salad. While his brother was a world-class chef, Seth was the opposite of handy in the kitchen. But even he should be able to make sandwiches, right?

He could go to the market and buy the ingredients for some BLTs. *You can't go wrong with bacon.* What if Tara didn't like mayonnaise? There were no peas or cooked carrots in mayonnaise, so he should be safe there. Besides, he would load the picnic basket with Comfort Zone's mouthwatering desserts. No matter how much he messed up on the rest of the stuff, the desserts would save the day.

But first things first, he needed a picnic basket before he could fill it. Did Aubrey and Landon own one? There was no time for him to go up to the house to check. He should just buy one when he went into town. What else did people bring to picnics? A picnic blanket. He'd better pick up one of those, too.

Seth pulled out of the restaurant parking lot and headed for Weldon. He knew where the market was, but that was about it. But the folks in the tiny town were so friendly and helpful, he could ask them about everything else he needed and be pointed in the right direction.

Excitement fluttered in his stomach. Was he having first-date jitters? He chuckled under his breath. When was the last time he felt really excited about something? He couldn't even remember. All he knew was that he was looking forward to having Tara all to himself.

CHAPTER FIVE

The sock elves not only stole her socks but every presentable piece of clothing she had. Tara had nothing to wear for her first date with Seth. She palmed her forehead and blew out a frustrated breath. It was a beautiful spring day, and she was tying herself into a knot over her *picnic outfit.*

She chose the park for their first date because it wasn't really a hangout point for anyone she knew. And it was spread out enough that she and Seth could have some seclusion. Basically, no one would see her, really, except for him, which made her problem beyond silly. Clicking her tongue, she grabbed a pair of black leggings and a loose blue tunic from her closet and put them on.

"There," she said to her perfectly pleasant reflection on the closet mirror. "Why did that have to be so hard? Is this Seth guy a big deal or something?"

She laughed at herself. He was *not* a big deal *or* something. Seth was the guy she was going out with on four dates. He was also the one leaving for Paris in a month. In a nutshell, he was like any other man she casually dated but had an even shorter shelf life. With no option of extending the arrangement. Her stomach dipped ever so slightly at the thought, and she ignored it. She was going out to be not-alone for an afternoon with a fine-ass man. Stomach dipping of any sort was not included. And definitely not recognized or analyzed.

She picked up her favorite lip stain but hesitated before putting it on. *Stop it with the overthinking.* She wore lip stain all the time. Tara wasn't doing it to look good for Seth. It just made her feel good.

"Relax. Quit analyzing every breath you take." With those parting words to her reflection, she grabbed her purse and jacket and walked out to the living room.

"You look nice," Jack said, wiping sweat off his brows with a small towel. He must've just come back from a run. "Going out?"

"Nice? What? Going out? No," she replied, cool as cucumber slices on ice. *Oh, for Gollum's sake.* "I'm just wearing what I normally wear on my off days when I run errands. That's where I'm going. To run errands."

"You are so weird sometimes." Her brother crinkled his nose with a hint of concern on his face.

"Weird? No . . . I'm always like this." She was freaking out. She didn't want her brothers to know that she was seeing Seth, but she was doing the opposite of not acting suspicious. *What the hell?* Sneaking around was her forte. That was how she kept her love life shrouded in mystery for her family. "This is me being normal."

"Yeah . . . normal. Okay. I'm going to my room now." Jack hurried away with a wary glance over his shoulder.

Tara raised her eyes to the ceiling. What was wrong with her? She was a single woman going on a date with a single man. It was ridiculous how nervous she was. Embarrassingly ridiculous. She yelled a loud "bye" and shot out the door before she gave a repeat performance of her bumbling-jackass act.

She was five minutes early, but Seth's car pulled up to her house. She should've told him to meet her a block away. He opened the driver's door and stepped out of the car. *Crap.* He was going to slow down their getaway.

"Get back in the car," she yelled as she jumped into the passenger seat. "Drive."

"Woah. What's the hurry? Did you just rob your own house?"

"Drive now. Ask questions later."

"All right." Seth shrugged, his lips quirking to the side. "Who knew a picnic could be so exciting?"

In response to her urgency, he floored the pedal and shot away from the curb with enough speed to shove her back into her seat. She laughed with unexpected exhilaration, and her heart flipped when Seth's deep laughter joined hers.

Once her house was out of view, he slowed down to something close to the speed limit and quirked an eyebrow at her. "So. What was all that about?"

"I didn't think this through very thoroughly."

"What? The picnic?"

"Yes. No. The fact that you and I are having a picnic together." She snuck a peek at Seth's face. A small frown formed between his brows. "It's not you. It's me."

"Seriously? I pick you up for our first date and you give me the 'it's not you, it's me' spiel?" He kept his eyes on the road, but a smile played around his lips.

"It's just that I don't want my family to find out about our dating arrangement. We're only seeing each other four times, and I don't want to complicate things."

Seth nodded, pursing his lips. "So you're having second thoughts about having a picnic at the park?"

"No. It's highly unlikely I'll see anyone I know there." She offered him a wry smile. "It's more about having you pick me up at my house. Silly little mistakes like that could blow our cover."

"I guess you're right. I don't need Landon to lecture me when he comes home. He thinks I'm a player, too."

"He *thinks* you are?" Tara cocked her head to the side and stared at his profile. "Are you saying you're not?"

"I'm saying there's more to me than you think. At any rate, he probably doesn't think I'm suitable for Aubrey's best friend."

"Well, tell him to mind his own freaking business. Aubrey's best friend can take care of herself just fine. Even with a renowned playboy."

"I'm not as bad as you think." Seth half groaned and half laughed. "I don't go through women like they're single-use items. They're human, real, and fascinating. Many of the models I've been seen with are truly just friends."

Tara waved aside his words. She didn't mind if he was a player. In fact, she preferred it that way. They were both looking for a good time. No complications. "Anyways, we're in agreement that the dating dare will stay between us, right?"

"Sure."

"We don't have to sneak around and meet at remote cabins or anything, but there's no reason to announce it to our family. Or friends. Aubrey might freak out if she knew that I was dating her little brother-in-law."

"Cut it out with the little-brother jabs. You're only two years older than me. I've dated women older than you, and they had no problem with me being younger than them."

"Okay, fine. I honestly don't want to date a man who calls me noona either." She should let it go, but she couldn't stop herself.

"So . . . you've dated lots of older women, eh? Did they, you know, teach you things?"

"They certainly had a willing student." He glanced sideways at her with a wicked smile. "Do you want details?"

"You're coming on to me." Tara gasped with feigned horror. "Is it because I'm an older woman?"

Seth burst out laughing, and almost missed a turn. "I've dated a few older women. They were beautiful and interesting. That's it. I don't have a fetish for older women or anything, so you can relax."

"Sure, you don't." She gave him an exaggerated wink, channeling her inner Lucy Ricardo. "Anyway, what I said about you being Aubrey's little brother-in-law is a fact. Aubrey and Landon seem so protective of you sometimes. Which is pretty odd. From what I've seen, your friend The Ego should shield you from trivial things like hurt feelings."

"Hey, stop making fun of my ego. You're hurting my feelings." Seth grinned. "Anyway, Landon has been protective of me ever since our dad left. He thinks I'm his responsibility. It must've rubbed off on Aubrey. But you're right. I don't need protection from anything . . . or anyone."

"But you do need protection from The Ego. You know, someone might kick your ass for that one day," Tara mused. "I have a sinking feeling that person might be me."

"Hmm. I'm not sure I totally dislike the idea of you kicking my ass."

"How masochistic of you. You don't know the power of my roundhouse kick."

"Ooh, sexy," he said with a shit-eating grin.

"You're playing with fire," she warned.

"That's so hot."

"Ugh. You're just . . . ugh." She threw up her hands and stared out the window to hide her smile.

Very pleased with himself, Seth drove the rest of the way humming under his breath. After a few turns, they found street parking across from the park. Tara stepped out of the car and shielded her eyes from the sun with her hand. The green of the grass and the bright primary-colored play equipment sparkled vividly beneath the spring sunshine. A contented smile lifted the corners of her mouth.

"Okay," he said, grabbing a huge picnic basket and a blue gingham blanket from the trunk. "Let's go pick a spot."

"This way. I'll take you to my favorite spot." She led him toward a tall tree with long, outstretched branches full of leaves. The tree had been around as long as she could remember, like an old friend, strong and steadfast. "I like to come here to read sometimes. It's quiet, and away from the main bustle of the park."

"Nice." Seth placed the blanket on the edge of the branch's reach half in sunlight and half in shade. "In case you got too cold in the shade, or too hot in the sun."

"Thank you." Tara soaked up his considerate gesture like a cactus planted in cracked earth, enjoying its first taste of rain.

"You're welcome," he said, his voice warm and his smile endearing. As their gazes met and held, heat swirled in the air between them.

"That thing is huge. Did you pack a dining room table in there?" Tara broke eye contact before she melted into goo, and got on her knees to peek inside the basket. "What did you bring?"

"Nothing much. I might've gone overboard with the jumbo-sized basket. I've never packed a picnic before," he said as he set out containers of sandwiches, brightly colored fruit salad, plates, and utensils followed by at least seven kinds of desserts.

"You call this nothing much? It looks like you've cleaned out

Comfort Zone and a poor, unsuspecting deli. Who's going to eat all those sandwiches?"

"No need to worry. I have a hollow leg for extra food storage, and you don't seem to be a lightweight either. I've seen you tuck away plate after plate of food."

"How rude. One does not talk about a lady's appetite." She held her offended expression for exactly half a second before giving into her smile. "Of course, you're right. And those look like BLTs. I'll be having about five of those. Thank you very much."

Seth paused setting the picnic to look at her appreciatively, and her heart did a loopy dance. He looked so handsome sitting there, setting out loads of delicious food for her. What could be better?

"I brought some sparkling cider and lemonade. I figured we can't drink in a public park, but we won't miss out on the fancy bubbles."

"Seriously, where did you get all of this? Doesn't look like anything I've seen at the delis in Weldon."

"Because it came from my kitchen. I *can* make a sandwich."

"It looks fantastic. I'm pretty impressed." She gave him a playful shove on his shoulder. "I guess this is my first taste of a date with Seth Kim."

"Only the first. There's plenty more to taste," he said in a low, delicious voice.

Tara's pants caught on fire. But she doused it with her icy cold will. If she was going to survive four dates with Seth, she couldn't let her attraction loose. She had a feeling that it would be insatiable.

"Neat. Can we eat?" she said in as casual a voice as she could manage.

"Yes, please." He handed her a plate with a half triangle of BLT and a scoop of lovely fruit salad. She picked up the sandwich and took a bite. The hint of nervousness on Seth's face made her heart go squishy. She had to remind herself a squishy heart was also not acceptable as part of the dare. *Remember to keep it casual.*

"This is literally the best BLT I've ever had," she gushed, taking another bite. The salty, savory bacon was abundant and crunchy without being tough. With the crisp lettuce, juicy tomato, and just the right amount of creamy mayo, the sandwich was heaven between sliced bread. "I guess the Kim brothers have a knack in the kitchen."

"Not in the least. Landon's the cook. Sandwiches are about the only thing that I can make, and throwing together a fruit salad isn't exactly cooking. I got fresh fruit, chopped them up, and tossed them together. I can't take credit for it tasting good."

"No way. Is this seriously happening? Am I truly witnessing Seth Kim being humble?"

"I'm being completely honest *and* feeding you. The least you can do is not insult me with your mouth full." Seth nudged her outstretched leg with his foot.

That little touch of his big toe meeting her calf felt like a heat pack being pressed against her skin. Trying not to be obvious, Tara stretched out her foot to nudge him back. Seth dodged her with a smirk.

"I am *not* insulting you," she insisted. "I really think humility is a good look on you."

Being a little sneakier this time, she successfully made contact with his calf. Her foot rejoiced. *Wow.* Was every part of his body as rock hard as what she'd just felt? Inquiring girl parts wanted to know.

"Was that a compliment?" Seth widened his eyes to cherub-level wonder. "I didn't even perceive it as such since it's so impossibly rare from you . . . like unicorns."

This time she went for a lightning-fast kick to his shin, her full plate bobbing on her thighs. But Seth moved quicker. He stopped her attack within inches from his shin with a strong grip on her ankle. She squealed and jerked reflexively. His hand felt like a molten iron clamp.

"Lemme go." She wiggled against his grasp. "You almost made me spill my food."

"*I* almost made you? You're the one who tried to kick me."

"Okay. Okay. I promise not to kick you if you let me go."

"Should I trust you?"

"Only someone gullible would trust me right now." In the same motion, she put aside her plate and delivered a playful kick to his biceps with her other leg. Startled, he let go of her ankle to block any further attacks. She didn't attack physically but couldn't resist one last jab. "See, gullible."

Pushing away his food, he lunged for her, pressing her torso into the soft blanket-covered grass. "I've learned my lesson."

He held her hands over her head, and she felt as though she'd had the wind knocked out her. Her heartbeat ratcheted up to a fast jog as awareness seeped into her veins like warm honey. All she had to do was lift her head off the ground a few inches to test whether his lips were as soft and plush as they looked. His gorgeous face was only a hand span away from hers, and he smelled like . . . pineapple and bacon. Her stomach growled.

"I'm hungry," she said breathlessly.

"So am I," he said in a low growl.

Her stomach growled more insistently this time. It was the perfect excuse to get out of a dangerously tempting position. "For food. I'm hungry for food."

Blinking rapidly, Seth released her wrists and helped her sit up. "Yeah. I meant for food as well."

She smiled slyly, preening with feminine pride. "You should eat something quick. You look like you're about to pass out from . . . hunger."

Without responding, he grabbed a triangle of BLT from the box and ate it in two bites. He was embarrassed. How sweet was that? Feeling content, Tara bit into her sandwich and glanced around the park. The green grass seemed to stretch on forever from their spot underneath the tree, and the blue sky looked almost within reach. She ate in easy silence, soaking up the moment. But in a few minutes, a gaggle of children's voices drowned the silence.

"School must be out early today," Tara said, watching a half dozen kids racing toward a tree near their picnic spot.

"Should we take cover?" Seth asked.

"Why? Are you afraid of little children?"

"Not afraid. I just don't know what to do with them."

"Well, you won't need to do anything with them," she reassured him. "Their moms are over there watching them."

Her heart dropped when she saw an acquaintance among the group of moms. Tara waved casually at her to avoid looking like she'd been caught doing something wrong. The woman waved back, saying something out of the corner of her mouth to one of the other moms. The pair looked toward them with obvious curiosity. Of all days . . . She never ran into anyone she knew here.

"Someone you know?" Seth asked, glancing over. "Are you sure we don't need to take cover?"

Tara laughed, her anxiety easing after the initial panic. "We don't really hang out in the same crowd, so I'm not too worried about her spotting us together. Besides, a picnic is hardly gossip-worthy."

"Good to know," he said. "Ready for dessert?"

"Which one? There are so many to pick from." In the guise of looking over the desserts, Tara scooted back to create more space between them. Although she wasn't overly worried, there was no harm in being extra careful.

"Why do you have to pick?" Seth grinned at her, eyes twinkling. "Just eat a few bites of every single one. I promise you there won't be any leftovers."

"I like the way you think." She rubbed her hands together, eyeing the desserts with renewed greed. "Why eat just one when you can eat them all?"

"Exactly." He methodically opened all the containers and lined them up in front of her. "Go for it."

Tara went for the slice of black-sesame and white-chocolate cake. The nuttiness and mild bitterness of the black sesames and the smooth sweetness of the white chocolate was a match made in heaven. The thick, dark cream, the soft white mousse, and the moistest genoise cake filled her mouth with incredible texture and a tornado of flavors. She'd eaten at least twelve dozen of them, but she still couldn't stop the whimpering moan that escaped her lips.

Her eyes had involuntarily slid shut. When she opened them, Seth was staring at her with such heat in his eyes that she stopped breathing. "You . . . you want a bite?"

"Yes."

That was the single hottest word she'd ever heard, and she was certain it wasn't the cake that he wanted a bite of. She wanted to jump him. Just literally straddle his lap and kiss the living daylights out of him. But she couldn't give into the temptation, especially with an audience nearby. Instead, she scooped up some cake on her fork and extended it to him, thinking it would be harmless. Seth leaned forward, wrapped his lips around her fork, and claimed the delectable morsel. He licked a speck of snowy confectioner's sugar from the corner of his mouth. Her lips parted and she forgot where they were. She wanted to flick aside his tongue so she could lick the sugar away instead.

He chewed and moaned much like she had, and warmth pooled at her center. She realized Aubrey named the cake Cloud Nine for this reason. It was foodgasmic.

She didn't know what she was doing. She certainly hadn't ordered her torso to stretch and lean toward Seth. When he moved to meet her in the middle, the lust in her veins sang *Hallelujah*.

Their lips were only inches apart, and she could feel his breath against her lips. The kiss that would quench her thirst was so close that her mouth watered. Their breath quickened in harmony, their inhale and exhale mingling and blending.

"Oof," he suddenly grunted, spinning away from her.

What the hell? Where was her kiss? Tara sat up when Seth scrambled to his feet and retrieved a soccer ball by their picnic blanket.

"My friend accidentally kicked the ball over here." A girl with corn-silk hair ran up to them, holding her hands out for the ball. "He's sorry, but he's too scared to come over himself."

"That's okay. It was an accident." Seth's expression smoothed into a gentle smile as he handed the ball to her. "It's very brave of you to come over to apologize for your friend."

"Thank you." With a wave she bounded away to her waiting friends.

Tara was much more annoyed than Seth that the rude soccer ball interrupted their kiss. The disappointment was brutal, and she was tempted to stab the ball with her fork to deflate it. Then it hit her. They'd almost kissed. *Holy heck.* A picnic could be brushed aside, but a kiss would provide enough fodder for town gossip. She went limp with relief that they were interrupted.

Even after the close call, watching Seth interact with the little girl so sweetly made her heart melt, making her want to flutter her lashes and moon over him. *Ugh.* She wished she could rub some dirt on herself and be rid of the warm and fuzzy feels. She was never this emotional. She blamed the lingering effects of Aubrey's wedding for her uncharacteristic sentimentality. Weddings were definitely going on her allergic-to list along with haikus and rainbows on rainy days.

Everything about their date so far was unexpected. He wasn't what she'd expected. He was kind, considerate, and endearing. The version of Seth in her mind was cocky, superficial, and entertaining. He was still cocky and entertaining, but superficial just didn't fit with her impression of him today.

The girl with the pale gold hair ran back to them and said in a breathless voice, "We need a prince."

"A prince?" Tara said, arching an eyebrow. Did she mean Seth? He did make a rather swoony fairy-tale prince. But the bigger question was whether Tara was willing to share. "What for?"

"To rescue, of course," the girl said with a *duh* expression. "None of the boys want to play the prince who's locked up in the tower. Now we have no one to rescue. Then what are we princesses supposed to do? Sit and wait for some clueless prince to come rescue us? No, thank you."

Seth pulled his eyebrows down to hide his grin and said in a serious voice, "Well, I'd be honored. I would love to be rescued by a beautiful princess."

The girl blushed and twirled a piece of her hair. *Gee, even a seven-year-old wasn't immune to his charms.*

"I'm Gwen by the way," she said by way of introduction.

"I'm Seth, and this is Tara."

"Okay. Come with me." Gwen grabbed Seth's hand and tugged

him to his feet. "I need you to climb up that tree and sit on one of the branches."

"Wait. What about Tara?"

"Yeah. What about me?" Tara asked. "Can I be a princess, too? I'll help you girls rescue the prince."

"No, we already have too many princesses." Gwen gave Tara a once-over. "I guess you can be the dragon that's holding the prince hostage."

"I like the sound of that." Seth's eyes twinkled with humor. "I think she'll make an excellent lady dragon."

"Meh," the girl said, drawing a huff of affronted laughter from the lady dragon. Tara obviously hadn't won over the little date crasher with her wit and charm. And she couldn't help noticing that Gwen still held tightly onto Seth's hand. "She'll be okay, I guess."

"Thanks?" Tara said as she bemusedly tagged along with the hand-holding couple leading the way.

Once she cut it out with the ridiculous possessiveness, her heart started puddling again. Seth was so wrong about not knowing what to do with children. He was fantastic with them, and it was so sweet of him to play the prince-in-distress for them.

"Sorry about the interruption," he said close to her ear. He'd broken away from the circle of children and came to stand next to her. "I'm sure they'll tire of us soon and let us return to our picnic."

"So you don't know what to do with children, huh?" She bumped her shoulder against his biceps, and he bumped her back.

"Gwen was sweet enough to let me join her group. I really didn't do anything."

Tara sighed. He was endearing her to death. "Well, here she comes to lock you up in your tower. Good luck."

"Are you going to let the princesses rescue me?" He tucked his chin and looked at her through his lashes.

The look alone could charm the pants off anyone within a mile radius. *I will fight off every single one of these adorable girls if you keep looking at me like that.* "Lady Dragon will do as she pleases."

With one last devastating smile, Seth was escorted to the tree where he would be imprisoned. Tara trailed after them again, guessing she needed to be stationed there as well to play the evil dragon. She had to admit, she was feeling the part.

He climbed the thick-trunked tree—aware that he was trying to impress Tara like a dumbass—and settled down on a sturdy branch hanging a few feet above the ground.

The rules of the game stated that the princess who defeated the lady dragon and her gremlin minions, played by the boys who refused to be the incarcerated prince, would win their happily ever after with the prince.

The game seemed like flag football with a fantasy theme at first. Then it evolved into something like freeze tag. The children wore belts with flags hanging off of them and chased each other around screaming murder. The gremlins roared and aggressively held their defensive positions, but when the ferocious princesses rained their wrath on them, they faltered.

The best thing about the game was that the battle raged a few feet away from the tree, and the prince could flirt with the lady dragon. Tara stood with her arms across her chest, leaning against the tree trunk, and watched the children with a gentle curve of her lips. She was nothing short of breathtaking.

"Do you think you'll have a change of heart and let me free?" he asked in a low voice.

"The question is, does Lady Dragon have a beating heart or one made of hard, jagged stone?" Her expression transformed into something mischievous and saucy that made his stomach fall and slam back into place.

"Would Lady Dragon turn into a beautiful princess if the prince kisses her?"

"Maybe the prince will turn into a dragon when she kisses him."

Seth wanted to jump down from his perch and kiss the hell out of his captor, whether he turned into a dragon or not. Tara came to stand below him and wrapped a hand around his calf, and he felt electricity jolt up his legs. He reached down and buried his hand into her long strands and tilted her head to meet his eyes.

"Come up here," he growled.

"Now you're commanding me?" she said imperiously, while color suffused her cheeks. "How dare you, trifling human?"

"I'm coming down." Releasing her hair, he swung one leg over the branch.

"No, you're not," she said, looking over her shoulder. "We have eyes on us, remember?"

"We're getting out of town for our second date," he said darkly, glaring at her for being unfairly beautiful. She blushed and opened her mouth, but whatever was on the tip of her tongue didn't get a chance to roll off.

"Ahh!" Gwen screeched, running toward them. "The dragon has put a spell on the prince. She's trying to eat him."

Tara snorted but turned to face the girl with a scowl on her face. "You dare disturb me? I will fly away with the prince. Leave me in peace."

She then stuck her arms out and flapped them around like great, sweeping wings and chased the little princesses around. They scattered, giggling and screaming. The gremlins forgot which side they were on and chased Tara around, approaching her as close as they dared and then retreating. Despite their standoffish attitude toward the evil dragon in the beginning, the kids clamored to her for more.

In the end, the kids went off for some snacks and juice. They forgot about the prince locked away in the tower altogether. Seth jumped down from the branch and strode over to Tara. She met him halfway, her face infused with pink after all the running around.

"So you defeated all my rescuers, huh?"

"They never had a chance." She smirked. "Besides, why should the princesses always get the prince? Dragons deserve happily ever afters, too."

"You're absolutely right," he said, taking a step closer to her. Seeing Tara like this made something in his heart clench tight, and he liked it. "Well, are you going to claim your prize?"

"My prize?" She widened her eyes much too innocently. "Oh, you mean the rest of our dessert. First one to the blanket gets to eat it all."

She took off before he could respond. Her long legs carried her quickly across the grass, and Seth barely caught up with her. He tackled her and dragged her down with him, landing on his back to break her fall.

"We have a tie," he said when she lifted her face from his shoulder. "We're going to share our dessert like civilized people."

"Are you sure about that?" Her triumphant grin had him twisting his torso to see where her outstretched arm went. Her index finger was poking into the picnic blanket. "Ha! I won. It's all mine."

He lay back down on the grass in defeat, but Tara didn't get off him right away. She smiled down at him for a moment before lowering her head to plant a kiss on his cheek. He nearly swallowed his own tongue. Weren't they supposed to appear platonic? *To hell with platonic.* He felt the caveman in him rise, and his fingers dug into her waist. Their eyes met, and their breath quickened. He lifted his head off the ground, and Tara lowered hers, her silky hair forming a curtain to one side.

"You guys. You guys." Gwen's clear, ringing voice interrupted them once more. *Dammit.* What happened to his alone time with Tara? "My mom says we have to go now. Thanks for being the prince, Seth, even though you really didn't do much other than sit on a tree branch. But, Tara, you were such an awesome dragon. I want to be a ferocious dragon next time. It'll be so cool."

"We had fun, too." Tara smiled warmly at the little girl.

"It was great meeting you," Seth said sincerely. She and her friends were too adorable. "Sorry I wasn't more interesting, locked away in the tree. Next time, I'll recite a poem or something."

"You're silly." Gwen giggled into her hand. "I have to go now. You could go back to kissing or whatever."

Belatedly, Seth realized he was still holding Tara firmly by the waist as she lay on top of him. Not that he minded. They should listen to Gwen and go back to kissing or whatever. But as anticipated, the moment was over and Tara scrambled off him and dusted imaginary grass off her leggings.

Needing a moment to gather himself, Seth sat down on the picnic blanket and set out the desserts for Tara. "You won fair and square, so here's your bounty."

"I'm not a total monster," she said, settling down across from him. "I'll let you have one bite."

"That's all right. I'm happy to watch you eat all the dessert," he said in a low, teasing voice. "Just remember to do it slowly."

"Shush for a minute. This is going to be fun." Tara rolled her eyes, but color blossomed on her cheeks. "There's this Korean food-fighter show where one contestant doesn't get to eat with the rest of his friends. But as he watches them eat delectable, mouthwatering entrée after entrée, he can choose to ask for one bite. Only one. Basically, he piles up a spoon with all the food he can fit on it, and shoves the giant spoonful into his mouth all at once. You'd be amazed how much food can be piled onto a spoon. Anyway, that's my offer. The one bite chance."

"That does sound fun." He grinned widely. Watching her lick and moan her way through all the desserts was tempting, but a bite of dessert was always welcome. He had his eyes on the brownie with salted caramel. "I'm game."

With a smile that lit up her face, Tara opened the container that held her first choice, Japanese cheesecake with a hint of yuzu. She tucked in fluffy morsel after fluffy morsel of the moist, light-as-air cheesecake with ecstasy on her face. His mouth watered with hunger and lust. She then moved on to her next indulgence, chestnut mousse cake.

"This is so good," she moaned. "Man, you're really missing out. You sure you don't want one bite?"

"No, thanks. I'm not that tempted." He was tempted. He wanted to bury his tongue in her mouth and taste the sweet nuttiness she held within.

"Your loss." Humming happily, she demolished dessert number 2.

She finally moved on to her third dessert, the salted caramel brownie. His absolute favorite. But he couldn't just watch this time.

He was so turned on, he couldn't sit still. With the children and their moms gone, they had this side of the park to themselves. It should be safe to have their date be more date-like.

"Let's change up the game a little." He looked at her with hooded lids, not bothering to hide his desire. "This time, I get to feed you."

"What? I'm—"

She stopped protesting when he plopped a forkful of brownie right into her open mouth. She tried giving him a narrowed-eye look, but once she chewed and the brownie melted in her mouth, her eyes slid closed.

Tara accepted the next mouthful eagerly. The air had stilled like a vacuum around them, and their breaths grew shallow. Every bite he fed her was exquisite torture, but he craved for more. Finally, he couldn't hold back a second longer, so instead of feeding her another forkful, he said, "One bite."

Before she could respond, he pressed his mouth against hers. The first touch was feather light, tentative. When she didn't pull away, he licked her bottom lip and was gratified by the parting of her lips. Like a man starved, he dipped his tongue into her mouth and found it to be a heavenly place of heat, flavored with rich chocolate and buttery caramel.

He moaned helplessly, never wanting his one bite to end. The tip of her tongue teased his, and her hands lifted to fist around his T-shirt, tugging him closer. He growled and pulled her onto his lap, splaying his hands on her back. When she whimpered and wrapped her legs tightly around his waist, his eyes nearly rolled back into his head. He'd imagined kissing her countless times, but this topped them all. It was almost too much.

This time there was no ball to interrupt them, but his annoyingly reasonable brain interrupted his lust-fogged thoughts. *We're in the middle of a park with nothing to shield us from view.* If he kissed her any longer, he might lose his mind and rip her shirt off.

He managed to tear his lips away from hers. "Tara."

She whimpered and fidgeted on his lap. He was beyond tempted to shut his brain down, so he could take her right there. And get them arrested. He placed a lingering kiss on the line of her jaw, then behind her ear, then finally on her forehead.

"If you keep kissing me like that, I'm going to take you in the middle of a park," he murmured against her skin, not quite ready to stop touching her.

"Holy shit." Tara practically jumped off his lap, her cheeks stained deep red, and scrambled away on her hands and feet. As aroused as he was, he couldn't ignore her resemblance to a crab. He held on to that image, trying to put the brakes on the launch sequence.

"I know." He raked his fingers through his hair. "It seems we're dabbling in some dangerous magic."

"Right? Caution: No kissing in public. Might rip each other's clothes off." She laughed shyly as she fanned her face with her hands.

"You're killing me. You know that?" he choked out, vividly imagining ripping her clothes off.

"No. You're not there, yet. You'll know when I'm trying to kill you," she promised, biting her bottom lip. He was doing it. He was going to jump her in the park. Then a slow smile spread across her face. "Softly. With my words."

"God. That's horrible," Seth said, laughing so hard he had to clutch his side to breathe. "You're supremely talented at telling dad jokes for someone who isn't a dad."

"See. You're fine now." She flicked a glance at his jeans. "If you're decent, we should pack up and get going. I think our Save the Prince game ate up our riverside-walk time. I need to get home."

"Home?" He didn't want to part with her already.

What happened to his plan to have her all to himself? Well, he chose to share her with a bunch of adorable kiddos. How could he have said no to that? But in hindsight, he regretted his decision just a little. He wasn't ready to let Tara go.

"Yeah. I told my brother I was going out to run errands. I can't believe I didn't have a better excuse. Sorry." Her shoulders drooped. "There are only so many errands I could hypothetically run."

"Let's get you home then." At least, she wanted to stay longer with him, too.

He grabbed the nearest container and began cleaning up the remains of the picnic. As he'd predicted, they'd eaten up pretty much everything he'd packed. Tara joined in right away. Every accidental touch of her hand and a bump of her elbow sent electricity striking down his spine. From the way her eyes shot to meet his, she felt the same spark.

They worked silently and efficiently and loaded everything back into his car within minutes. The air in the car was charged as he drove her back home. He snuck a peek at her, but looked away blushing when their eyes met. *Christ.* He was acting like a love-sick kid.

"Can you pull up here? I'll walk the rest of the way," Tara said, a block away from her house.

"You're taking this sneaking-around business pretty seriously." He shifted the gear into park, and turned to face her.

"You better, too, if you don't want our next date to be dinner with my family." She unbuckled her seat belt. "Like you promised, I had fun today. Thank you for the lovely picnic."

"My absolute pleasure." He sat awkwardly for a second, wondering if it would be okay to kiss her again. But he remembered their kiss in the park and settled for a quick peck on her cheek. He wouldn't be able to handle anything more if the goal was to let her go home. "Bye."

"Bye." Tara placed a sweet lingering kiss on his cheek in return.

He clenched his fists, fighting the urge to pull her against him, and watched her get out of the car. Long after she disappeared from the rearview mirror, Seth exhaled and unclenched his hands. Then he reached over to crank up the AC.

If he wanted any chance of sleeping that night, he better hit the gym hard.

CHAPTER SIX

Tara tossed and turned all night, sleeping fitfully and dreaming of brownies. She woke up groggy and cranky the next morning, not at all certain what she was feeling.

Her phone chimed when she stepped out of her bathroom, wringing her hair with a towel. She adjusted the towel around her and checked to see who it was.

SETH: If you tell me you slept like a baby, I'm gonna have to take you down.

She laughed, her crankiness immediately relaxing its hold on her.

TARA: Let's just say I woke up craving brownies.
SETH: That brownie was the most delicious thing I'd ever tasted.

Heat flared to life in her vagina, and Tara checked to see if her towel had caught on fire. No arson attempt had been made on her person.

TARA: Are you in bed?

SETH: Yes.

She squeezed her thighs together.

TARA: Lazy. It's past eight. Get up.
SETH: Like I implied, I didn't fall asleep until four in the morning.
TARA: What are you wearing?
SETH: I thought you wanted me to get up?
TARA: I do. Get out of bed and tell me what you're wearing.
SETH: I don't wear anything to bed.

She needed another shower. A cold shower.

TARA: So you're naked? Right now?
SETH: Yes.

Why was she torturing herself like this?

SETH: Hello?
TARA: I'm here.
SETH: Your turn.
TARA: My turn what?
SETH: Tell me what you're wearing.

It was time to torture *him* a little.

TARA: A towel.
SETH: Is it a small towel? A tiny hand towel?
TARA: Oh, for heaven's sake. It's off. Happy now?
SETH: Fucking hell.

Delight raced across her bare skin. It felt so fantastic to be wanted by him.

TARA: Okay. I need to get dressed, and go to the brewery. Have a good rest of the morning.

The ellipses flickered and stopped. Flickered and stopped.

SETH: You, too.

Tara stepped out of her house with a smile on her face, and it stayed with her as she sped to work on her bike. She was going in early to start a new batch of ale. She'd always loved this part of her job, but sexting with Seth first thing in the morning added to her excellent mood.

Alex was already at the back, pouring the grist bill for their India Pale Ale into the mash tun.

"Hello, brother dear," she said with a wide smile on her face. "Let me get geared up and join you."

"Please do." He shook the bag over the tun, emptying out the last bit, then turned around to pin her with a quizzical look. "Why are you so chipper today? You're practically glowing."

"Because it's our brewing fun day," she replied, dialing back some of her cheer. She glanced sideways at Alex as she pulled on her rubber boots. She lived and worked with her brothers. They were way too attuned to her moods. Worse yet, they could always sniff out her bullshit.

"Sampling day is your über-happy day. You're disproportionately cheerful for brewing day."

"What? Are you telling me to dial down my happiness?" Tara

conjured an exaggerated injured look. "What kind of brother are you?"

"Sorry." Alex eyed her suspiciously but didn't continue his line of inquiry. "Be sampling day happy on brewing day. It's a free country."

She'd always been able to separate her dating life from her real life, but thoughts of Seth were crossing the line. His sweet, considerate side had punched a hole through her armor. What happened to the superficial playboy she'd signed up to date? And that kiss. After only one date, he was getting under her skin. Had she underestimated the effect he could have on her?

"Which grains should I bring?" she asked, scattering her inconvenient thoughts.

"The base malt is already in. We just need to mix our specialty malt."

"Well, this one's your recipe, so take the lead. I'll assist." They usually helped each other on brewing days—an extra pair of hands were always welcome—but the main brewer of the particular batch manned the helm. "Speaking of assisting, where's Jack?"

"It's accounting 'fun' day for him," Alex said, cringing in distaste. "I can't get used to how much he enjoys that part of the business."

"If it weren't for him, the brewery wouldn't be what it is today." Tara automatically defended Jack. "We're lucky to have his brilliant business mind on our side."

"I know that. But the word 'number' . . ." Alex shivered dramatically.

"Was derived from the word 'numb,' meaning the bringer of numbness," she rattled off in monotone. "And we must avoid brain numbness at all costs."

"You got it." He beamed at her like she was his star pupil. "Let's get on with the real fun part of the business."

They filled the mash tun with various bags of malt, working in companionable silence. And her mind wandered predictably to Seth. *I wonder what he's doing right now.* He couldn't possibly still be naked. But he was in her mind. He was taking photos naked. Building Landon's website naked. And having lunch naked.

Tara was in trouble. She was troubled. How could she be working with her older brother in the sacred duty of brewing while unsanitarily daydreaming about naked men? Well, in her defense, it was only one man.

Once the mash was lautering, she and Alex took a lunch break. While they ate their roast beef sandwiches on pretzel rolls—the spicy mustard gave it the perfect amount of zing—Tara fidgeted with her phone, turning on the screen every twenty seconds.

"Now you look all sullen. Brewing day really isn't as fun as sampling day, is it?" Alex said affectionately.

"It's not that. I . . . promised Aubrey that I'd help Seth with building Landon's restaurant website." Where the hell did that come from? And why hadn't she thought of it sooner? It gave her the perfect excuse to spend more time with Seth. "But we've been so busy lately, I feel like I've been neglecting my duties."

"I can handle the rest of the brewing if you want to go work on that until the pub opens."

"Really? That would be so great." Tara squished two bites' worth of sandwich into her mouth and washed it down with some root beer. "Thanks, Alex. I'll see you in a few hours."

"And there she goes like the wind," he said wryly.

She was full of shit. No one had asked her to help with the website, obviously. It was just an excuse to see Seth sooner than later. She didn't question why she wanted to see Seth badly enough to fabricate an excuse to do it. Their date had been fun, and she wanted more of it. Girls just wanna have fun and all that. No big deal.

It was just about one o'clock, and she pedaled her bike to Comfort Zone and parked it outside. Why was she so excited? It wasn't like her excuse allowed her to see Seth immediately. She needed some coffee and sweets to fuel her brain. She had to plan how she could offer Seth her help without seeming like she was desperate to spend more time with him. She walked into the busy bakery and seated herself at the counter. Justine and Lily were both in the back, but the new part-timer recognized her.

"Hi, Tara," she said brightly. "What can I get for you?"

"Can I just get a cup of Americano for now?" she asked, her thoughts elsewhere.

"Sure thing."

She took a big breath and pulled her cell out, but after a moment's hesitation, she put it down on the counter. She couldn't just text him. He didn't need to know how much she wanted to see him.

She stared down at her phone for a long while, both excited and uneasy about luring Seth out. There was a desperation there she remembered. The last person she'd felt that way about was her college boyfriend. Even though she'd seen Jason the day before, the hours had seemed to stretch miserably long until she'd gotten to see him again. Her heart had ached just like it did now as she waited for the next time she met Seth.

It was unacceptable for her to feel that way about him. About any man. Tara had learned her lesson the hard way about what lay that way. Such emotional vulnerability could open her up to the kind of hurt she never wanted to endure again. But this was different. She made a conscious effort to draw her shoulders away from her ears.

There was no need to panic. No harm could come of her seeing Seth. He was flying off to Paris in less than four weeks. Things couldn't possibly lead to a toxic relationship. She wouldn't let it.

The dating dare was all about fun and forgetting her woes. Seth had a way of making her feel seen, respected, and valued. The hollowness that had been eating away at her since Aubrey's wedding was receding, and she felt far less alone thanks to his entertaining ways. She simply enjoyed spending time with him. That was all. Nothing more.

"Tara, when did you come in?" Justine walked out of the kitchen wiping her hands on a pristine white towel that she tucked into her apron once she finished. "Why didn't you come back to say hi?"

"Oh, I knew you guys were busy with your afternoon bake. I didn't want to distract you." Tara got off her stool and went around to give Comfort Zone's sous-chef a big hug.

"Well, you're always welcome in the kitchen whether or not Aubrey is here. I miss her already, and it'll help if you came in to chat with us. Lily still barely talks." Justine laughed. "She would rather scowl or roll her eyes at my attempts at jokes."

"She probably misses Aubrey, too." Tara missed her best friend like a toddler missed her binky. "Why don't you stop by the brewery tonight. We can catch up."

"I'd love to." The lovely baker's smile widened. "Can I get anything for you?"

The salted caramel brownie was the first dessert to pop into Tara's mind, and she blushed furiously. No. She wasn't going to order that, or else she would be daydreaming about their kiss for as long as the taste of the brownies stayed in her mouth. She needed to plan, not daydream. "I'll have two . . . no, three . . . cherry-almond cookies."

"I have a fresh batch coming out in five minutes. I'll bring it over when it's ready." Justine winked at her.

"Ooh." She rubbed her hands together in anticipation. "I'm going to snag that corner booth."

Just then the part-timer returned with a steaming mug of Americano and Tara carried it with her to the cozy diner-style booth. She planned on hunkering down for a while to iron out her plan, and the booth was much more comfortable. Her eyes slid shut with her first sip of coffee. The warm aromatic brew wrapped her in a comforting hug.

"Tara." Seth's voice appeared from somewhere over her head. Was she imagining things now? She slowly turned to find a tall gorgeous man with windswept hair standing by her booth, grinning at her as though she was a surprise birthday present. "This must be my lucky day."

"What are you doing here?" Her heart squeezed tightly as though the burst of joy at seeing him was too much for her. It was all she could do not to throw her arms around his neck and hug him. It was disconcerting as hell.

"The contractors put in the bar this morning, and I wanted a little break from the wood dust." Then he pointed to the laptop case he held in one hand. "And I really need to work on the restaurant's website."

How was this happening? Her chance to offer him her help just fell onto her lap. Hiding her glee, she asked casually, "How's that going?"

"It's going," he said a bit glumly. "I've been more focused on getting the photographs ready."

Time to make her move. "Did Aubrey mention that I have a degree in graphic design?"

"Do you, now? Well, isn't that handy." His eyes lit up. "Are you volunteering to help me on Landon's website?"

"Actually, Aubrey asked me to help out if I can. I've just been so busy." She was lying through her teeth, but this was about saving face. He mustn't know how much she wanted to spend time with him.

"I would love it if you could lend a hand," he said with puppy-dog eyes as if she'd say no.

"Well, you're in luck. I have some time before I need to go back to the brewery."

"Oh, thank God." His shoulders sagged in relief. "I really appreciate your help."

Muahahahaha. She had him.

But her excitement turned to self-consciousness when he slid into her side of the booth and stopped a hand's width away from her. She only had to shift her leg a tiny bit for her thigh to press against his. The bakery turned sweltering hot.

"Um. Wouldn't you be more comfortable on the other side of the booth?" She cursed her pale skin as heat spread on her face.

"No, I'm perfectly comfortable here," he said with a knowing grin.

Damn him. She caved and inched away from the warmth of his body, mumbling something about personal space.

"I need to sit beside you so we can share my laptop," he explained, his eyes still sparkling with humor.

"You're right. This is much more practical," Tara agreed in a no-nonsense voice. She refused to let him see how much she wanted to jump on his lap and call him Santa baby.

Shit. I need my head examined.

S eth failed to mention that he came to Comfort Zone on the off chance that Tara might be there. There was no need to weird her out. He hadn't been able to stop thinking about her all day. So he'd packed up his laptop and come to the bakery with the intent of camping out as long as he could. That sounded desperate even to his own ears.

But he wasn't really desperate. He just wanted to spend more time with her, because he'd had such a good time when they hung out. With her to distract him, he wouldn't be impatiently counting down the days until he could finally go to Paris. That was why he'd celebrated with a mental fist pump when she offered to help him with the website.

Sitting so close to her with her tantalizing scent assailing his senses was delicious torture. He wanted to do so much more than sit demurely next to her. Though she didn't act like it, he would like to think that she was as affected by their proximity as he was. Or were her cheeks always so rosy? He couldn't take his eyes off of her. The curl of her long lashes, the tip of her pert nose, and the lower lip snagged by her teeth as she peered into the laptop screen. Poor lower lip. He should lick it better.

"You really meant what you said about focusing on the photographs." She glanced sideways at him. "You've basically registered the domain name and created a landing page."

"We still have close to a month left. I thought it important to have all the content well prepared before I started," he said. "Plus, I was procrastinating."

Tara snorted. "Lazy ass."

Before he could respond, Justine came to their booth and placed a plate of fresh-baked cherry-almond cookies on the table.

"Hey, Seth," the baker said with a welcoming smile.

"He's here . . . that is . . . with me . . . so we could work on Landon's website together," Tara blurted, looking like her teacher caught her drawing a caricature of him. "I have a degree in graphic design."

"Okay. Cool." Justine smiled at Tara and turned back to Seth. He straightened his features to hide his amusement. "Don't tell me you already finished all those goodies you picked up yesterday."

"We did finish it all," he said. Tara kicked him in the ankle. "I mean, *I* finished it all. You know I can't get enough of Comfort Zone's desserts."

"I don't know where you put it all, but I'm glad we have such a loyal customer." Justine looked askance at Tara. "Are you sure this will be enough? I don't think he'll leave you any."

"Don't worry. I can hold my own," Tara said, pretending to size him up. To better accommodate her perusal, he opened up his chest and flexed subtly. "*Nobody* messes with my dessert. Not even Cookie Monster here."

"As she just made clear, those are *her* cookies." Seth watched Tara tug the plate of cookies closer to her. He wanted to kiss the adorable woman right then and there. "I'll take a half-dozen brownie cookies."

When Justine walked back into the kitchen, he turned to face Tara. "What? No salted caramel brownie?"

To his satisfaction, Tara blushed to the top of her roots. And her eyes dropped to his lips and stayed there. Oh, she remembered the kiss all right. His heart pumped at his own memory, and his blood rushed south.

"It was a bit too sweet for my taste." Tara paused and met his gaze. "I like a little more . . . bite."

It was Seth's turn to blush. He was so fucking turned on. If she wanted a bite, he could give her a bite. In fact, he wanted to bite her plush lips and earlobes and scrape his tongue across . . . He needed to get a grip. Jumping on her at Comfort Zone would be equivalent to making a town-wide announcement that the two of them were dating.

He cleared his throat and stared hard at the computer screen. "Where do you want to start?"

"The beginning, obviously." Tara let him change the subject, probably putting a tally mark by her name on the scoreboard. "What were you picturing for the website? Do you have a theme for it?"

"It'll be easier if I showed you some of the pictures I took." Seth turned the laptop toward him and opened up the photo album for the restaurant. "This is one of the pictures I took today. I wanted to capture the warm, welcoming air of the restaurant without giving it a blurry, rounded-out look. It was important to keep the photo sharp and focused like life heightened. The website symbolizes Landon's dream but shouldn't have a dreamy affect. I want his dream to feel real and alive."

"Wow. These are amazing, Seth. And the restaurant is coming along so beautifully. Oh, I love the new floors." Tara continued scrolling through his pictures, and his chest puffed out with pride. It felt damn good to have her compliment his work. Why did everything she did feel so . . . extra? "I'm getting a feel for what you're saying. You show the restaurant in its best light. It doesn't have a sleepy feeling. Instead, it pops and feels edgy through your lens, and that's what the website should look like."

"You got it on the nose. We make a good team." He reached over and took a sip of her coffee. "Mmm. I love Americano."

"Hey, get your own." When he set the mug down in front of her, she wrapped both her hands around it and gave him a sideways glare.

"I already had three cups of coffee today. I need to slow down a bit."

"Fine, we can share," she said with a calculating look. "But I get one of your brownie cookies."

"*I* have no problem sharing." He leaned in close and said, "You're the one who hogged the desserts yesterday."

"I didn't hog anything," she said haughtily. "I won fair and square."

"You call that fair and square? You got a head start."

"And your legs are longer."

"I guess I shouldn't complain," he relented, and changed tactics. "You did give me one bite of the brownie."

"Would you please stop talking about the brownie?" She looked around the bakery as though someone might be listening.

"Why are you so nervous? Who here would understand what that bite of brownie means?"

"What does it mean? Do explain."

"For a start, it was the best damn first kiss I ever had," he said earnestly. "Don't you dare deny it."

"Agreed. And?"

"I know I'm leaving the country soon, but this attraction between us is extraordinary. We can't keep fighting it."

"Can't or won't? Wouldn't giving in to our attraction complicate things for us? With Aubrey and Landon in our lives, can you be certain that we'll be able to see each other again without it being weird?"

"We're adults, Tara. We both know what we're going into, so there won't be any hurt feelings. We'll be able to remain friends. I won't make it weird. I promise."

Tara stared at him for a long moment before she shook her head. "Why are we even talking about this right now? We're supposed to be working on this website."

"Wait." Seth sat up as a sudden thought occurred to him. "Does this count as a date? If you're counting this as a date, I'm leaving right now. I never agreed to a working date."

"Seriously?" Her wide eyes looked too innocent. "We're sharing a cup of coffee and having dessert together. It sounds like a date to me."

"This is not a date. Coffee and dessert aside. We need to have a meal together for it to be a date. That's the rule."

"You're making that up."

"It was my dare, so I get to make up the rules." He didn't mind one bit that he came across as supremely immature.

"Fine. This isn't a date." Tara rolled her eyes. "Keep your pants on."

"Is that your rule?" he teased, lightly bumping her with his shoulder. "I have to keep my pants on when we're not on a date?"

"You are so immature." Fighting a smile, she turned her attention back to the photographs. "How can someone so childish create such beautiful things?"

His heart thundered in his chest. As a kid, he'd always worn his heart on his sleeve and put his everything into his art. He chose photography as his profession because it put a barrier between his art and what the world saw. Unlike his art, photographs filtered out most of his inner self. But something in Tara's voice told him that she was seeing more than he meant for her to see.

"The setting itself is beautiful. All I did was capture it," he said warily.

Tara kept scrolling through the photos and Seth belatedly remembered the photos he'd taken of the light—when the light and shadow danced to create a small window into another place. He'd been tempted to place them into a separate folder, but he hadn't wanted to admit that they were special to him. Because they weren't. They were just some pictures that he'd enjoyed taking as a photographer. Pictures of the restaurant, which belonged in the restaurant folder.

But now, as Tara drew closer to them, Seth had the urge to snatch the laptop away from her. Despite his effort to minimize their significance, he had to face the fact that they were more than just pictures to him. And he didn't want to hear her laugh at his pictures of wood dust. *Goddammit.* He was overreacting. He'd just played with the light a bit. That was it. They were nothing.

A sharp gasp from Tara ripped him out of his anxious musings. Her lips were slightly parted and her eyes were wide with wonder. With trepidation, he lowered his gaze to the screen to find the first photo of the enchanted light he'd captured.

"Seth," she whispered, her voice so soft that he could hardly hear her. "This is . . . What is this?"

"It's nothing." His heart plummeted as he prepared for her laughter. He reached for the laptop and tried to shut it closed, but Tara pushed his hands aside and blocked the laptop with her shoulders.

"Hey, stop that," she said, her eyes never leaving the screen.

As he sat beside her, the blood draining from his face, she scrolled through more of his photos from that day.

"Seth," she said again, clutching at the front of her shirt. "These are . . . They're alive."

Something fierce burst into life inside of him. She didn't laugh. Her surprise . . . her awe. It wasn't because she thought his work was ridiculous. She liked it.

"It . . . I . . . sometimes . . . something comes over me," he said in a low, halting voice. "It feels as though I'm transported to another place. Maybe a different dimension. Everything around me changes but is the same. It just becomes filled to the brim with life and beauty. My camera captures the other world, and that's why those photos look . . . different."

What the hell was he going on about? Even he could tell how

odd that might sound to someone. His heart thundering, he slowly turned his gaze to Tara. She was staring at him with admiration and wonder in her eyes.

"I've seen your work. Your fashion magazine photos. They are so vibrant and full of life, and they always convey what you want to say through them. I'm no professional, but even I could tell that you have talent," she said, not breaking eye contact. She was so close. Sometime during their struggle with the laptop, Tara had gotten closer to him, her leg and hip pressed against him. Her warmth and her scent assailed his senses, but he could only listen to her words. "But these . . . these are more than just pictures snapped by a talented photographer. They touch my soul and steal my breath. They're works of art."

He wanted to kiss her. He wanted to taste those precious words, not just hear them. His veins pumped with an inexplicable emotion, too hot and sharp for his body to contain. Was it joy? Was it lust? Maybe a combination of both, but it intensified to the point where his nerves lit up. He clenched his fists until his knuckles turned pale, his bones pushing against his skin. He couldn't kiss her now.

But it was too much. It was the first time since his one-and-only exhibit that he'd shared a part of his art with anyone. These photos were mere shadows of what he wanted to do with them. They were the barest outline. Still, he'd shown her a part of himself that he'd guarded with his very being.

"Come with me." He hardly recognized his own voice. It was so low it rumbled in his chest.

"What? Where?" she said. He shifted to the edge of the booth and took ahold of Tara's hand. "Wait. Our stuff—"

"Leave them. We won't be long."

Tara tugged her hand free but followed him closely. Once outside, Seth grasped her hand again, and moved quickly to the alleyway behind Comfort Zone. He stood close to her but shoved his hands into his pockets so he wouldn't grab her.

"Please. I need to kiss you," he rasped. His whole body was on fire, and his mind screamed just one word. "Tara."

She placed her hands on his shoulders and pushed herself up on her toes. That was all the answer he needed. He backed her against the wall and planted both his palms above her head, and crushed his mouth against hers. A sound between a moan and a groan tore from him.

She tasted so good—like cherries and coffee. He used his tongue to lick her softly parted lips, coaxing her to open wider. She tilted her head to give him full access. *God.* He delved into her, soaking up the wet warmth of her mouth and the sweet sound of her moans. He pressed his body against hers, letting her feel the extent of his arousal. She made a throaty sound of approval and ground her hips against him. He hissed against her mouth, rational thought a thing of the past.

When her hands snuck under his shirt to roam over his chest and stomach, he jerked helplessly against her touch. He smoothed his hand down her arm, then cupped the fullness of her breast. She pushed herself against his palm, asking for more. He brushed his thumb over her peak, and she mewled. She actually fucking mewled like a fucking kitten.

His hand slid down her thigh, and he brought her leg around his waist and pressed his hardness into her center. It was only when she cried out that he remembered they were hiding behind his sister-in-law's bakery, and someone could lumber down the alleyway at any moment. *Shit.* He was so close to taking her against the wall after promising her that he would keep their relationship a secret.

"We need to stop," he said, tearing his lips away from Tara.

She growled and pulled him back, and he kissed her helplessly for a few desperate seconds, then lifted his head again. When she finally opened her eyes to look at him in a haze of desire and confusion, it took all of his willpower to step back from her.

"If we're still keeping our dates a secret, I shouldn't take you against the wall in an alleyway," he said as he fought for breath.

Tara's eyes widened with something like alarm, but when she blinked, it was gone. It was with a measured albeit winded voice that she said, "Dammit. I can't believe I forgot what happened the last time we kissed in the park. I shouldn't have kissed you."

"I kissed you. I dragged you out here with the single-minded intention to kiss you."

"You think I didn't know that?" Tara pressed the back of her hands against her flushed cheeks. "Fine. We both wanted to kiss, but we both should've known better than to kiss like this in public."

"Now what?"

"What do you mean now what? We're going to pretend like we had an important business discussion and go back inside Comfort Zone. We'll finish our dessert like civilized people. Then I'll leave and go back to the bar. You could stay a bit longer to work on the website, then leave as well."

"You're going back to the bar?" He couldn't hide the disappointment and longing in his voice.

"I have to," she said, placing her hand on his arm. He clasped his hand over hers. "I can't play hooky to go to bed with you. Not when we're trying to be discreet."

"Of course not," he said valiantly. "Let's get back before too many people notice we've been gone."

What he actually wanted to say was *to hell with discreet*. He wanted to throw her over his shoulder, run to Lola's like Flash on a sugar high, and make love to her until neither of them could walk. At times like these, it would've been nice to really be a bad-boy player.

CHAPTER SEVEN

*L*ast evening, Tara was blessed with a maximum-capacity bar so she didn't have a minute to spare for her thoughts. Otherwise, she would've obsessed over her alleyway kiss with Seth all night. But this morning, there was nothing stopping her from obsessing while walking through the aisles of the drugstore.

Even though it had still smelled like cinnamon and vanilla from Comfort Zone, the narrow alley had felt far away and a little . . . dangerous. It was hot as hell. She'd forgotten everything but the feel of Seth's lips against hers. Her body had cried for more, and if he hadn't pulled back, she might've had him right then and there.

She had never felt this all-consuming, physical need for someone before. Not even with Jason. Her memory of sex with him felt like a watery silhouette compared to what happened when she and Seth kissed. But even the lukewarm desire she'd felt for Jason had given him too much control over her.

She wanted to run. This was precisely the kind of situation she'd been avoiding since she left Jason. Relationships were a trap, confining and stifling. She treasured having her space and a life of her own separate from anyone else. When she was with Jason, she couldn't even study on her own or with her friends. He insisted she study in his room even when he wasn't doing schoolwork himself. He acted as though he had the right to micromanage everything she did . . . everything she was. She was constantly watched and measured, but she always fell far short of expectations.

If she gave into her attraction for Seth, would he begin demanding more of her? More of her time? More of her affection? If she fell for him, she would do anything to make him happy. Nausea churned in her stomach. She would be lost. But what if she was so badly broken that *she* turned into the one to confine him within her expectations—the one to constantly demand more until he believed he wasn't good enough. For a moment, terror swept through her. Then she remembered he was leaving in less than a month.

Seth moving away was the best thing about dating him. It was insurance against the relationship trap. She was safe with him. She could handle a playboy out for a fun time, especially since that was exactly what she wanted, too.

Tara tore her mind away from Seth. For something that was supposed to be uncomplicated, she sure thought about it a lot. She looked around the store where she'd come for a reason. What was it again? Oh, yes. Her favorite citrus-scented shampoo. How did she end up in the diaper section anyway?

She wound her way down the aisles until she reached the shampoo section and stopped short. Her mind's constant companion was perusing the shelves. She was getting really good at conjuring him up. Her heart took off on a sprint, and she resisted the urge to fly into his arms. Was this how it was going to be every time she saw him?

As though sensing her presence, Seth lifted his head, and a slow, happy smile spread across his face. "Fancy meeting you here."

"Run out of your athlete's foot medicine, did you?" She arched her eyebrow, stamping down her answering smile.

Seth burst out laughing. He genuinely seemed to enjoy her sharp tongue. Was he a glutton for insults or something? "Actually, I ran out of shaving cream a couple days ago."

"I can tell. I thought you had a five o'clock shadow yesterday, but you have the beginnings of a beard now." Without thinking, Tara reached out and ran her hand down his rough cheek. "I kind of like it."

"You do?" His eyebrows shot up. "Do you want me to grow it out?"

"It's your face." She backtracked, chiding herself for acting way too familiar. It didn't matter what she liked. "Do what you want. It doesn't affect me."

"Well, it actually does." He stepped toward her and spoke close to her ear, "Think about how it would feel against your thighs when I taste you."

She gasped, and her hand fluttered to her chest. She actually freaking did that. Like some Victorian maiden. *What the fuck.* She cleared her throat loudly, planning to give him her best comeback. What came out was, "Um . . . abba . . . wha?"

"You don't have to decide now." He laughed quietly, his hot breath tickling her cheek. "I'll grow it out for a couple more days while you mull over it."

"I can't believe . . . you don't think . . . ugh." She backed away from him so she could think and breathe. "The Ego."

Seth shrugged happily and peeked at her basket. "Dark chocolate? Is that what you came in for?"

"No, I need some shampoo." If she was honest with herself, the shampoo really was an excuse to come in for the chocolate.

Seth cocked his head to the side, intensely interested. "Which shampoo do you use?"

"Um, nothing fancy. Just a drugstore brand." She glanced sideways and pointed to it. "This one."

He promptly reached for a bottle, popped open the cap, and inhaled deeply. Then he glanced down at the shampoo with disappointment. "No, this isn't it."

"What are you talking about? I should know what brand of shampoo I use."

"Your hair smells similar to it, but there's something more." He reached out to wrap a piece of her hair around his fingers and sniffed. "It's been driving me wild, trying to figure out what it was."

"My conditioner is the same fragrance. I don't put anything else on." Something about knowing that Seth spent his free time thinking of how her hair smelled was quite gratifying.

"There's this sweetness underneath the citrus." He absently rubbed her hair between his fingers, effectively holding her in place.

"Sweet?" There was an erotic undertone to his musing. Or maybe it was just her. She was getting very, very turned on. "Oh, that must be me."

"Yes, that's it. It is you." Seth's eyes snapped up to meet hers, and held her gaze for a long moment. "Something uniquely you. I won't be able to enjoy this scent anywhere but where you are."

You sure as hell won't find it in Paris, she nearly said. But what would that accomplish? It wasn't like she didn't want him to leave. "You're imagining things. It's citrus shampoo. On sale for seven ninety-nine."

Seth finally let her hair slip through his fingers. She moved to walk past him, but he walked alongside her. "So what's on the agenda today?"

"Running errands. Maybe doing the laundry. Then the late shift," she counted off on her fingers. "A truly exciting lineup. Why do you ask?"

"I thought . . . maybe you could help me find something."

"Find what? At the drugstore?"

"Flowers. I need wildflowers."

"Have you been to the florist?"

"Not yet, but I can use your opinion. Will you come with me?"

"Okay. Why not." Inside, she wanted to bounce on her heels. Another nondate with Seth? *Hell, yeah.* "I guess laundry could wait until tomorrow."

"I'm honored," he said dryly. Then his eyes focused on something over her shoulder. "I see the shaving cream. Let me grab that, then we can go. Unless you have more shopping to do."

"No, I'm good." Then she remembered she was running low on tampons. "I lied. I do need something. Then I'll be done. I can meet you at the register."

"That's okay. I'll go with you."

"Suit yourself," she said.

She walked over to the feminine hygiene section, expecting Seth to mumble an excuse and run to the register.

"Whenever I see an ad about maxi pads with wings, I always imagine them flying around the living room," he said with a light laugh. "Like the Hogwarts acceptance letters in Harry Potter."

"That's because you're a strange one." But Tara couldn't help snickering at the imagery. She might never be able to unsee that now. "Okay. I'm done. Let's go pay for our stuff."

He stepped to the side with his arm outstretched. "After you."

"Why, thank you. I've never experienced such gallantry at the feminine hygiene aisle before."

Seth chuckled, the corners of his eyes crinkling. As they stood in the checkout line, they smiled and peeked at each other. Like a sappy couple. Which they definitely were not. A couple. Especially a sappy one.

Once they finished paying, he came to stand beside her. "Do you want to drop your car off at your house? It makes sense to drive in one car."

"I actually rode my bike here." She thought for a moment. It wasn't as though anyone would steal it. "It'll be fine where I parked it."

"We could take it with us. I have a bike rack."

"That works, too."

Tara led him to where her bike was parked. He lifted the bike and secured it like it weighed nothing, his muscles shifting and bulging. It was quite a show but altogether too short.

"Thanks," she said, her eyes still roaming his chest and arms.

"My pleasure," he replied with a cocky smile.

She snorted and shook her head. The Ego probably nudged him to flex extra hard for her. Not that she was complaining. Seth was half-way to the passenger door when she opened it herself and plopped down on the seat. It made no sense to wait for him to come around to open the door for her when she too had hands and limbs. He didn't seem to mind. He shrugged and retraced his steps to the driver's side and got in the car.

"Which way to the florist?"

Tara pointed to the right. "It's around that corner and two streets down."

"That's really close. Maybe we should've walked."

"Yeah, but I wasn't sure if you planned on buying a trunkful of wildflowers or something."

"Not quite a trunkful, but I do want a nice-sized bouquet." He slowed to pull into a spot in front of the flower shop. "Or maybe a huge one. I'm not sure. I have a rough concept in my head for the shot, but I'll know which flower is the right one when I see it."

The bell tinkled merrily when they stepped into the lovely flower shop. Tara always felt a little happier when she was in there. The gorgeous palette of nature's colors and the heady fragrance of the flowers made it seem as though all was right in the world.

"Hey, Rosie." Tara waved cheerily at the florist/owner.

Seth leaned down and whispered, "Rosie?"

"Shush. She was meant for this job. That's all."

"No, I think it's cool."

"Tara?" The florist rushed out from behind the counter and wrapped her in her arms. "It's good to see you. I haven't seen you in weeks."

"It's good to see you, too. Rosie, this is Seth, Aubrey's new brother-in-law."

Seth extended his hand. "Nice to meet you."

Rosie blushed like her namesake flower, placing her hand inside his with a breathy giggle. "It's so nice to meet you."

So nice? Was she flirting with Seth? A fleeting image of herself bending down to bite Rosie's hand struck Tara. *Down, green monster.* They were just saying hello, for llama's sake.

"Rosie was two years behind me in high school," Tara said in an odd, high-pitched voice. "Go, Weldon High."

"Yeah, she was one of the few upper classmen who acknowledged my existence." Rosie smiled fondly at her, and Tara felt as small as a pussy willow for her brief bout of jealousy.

"I can see her doing that," Seth said to Rosie while smiling warmly at Tara.

"She's exaggerating." It was Tara's turn to blush. "Anyways, can we look around the store? Seth here is looking for some flowers that he'll know when he sees them."

Rosie blinked rapidly but held on to her smile. "O-kay. Feel free to browse and let me know if you need any help."

The store was small, but every nook and cranny held beautiful arrangements and potted plants. Seth was quiet as he searched for the right flowers, and Tara walked beside him, enjoying every hidden treasure she spotted.

Her favorite was a small bouquet jam-packed with the colors of spring—yellow, pink, green, white, with droplets of orange-colored berries dotting the surface. Without thinking, she reached out for it. She just wanted to hold it for a second.

"That's beautiful," Seth said, reminding her how close by her side he'd been standing. "Do you like it?"

"I do. Something about it is so joyous and whimsical." She smiled as brightly as the bouquet.

"May I?" He stretched his hand toward the arrangement she still held.

"Sure," she said, handing it to him. Maybe he was as enchanted by it as she was.

To her surprise, Seth strode purposefully to the register and extended the bouquet to Rosie. "Could you ring this up for us?"

"Was this what you were looking for?" Rosie asked. "I'm very happy with how this turned out."

"It's very well done, but it actually caught Tara's eyes more than mine."

"Hey, what are you doing?" Tara came up behind Seth and placed a hand on his arm. So warm and firm. She wished she could wrap her hand around it and squeeze to feel how muscular he actually was. *Stop acting like a glutton, and focus.* "You don't need to buy me those."

"I don't need to, but I want to. You're taking time out of your day to help me. These are merely a token of my appreciation."

Rosie's eyes hopped from Seth to Tara. If Tara made a big deal out of it, it would look suspicious. Besides, it really wasn't a big deal. He was just buying her flowers to thank her for her help. It didn't matter that she never accepted flowers from men. They were too hard to explain to her family. But this time, she didn't want to refuse. She really loved the bouquet, and if she were honest with herself, the giver wasn't half bad himself.

"Thank you," Tara said softly, her heart dipping at his sweet gesture. "But I don't think I've been any help so far. Have you found your flowers?"

"Actually, that bunch behind the counter looks promising." He pointed out a bundle of tiny lavender blossoms.

"Oh, those." Rosie walked back to retrieve them. "I actually brought them from my backyard."

"Do you have more of them? I need about seven to eight bundles of them."

"I'm afraid not," the shopkeeper said apologetically but brightened suddenly. "Actually, these are in bloom in abundance in the hills behind the high school. Do you know where I'm talking about, Tara?"

"*Now* I remember where I've seen these before." Tara snapped her fingers. "Yeah, I know exactly where you mean."

Rosie processed Seth's credit card and returned it to him. "I'm sure you'll find all the flowers you need there."

"Thank you so much, Rosie," he said warmly, and the florist fluttered her lashes.

If Tara didn't like her so much, she would've rolled her eyes, but women had to stick together. *I mean, who can resist that smile and twinkling eyes?* Other than her, she meant. True, she'd kissed the man a couple times and wanted to climb him right now, but she had successfully resisted jumping into his bed so far. She considered that a huge accomplishment, and a testament to her superhuman willpower.

"Milady," he said extending the flowers toward her.

"You're so corny." But she accepted the bouquet and added, "Thank you, kind sir."

The speculation in Rosie's eyes grew more certain, and her smile turned wily. "Should I give you guys some privacy?"

"No, thanks," Tara couldn't hold back her eye roll this time. "We have business we need to attend to. Ready to go tramping through the hills, Seth?"

"Just lead the way," he said enthusiastically.

Waving their goodbyes to Rosie, they got back into his car and headed toward her alma mater. She rarely went by there anymore, but every time she saw her old high school, she had mixed feelings. On the one hand, she'd hated high school with a vengeance. The mindless drilling of required courses and the suppression of individuality—studying something she had no interest in just because someone told her to—were both suffocating and excruciatingly boring. On the other hand, she loved the friendships she'd developed and the different interests she'd been exposed to through them.

But always prevalent and consistent during those awkward teenage years was her overwhelming insecurities when it came to boys. She was invisible to them. Unattractive. Uninteresting. She was a late bloomer, so she had no boobs to speak of until the summer of her senior year. By then, her love life was too abysmal to salvage, as was her self-confidence. And the fact that she was getting attention only because of her breasts pissed her off to high hell. Her insecurities followed her to college. It was no wonder she lost her mind with gratitude when, for the first time in her life, a boy liked her back.

The first taste of love had been as sweet as ambrosia, heady and electrifying. But that was before the feelings of inadequacy and guilt set in. Nothing she did for Jason was enough. As his demands on her grew, so did his disappointment in her. The harder she tried, the more he criticized her . . . belittled her. By then, love wasn't warmth and happiness, but anxiety and defeat. She had no plans to make herself go back to that time. She wouldn't risk falling in love again. With anyone.

"Turn left here," she shouted, jerking back to the present. She was so lost in her thoughts that they almost passed the small road that led up to the hill.

"Whoa." With his great reflexes and a responsive sports car, Seth was able to make the turn.

"Sorry about being a lousy navigator," she said sheepishly.

"No need for that." He stole a quick glance at her before focusing back on the road. "Okay. Do we just follow this road from here on?"

"Yes."

And that was what Tara intended to do as well. She would keep walking the path she had been on. The safe road where no love existed. Where no pain existed.

The field near the edge of the hill was tightly packed with the flowers he'd admired at the florist. The late-morning sun shone softly down on the lavender-colored blossoms, lighting everything to a crisp clarity. Tara stood a few feet away, running her hand over the tall grass.

She'd grown quiet in the car on their way over. Seth had no idea why, but his eyes kept following her, observing her in a rare solemn mood. Her ever-present smirk was smoothed out, and her lips looked wider and fuller. Her sharp, ever-watching eyes seemed faraway, and a single furrow marked the space between her eyebrows. He wanted to smooth it out with words and touch, but he held himself back.

This still and pensive Tara was achingly beautiful. But Seth didn't know where she'd gone, and it bothered him not to know. How could he, though? He'd only just started getting to know her. Even though he found new facets to the fascinating woman whenever they spent time together, it wasn't enough. He wanted more. He was hungry to know everything about her. Her hopes, fears, and dreams. What made her happy. His heart thumped against his chest with his fierce desire to make her happy.

The realization hit him physically, making him take a step back from Tara. *Where the hell did that come from?* Sure, he wanted to give her a good time, but it wasn't his job to make her happy. That wasn't what this was about. He was leaving in three weeks. If he made her happy, wouldn't his leaving make her sad? His chest felt tight and sore at the thought. He couldn't bear the thought of causing her any kind of pain.

He had to be honest with himself. Being with Tara felt . . . different. It didn't feel like the comfortable camaraderie he'd shared with his friends with benefits. It didn't feel like fondness and respect. The respect was there—perhaps more strongly because it was her—but he felt a connection to her he hadn't felt with anyone else. Not even Jessica. The way his heart stuttered every time he set eyes on Tara. How making her laugh made him want to stick his chest out and crow. How everything she said and did was . . . more. He was developing feelings for her that he swore never to feel for anyone ever again.

He didn't know how he felt about it. Paralyzing fear? The desperate urge to run in the other direction yelling *never again*? Nope. After years of hiding behind the defensive wall he'd erected, the gaping holes Tara punched through it didn't alarm him. The closest thing to how he felt was *huh, how 'bout that.*

"So, do you want to pick some and take them back to the restaurant?" Tara broke the silence.

"No, I don't think so." He looked across the field, taking in the stunning ocean of flowers. "Even the biggest bouquet wouldn't do them justice, and snapping away their vibrant life doesn't feel right either."

"Maybe you're right." She walked out to the clearing on the edge of the hill and stared out at her town. "I'd forgotten how beautiful this place was."

In that moment, the sun hit her from exactly the right angle, and the world changed around her. She turned into something unquantifiable. Solid but transparent. Glowing but shadowed. Sharp and smudged.

"Stay right there," he said and rushed to his car. He popped open the trunk and pulled out his camera.

"What? Why?"

"Just don't move. Please." He ran back to where she was standing, and took shot after shot before she could even speak. "You could sit or stand or crouch, and look anywhere you want. But do it in that spot."

Tara blushed slightly, tucking her hair behind her ear. "All right. I guess."

Time stood still. A hundred years passed. She was ever present and ever changing, and he couldn't breathe. The light shifted but it didn't diminish her beauty. It merely re-created her into something else.

When he came back enough to notice his surroundings, he was lying flat on his back with his head on the dirt. He adjusted the lens and took the shot he believed he meant to take. Tara was sitting with her knees drawn to her chest and her arms wrapped around them.

She was staring out into the panorama. This time, she didn't seem pensive or faraway. She seemed serene and content.

"I'm sorry," he mumbled, shifting to a sitting position beside her. "How long have you been sitting here?"

"A few minutes. I was standing most of the time." She pulled out her phone and checked the time. "About thirty minutes, I think."

"Sorry," he said again. "And thank you."

"You were right here. So intensely focused on what you were doing." Her expression grew thoughtful as she studied him. "And yet you felt so distant. Like you weren't here at all."

"I was with you. I was with you through it all. Even when you changed from one vision to the next." His gaze drifted away as he searched for a way to describe what happened to him in the last half hour. "I saw you in watercolor. I saw you in pastels. I saw you when you were nearly transparent. You're all I saw."

His head swiveled toward her when he heard her sharp intake of breath. Had he said too much? Did he even make sense?

"Will you . . . will you let me see the pictures?" she asked with a slight tremor in her voice.

"Of course." He couldn't help but reach out and cup her cheek. "Anything you want."

With a soft sigh, she turned her head and kissed the palm of his hand. A shiver ran through his body, and Tara's eyes darkened. Pushing up on her knees, she buried her hands in his hair and tugged him close until their lips met. It wasn't like any other kiss they'd shared. Sure, there was passion, but this made him feel cherished. It was as though she saw something in him that was precious, and she poured out her awe and pleasure into the kiss.

He drank what she offered, savoring every drop of her tender affection. He wanted this. Very badly. Seth realized he cared about Tara, and wanted her to care about him, too. Again, it wasn't a feeling of fear or wariness that overcame him, but one of eagerness and anticipation. Helpless against the pleasure, he deepened the kiss, pulling her tightly against him. She moaned and ground against him as tenderness gave way to desperation.

Seth wanted to push her against the soft earth and make love to her, but he couldn't be that reckless. Nor could he wait much longer to have her. "Come home with me."

Tara froze, then slowly drew back. He relaxed his arms but didn't let her go.

"I . . . can't," she said with a faint frown.

"Why?" She wanted him as much as he wanted her. There was no question about that. Why was she keeping him at arm's length?

"Well . . . I didn't plan on counting our chance meeting as a date." She spoke in a rush. "And you remember the rules, right? You have to keep your pants on during nondates."

"To hell with the rules," he growled.

Tara scrambled back, and Seth let his arms drop to his sides. She got to her feet and looked everywhere but at him, clearly panicked. What was she afraid of? Then a thought rushed into his head. No . . . she couldn't be, but maybe . . .

"Tara," he said carefully so as not to startle her. "Have you . . . are you a . . . virgin?"

"What?" Her eyes seemed to bug out of their sockets. Then she burst out laughing.

"What's so funny?" His eyebrows drew down into a frown because he had a feeling the joke was on him.

"Oh, my gosh. I can't even." She wiped her eyes with the back of her hand, and straightened up with her hands at her waist. "Was that the only reason you could think of? That I wasn't jumping eagerly into your bed because I was a frightened virgin. Oh, no. The one-eyed monster."

"All right. Enough of that." She had a point there. Heat rushed up until his cheeks and neck were pulsing with it. Maybe his ego really was a bit inflated. "Look, I was just trying to make sense of why you seemed so nervous every time things got heated."

"I don't know what you're talking about." She averted her eyes again, the merriment dimming slightly. "I don't need a reason to not sleep with you."

"Fair enough." He got to his feet, swatting dirt off his pants. "But what more reason do you need to sleep with me?"

"I have a reason to sleep with you?" She raised a perfectly arched eyebrow.

"You want me." He smirked. "Desperately."

"Fair enough." She smirked back at him with as much ego as he'd exhibited. "But what's the rush? We've only had one date so far."

"As you well know, I'm leaving in little over three weeks. I'm in a rush," he said with a subtle growl. "I'm losing my fucking mind from wanting you. You do realize that, don't you?"

"Yes." A lovely pink blush blossomed on her cheeks.

God, she is so beautiful.

Then she glanced at her watch and genuine regret washed over her expression. "As fun as this was, I have a little thing called a job."

Seth shoved his hand through his hair. "Of course. I've taken up too much of your morning already. I really appreciate your help. I got some amazing pictures today."

"I'm not sure if it'll be much help for the restaurant website," she said shyly.

"Don't worry. I got some shots of the flowers, too." He paused. She'd asked to see the photos, but he wasn't ready to show them to her yet. "Oh, and I'll go through the pictures I took of you, so you can see them the next time we meet to work on the website."

But more important than the nondates, he needed to schedule their second date, so he could seduce the hell out of her.

CHAPTER EIGHT

He's leaving.

Tara reassured herself every time her heart tripped on the peaks of her anxiety. No matter what happened between them, her autonomy was safe. She had nothing to fear. So what was holding her back? Nothing. Nothing at all. It was a go. Green light to show Seth the time of his life.

Wait. Time out.

Why was she giving herself a pep talk to have sex with Seth? She was starting to annoy herself. If it happened, it happened. She should just be in the moment and go with the flow. When it came to Seth, she second-guessed herself at every turn. The beauty of the dating dare was the uncomplicated simplicity of it all. But she was ruining it by overthinking her every action.

"Stop being such a loser," she chided herself.

"What was that?" Jack looked askance at her.

Shit. Did I say that out loud?

"Oh, nothing." She sighed. "Just talking to myself like a lonely old lady."

"Just the usual then."

From his crouched position, her brother shot her a teasing smile before returning his attention to the table he was holding up with one hand. She felt a twinge of envy at how fit he was and surreptitiously flexed her arm. The barest definition showed up. She made a face and lowered her scrawny arm back to her side. But then again, that was why Jack was the one fixing the wobbly tables in the hall and not her. *Thank you, scrawny arms.*

"Are you almost done with that?" she asked, walking around the bar to stand over him.

"I think I have just one more to fix after this." He squinted up at her. "Are you offering to help?"

"Sure, I'll help."

"I was just testing you. You passed." He stood to his full height and stretched his back, twisting left and right. "How about I get the last table and you make us some food?"

She pulled out her phone from her back pocket to check the time. It was past four. She noticed a text from Roger, but after a split second of hesitation, she deleted it. Texting with him while she was with Seth didn't feel right. She didn't analyze why she felt that way.

"On it. You good with kimchi fried rice?" They needed to have their dinner before they opened at five.

"I'm always good with kimchi fried rice. And can I have my egg sunny-side up?"

"Duh. Of course." Like she wouldn't know her brother's preferences. Jack liked his sunny-side up, Alex liked his over easy, and Tara liked hers over medium. "Coming right up."

She took care to make fragrant green-onion oil as the base before adding the kimchi to the lightly sizzling pan. Once the kimchi was nearly translucent, she mixed in a spoonful of chili paste for its pretty red color and extra spice, then added some day-old rice into the mouthwatering sauté. After the rice and the sautéed kimchi were thoroughly combined, she lowered the heat to let the rice crisp on the bottom. While it did that, she fried up made-to-order eggs. Tara scooped up the finished fried rice into a rounded bowl, pushing it down compactly, then upturned it onto the waiting plate, and repeated. She lovingly placed the fried eggs on top of the perfect domes of deliciousness, then sprinkled some toasted sesame seeds on top.

"Voilà," she said with a chef's kiss and carried the plates to the small table in the kitchen. Then she poked her head out to the dining hall. "Dinner is served."

Tara waited, spoon in hand, for her brother to join her. She was beyond ready to pop her yolk and take that perfect first bite.

"This looks amazing. As usual," Jack said, taking a seat across from her. "Your kimchi fried rice is the best. When are we going to add it to the menu?"

"I'm the brewer, not the cook. The kitchen is still Mom's domain."

"Don't you think it's getting a bit too much for her?" he said between bites.

"Oh, my galloping horses. If you say that in front of Mom, you won't even get a chance to say, 'I'm too young to die!' " Tara joked, but she really didn't like thinking about her parents growing old. Where they became the vulnerable ones who needed to be taken care of. They were her anchor. "She's not even sixty yet. She has at least forty more years in her."

"I guess you're right." He'd already finished off his plate. "Besides, I am too young to die."

"Who's too young to die?" Their mom bustled in from the side door. "Oh, Lord. Is someone sick?"

Tara shot a glance at Jack, bringing her thumb and index finger just a hair's width away from touching. *Thiiiis close,* she mouthed to him. Then turned to her mom, who was preparing to get agitated.

"Mom, have you been binge watching that morning K-drama? No one is dying."

"But I heard Jack say something—"

"It was just a figure of speech," Jack said, clearing his dishes to the sink.

"Fine, but don't any of you dare keep secrets from me. If you do, I'm just going to assume the worst."

The guilt poking at her made Tara shift from foot to foot. "Course not."

"You know I'm an open book, Mom," Jack said, but something in his voice made Tara shoot him a look.

Was he hiding something, too? She tried to catch his eyes, but he wrapped a black apron around his waist and walked out to the bar. After pondering the possibility for a moment, Tara let it drop. She had too much going on in her confused mess of a brain right now to pursue a conspiracy theory against her sweet older brother.

The after-work crowd steadily filled the pub with chatter and laughter, and Tara smiled with the satisfaction. The brewery was booming, and if she had anything to do about it, it would only grow more. The seasonal brews they'd introduced were being well received, and more craft-beer aficionados were taking notice of Weldon Brewery. Slowly but surely, they would leave their mark with the quality of their brews.

Her cell phone vibrated in her back pocket, but she stubbornly ignored it. The pub was too busy for her to be distracted. Besides, she had a feeling she knew who it was, and he would be the biggest distraction. She'd already spent half the afternoon driving herself nuts with questions about what was happening between them. But every time she saw anything close to an answer forming in her mind, she shied away from it. The morning on the hill had felt as though it was more than a casual nondate. Something had changed between them. It was lust. Their desire for each other had reached another level. Like nuclear level. That had to be it.

"Hello, gorgeous." An unfamiliar man approached her at the bar with a slimy smirk that begged to be punched off his face. He appeared to be in his early twenties, brimming with the false confidence that came from the misguided belief that he was invincible. Oh, the follies of youth.

She caught her brother's eyes at the other end of the bar. His face was set in stone, which she recognized as the calm before the storm, but when she gave him a subtle shake of her head, he reluctantly turned his back to her with a frustrated huff. Her brothers and she had an agreement. They weren't allowed to interfere unless she was in physical danger. She couldn't have them bodily throw out every customer who hit on her. It was easier for her to handle things without the complications of testosterone overload.

"What can I get for you?" she asked with polite indifference.

"You can start by giving me your number." He thought he was oh so clever.

"My number's not on the menu." She pointed helpfully to the chalkboard menu above her head. "Why don't you try again?"

The guy's cocky front crumbled a little, but he pulled himself together for a second try. "Playing hard to get? Not a problem. I'm a patient man."

"A man. Right. Just to be sure, may I see your driver's license? You look a bit young to be sitting at the bar."

His eyes flared with indignation and injured pride. "You gotta be kidding me."

"Nope. Not at all. ID please."

He took out his driver's license and threw it on the counter.

"Great." She squinted her eyes and inspected every minute detail before handing it back to him. "Thank you. May I recommend a customer favorite?"

"Sure." He retrieved his license with a sullen expression, likely realizing he didn't have a chance in hell of picking her up.

Once she sent away the mildly embarrassed customer with a stellar brew, she patted herself on the back for a job well done. *Situation handled.* And because she was a bratty little sister, she arched an I-told-you-so eyebrow at Jack, flashing a cocky grin.

The rest of the evening passed in an uneventful but busy blur, but her phone had burned against her butt the entire night, refusing to be forgotten. *Damn Seth with his handsome face and hard body.* With only a few lingering customers left in the hall, she couldn't resist anymore and pulled out her phone.

SETH: Ready for our second date?

Tara's heart lodged itself in her throat before dropping down to her stomach. *A date? Where he doesn't have to keep his pants on?*

TARA: Sure. Why not?

She was overheating. Why wasn't he responding? It was past ten. Maybe he was asleep. She wanted to kick herself for not answering his text earlier. Full stop. Was she this desperate? Apparently.

When ellipses finally appeared on the screen, she squealed before she could stop herself. *Bye-bye, self-respect.*

SETH: Busy night at the brewery?

TARA: Weldon Brewery is always busy. Thank you very much.

SETH: I didn't mean to text you while you were working. I just thought of you and didn't notice the time.

Damn. That was too sweet. *Sucker alert. Sucker alert.* Had she forgotten that she was dealing with a player? *Yes.* Lately, she frequently forgot that he was. He didn't fit neatly into the playboy category like she'd thought. He was much too kind. Much too considerate. She didn't know how to feel about that.

TARA: Don't worry about it. That's what text messages are for. You text when you want, and I text back when I want.

SETH: Still, I won't make a habit out of it. But now that I have you, is there something you particularly want to do for our second date?

Yes. I'd like to have sex. That was what she wanted to do on their date. There was no use denying it. She'd wanted him since he agreed to play the prince in the tower for a little girl at the park. No, maybe even sooner than that. Like the night of the wedding. *How can I say that without making a complete fool of myself?*

TARA: Can you ski?

SETH: Like James Bond.

TARA: Watch yourself now. The Ego is stirring.

SETH: Hahaha. So skiing?

TARA: Yeah. I have this weekend off and it's the last week of ski season in Mammoth. We could leave early Saturday morning and come back Sunday evening.

She held her breath as the ellipses rolled and rolled on the screen.

SETH: Sounds fun. I'll take care of the accommodations.

She wanted to clarify that he was to get only one room. With one bed. But that would sound like she was throwing herself at him. Besides, Seth wasn't a naive virgin. A woman didn't propose a weekend getaway to stay in two separate rooms.

TARA: Then I'll get the lift tickets.
SETH: Awesome. More details to follow later. Good night.
TARA: Good night.

She was so excited about their date that she doubted she would get much sleep for the rest of the week. She could only hope that thoughts of their first night together would keep Seth up at night as well.

Seth parked a block away from Tara's house as instructed and hoped that he wouldn't have to wait long. He didn't want anyone to report him as a suspicious man parked on their street in the cover of darkness. But more importantly, he couldn't wait to see Tara. He shifted in his seat but couldn't get comfortable with so much restless energy coursing through him. Maybe he should sprint back and forth down the street. The neighbors would definitely report him if he ran around the street like his pants were on fire. Well, his pants *were* on fire, figuratively speaking.

An overnight ski trip with Tara. He was looking forward to spending time with her, skiing and sipping Irish coffee. But tonight . . . he couldn't even let himself think about it. The things he wanted to do to her. He was one dirty-minded bastard.

Before he got himself too excited, he spotted Tara walking toward his car with a small duffel bag. He hurried to her and took the bag off her shoulder. Then, because he couldn't help himself, Seth placed a soft kiss on her lips in a rush of affection. It was so good to see her. When he pulled back, Tara's eyes were wide with surprise and her lips were curved shyly at the corners.

Impromptu, lust-driven makeout sessions were one thing, but easy affection was somehow more intimate. It was as though they were a couple, who had the right to kiss each other whenever they wanted. He liked the idea of them as a couple, even if only for a few weeks. It felt right.

"Hi," he whispered. The muted neighborhood, quiet and sleepy in the dark morning, compelled him to make as little noise as possible.

"Hi," she whispered back.

Seth led her to the passenger's side and opened the door for her. Once she was settled, he stowed her bag next to his in the trunk and slid into his seat. "Are you ready?"

"Yes." She squirmed in her seat, unable to contain her excitement. "I made us a road-trip playlist."

"Aww, are you giving me a mixtape, Tara? Does that mean you *like* like me?"

"Be quiet and drive. And behold the mastery of my playlist." She sighed and relaxed into her seat as the first strains of Vivaldi's *Four Seasons* permeated the air.

The familiar melody was soothing in the stillness of the early morning. Seth smiled his appreciation at Tara, then turned his attention back to the road as he led them toward the highway.

Their road trip began in earnest with the soulful voice of Ed Sheeran singing to mellow, acoustic music. As Weldon disappeared behind them, they listened in companiable silence as more evocative music filled the car. Soon dawn stained the sky with indigo, purple, and pink, and they cruised down the nearly empty freeway.

"This isn't just a playlist," he said. "It's like the soundtrack to our road trip. If we were in a movie, this song would be playing in the background right now."

"You understand my genius." She smiled brightly. "Since you insisted on driving, I wanted to do something to make the long drive more enjoyable."

"Thank you. That's very thoughtful of you."

"You're welcome," she said softly. "I'm glad you like it."

He tucked away the warmth of the moment before consulting his navigator to make sure he'd switched to the right freeway. "Do you ski often?"

"Not really. Just once a year or so. I'm too busy with the brewery, and it's hard to get away." She shifted and turned to face him. "How about you? For you to ski so well, you must go often."

"Yeah, I try to go at least three or four times a season. And when things work out with my schedule, I like to go for a weeklong trip to Utah or Colorado. The snow is pristine out there."

"I should confess now that I'm a modest intermediate skier. I'm afraid I won't be joining you on the black diamond courses."

"On our last date, we let the princesses and goblins interrupt our date. I'm not letting anything split us up today," he said resolutely. "We'll warm up on the intermediate courses, and when you feel more confident, we can hit the advanced slopes. You'll love it."

"But I've never gone on one before." She sounded uncharacteristically timid.

"Well, today will be perfect for your first time, since I'll be right by your side if you need help. But I have a feeling you'll rise to the challenge."

"Hmm. I'll think about it," she said, her eyes sparkling with curiosity.

"You know you want to." He grinned widely, because it was true. Now that he'd presented her with a challenge, she wouldn't be able to rest until she conquered it.

"Maybe," she said. "Oh, are we going to stop at Bishop? The bakery there has the best bread."

"I know exactly which one you're talking about. Let's grab some sandwiches for lunch there so we could hit the slopes as soon as we can."

"Sounds like a plan."

Then they had to stop talking because "Bohemian Rhapsody" came on.

They made good time to Mammoth, even with the stopover at Bishop. It was too early to check in, so they dropped their bags off at the hotel and headed outside with their sandwiches.

"Should we save these until lunch or do you want to eat them now?" Seth was hoping for the latter choice. He was starving.

"Let's eat them now. It's past ten, so we'll call this brunch and ski straight through the afternoon."

"You read my mind."

They sat at a bench outside their hotel to eat their brunch, then went on to get geared up at the rental shop. Seth wasn't very happy with his rental gear, but he'd already packed up his ski gear to be shipped to Paris. These would have to do. At least Landon's ski jacket and pants fit him.

"Do your boots feel okay?" he asked.

She walked back and forth a few times and nodded. "Yeah. They're good. Let's go."

When they were ready, they huddled into the gondola to reach the ski slopes. It was always fun to watch the rooftops of the ski chalets grow smaller while climbing to the top.

Tara sat in the middle of the bench across from him and looked around at the changing vista.

"Did I tell you that gondola rides are one of my favorite things about skiing?" Seth said. "It makes me feel like a little kid on a Disneyland ride."

"Kind of like riding on the flying boat in Peter Pan's Flight." A soft smile touched her lips.

"Exactly. That's my favorite dark ride."

"Plus, it's in Fantasyland with Sleeping Beauty's Castle and the Mad Hatter," she said, her features brightening up.

"The Mad Hatter? Is that some kind of *Alice in Wonderland* ride? I've never heard of it."

"No, it's a store filled with wondrous things like Mickey ears and tiaras."

"So which one do you like to wear?" he asked.

"The Minnie ears, of course."

Seth chuckled, enjoying seeing yet another side of Tara. "I wouldn't have pegged you for a Disney fan."

"I'm not peggable."

"It seems you're not."

When they got off the gondola, they stepped into their skis and headed for the lifts to the intermediate courses.

"I always get nervous getting on the lifts," Tara said with a slight tremor in her voice, and there was a pallor to her skin that hadn't been there a moment ago.

"It's your survival instincts," he said matter-of-factly, smoothing out the frown that tugged at his eyebrows. He didn't like seeing her worried but she deserved better than meaningless reassurances. "We're going to sit on an open chair and go up the mountains. It's perfectly safe, but also a little reckless when you think about it."

"We humans happily take unnecessary risks as long as it's fun." She smiled, some color returning to her cheeks.

"That's what separates us from the animals," he deadpanned.

Tara was still laughing when they plunked down on the lift. He hoped he'd successfully eased her nervousness. When the lift began its ascent, she tensed for just a few seconds then relaxed enough to gently swing her legs back and forth.

"Comfy?" he asked.

"Better." She blew out a long breath. "Oh, look. We're almost at the part where we jump off of a moving suspended chair and drop to the ground."

He chuckled. Humans really were outrageous creatures. They landed lightly on the snow without mishap and glided away from the lift. The course was pretty straightforward and without many challenges, but going down the hill with the wind rushing in his ears was going to feel great.

"Ready?" Her body coiled back like a spring. *Hmm.* He suddenly doubted her claim of being a *modest* intermediate skier.

"Here we go," he said and pushed off with Tara close by his side.

The graceful flow of her movements proved his thoughts right. She skied beautifully. He stayed close to her and didn't pick up speed. He was serious about not being separated from her. He didn't want to let her out of his sight. As though she was testing him, Tara swooshed downhill, suddenly picking up speed. With a hoot, he sped up to join her.

She curled herself tighter as they approached the bottom of the hill, and he couldn't help himself. Maybe he wanted to show off like a peacock during mating season. He zoomed past her and stopped in a smooth arc at the bottom. Quickly, he pulled out his phone from his jacket pocket and pretended to scroll through messages.

Tara slid expertly to a stop beside him a few seconds later. He glanced up from his phone with surprise. "Oh, there you are. I thought you'd gone for some refreshments."

"Show-off," she said, and laughed. "You really can ski like James Bond. I thought maybe it was just The Ego talking."

"And you're no intermediate skier."

"I really am. I've never skied on the advanced slopes."

"That doesn't make sense." Seth cocked his head to the side, truly puzzled.

"I have this irrational fear of sliding off the chairs, and landing on the snow way below like a crumpled doll," she said, staring down at her boot-covered toes. "That's why I get so scared getting on the lifts. But to go to the diamond courses, you have to take multiple lifts, going even higher."

"But it's not the heights because you did fine on the gondola ride."

"Because it's fully enclosed. The lifts are so . . . open."

"What if I promise you, I'll never let you fall? I'll hold you tight the entire ride and not let go." He leaned closer to her so she would look at him. "I'll be your personal seat belt."

Her eyes widened and her lips parted, and she seemed almost mesmerized when she said in a breathless whisper, "Okay."

He'd had no ulterior motive other than to make her feel safe, but her reaction heated his blood to a quick boil. The depth of emotion she brought out in him was unnerving, yet thrilling. He wanted to laugh with her, to protect her, and make love to her with an intensity that surprised him. But he liked it, and hungered for more than a little taste of it.

Suddenly, the beginning of his *new chapter* in Paris loomed like a ticking bomb, ominously counting down the time he had left with Tara.

CHAPTER NINE

Oh, my Groot. We're up so high. So very high," Tara squeaked. Seth was sitting right beside her with his strong arms wrapped around her. Her personal seat belt. So romantic. Yet, her freak-out kept climbing. "Are you sure you're not defective?"

"Tara."

When she turned to face him, he crushed his mouth against hers. One moment she was scared and the next moment, she wanted nothing more than to climb onto his lap. She opened her mouth wider to give his tongue easier access. She moaned softly. Then she was rudely—but gently—set apart from him.

"Ready to jump?" he asked in a husky voice.

"What are you talking about?" she said, completely confused why he'd stopped kissing her.

"We're almost at the top."

"What—oh." She'd forgotten she was even on a lift. He'd kissed her to distract her from her fear. And boy, had it worked.

"Ready?" he asked again.

"Yeah. Sure. I'm ready."

Then they dropped together onto solid ground. Well, not exactly solid. The snow was softer up here since they didn't groom the slopes and fewer people ventured up this high. She loved how her skis sank into the powdery snow.

The air around them felt eerily calm. There were other skiers and boarders on the slopes, but their voices sounded far away and muted. The anxiety she'd felt moments before melted away, and anticipation raised goose bumps on her arms.

"Oh, Seth. It's so beautiful here," she whispered. The tall, viridescent trees behind them stretched to pierce the crisp blue sky, and the glistening powder down the slope cast a crystal-like glow to the entire picture. It was as serene and magical as a dormant snow globe.

"I knew you'd like it." He chuckled softly. "Let's take this one easy, so you can get a feel for it."

"After I get a feel for it, I'm going to redeem myself and beat you to the bottom."

"Sure, you will." His smirk was all cocky arrogance. It was so annoying how much it turned her on.

"Yeah, you're such a big, tough man that you managed to beat an intermediate skier by a few seconds."

"What can I say? Winning is a thrill no matter how small the challenge."

"I may not be able to beat you, but I'm going to be on your ass all day. You won't be able to shake me off."

"Promise?"

Grrr. He was infuriating. And oh so entertaining. With a delighted laugh, she pushed off ahead of him. Skiing down the pristine snow and challenging her skills was a sweet high. The air was colder up here and the wind stung her cheeks as she picked up speed. When it got too fast for her, she swerved left and right, drawing long zigzags on the snow.

Seth skied ahead of her but always slowed down and waited for her, so she never lost sight of him. Despite his insistence that she would love the diamond slopes, he was watching her carefully. She liked this protective side to him. She loved her parents and older brothers, but they sometimes made her feel claustrophobic with their overprotectiveness. Seth gave her space and didn't hover, but still let her know he was there for her.

They skied the last stretch of snow side by side, and slid to the bottom of the hill together. Tara was breathless from the exertion and excitement. She threw herself into Seth's arms, and hugged him tightly around his shoulders, not caring that their skis were tangled up.

"That was amazing." Her voice was muffled by his jacket. "Let's do it again."

"Are you sure you don't want to take a break first?" he asked as he untangled them before they toppled over.

"No way. Not even spiked hot chocolate can tempt me away."

"And you're up for another lift ride?"

"I found your strategy on the last ride very satisfactory."

A wolfish grin spread across his face. "I think I could manage it again."

As soon as her butt landed on the seat of the lift, Tara wrapped her arms around Seth's neck and kissed him. There was no reason to wait until her panic rose. With a sexy chuckle that rumbled in his chest, he kissed her back like he meant it. His laughter turned to a groan when she traced his bottom lip with her tongue, and it was her turn to smile in satisfaction. She loved that she could make him desperate with a flick of her tongue.

This time, she pulled away from him as they approached the end of the ride. Seth tried to tug her back with a frustrated growl, but she gently pushed him away. "It's time to get off."

Seth shook his head as though he needed to clear it, and jumped off with her. The peaceful calm was broken by the raucous laughter of a group of teenage snowboarders. Tara shrugged. It was getting later in the day, so the hills were becoming a bit more crowded. The kids wouldn't be a distraction once they started down the slope.

They pushed off without delay. Tara kept pace with Seth this time, the terrain a bit more familiar to her. He glided effortlessly beside her, as though skiing was as natural as walking to him. He was holding back so he could stay with her. She wanted him to enjoy himself as much as she was enjoying herself, so she picked up her poles and curled in on herself.

"Later," she yelled and zoomed away.

"Not a chance." Seth's laughing voice reached her ears as he sped past her.

Happy that he was finally throwing himself in, Tara slowed down a bit so she wouldn't smash into a tree.

It happened so fast she wasn't quite sure what hit her. She knew she'd successfully avoided the trees, but then why was she lying flat on her back? Seth had apparently slowed down to wait for her because he was by her side immediately.

"Tara. Are you okay?" He clicked off his skis and knelt by her side.

"Yeah, I think so," she managed to say.

When she heard someone groan to her side, she swerved her head to find one of the teenage boarders gathering herself off the ground. Tucking her snowboard under her arm, she walked over to Tara.

"Oh, my God. I'm so sorry. I slipped and the edge of my board caught your ski."

Seth had her sitting up now, so she was able to answer with some dignity. "That's all right. It was an accident."

"I'm still sorry," the teenager said.

"Ow," Tara yelped and the *that's okay* that had been on the tip of her tongue got waylaid in a cloud of pain. It felt as though a pair of metal clamps were attempting to crush her ankle and doing a decent job of it.

"Shit. I'm so sorry, Tara," Seth ground out, sounding frustrated and angry with himself. "I need to remove your boot to see how badly you're hurt. I don't know if I can do it without hurting you. Can you hang on while I take it off?"

"Yes, I'll hang on," she said, bracing herself. If the pain she'd felt when he unlatched her ski was any indication, this was going to hurt like a bitch.

"I'll help," the girl volunteered and grabbed her right leg to steady it as Seth gently worked her boot off.

She couldn't help it. She whimpered, biting down on her lip.

"Fuck," Seth said, turning worried eyes to her. Then his continued efforts drew a moan out of her. He stopped immediately. "Fucking hell."

"Oh, God. I'm so sorry," the snowboarder said again, wringing her gloved hands.

"I'm okay. Keep going," she said to Seth, setting her jaws to prepare herself.

Tara tried to stem the tide of tears streaming down her face. She didn't want to upset Seth anymore, and the poor girl was near tears herself. She took a deep breath to stop herself from grimacing. When her boot was finally off, cold sweat drenched her face and back from enduring the pain.

"Goddammit," Seth cursed under his breath. "Your ankle is too swollen for me to tell if it's broken or not."

"Crap," Tara sighed. "We don't have cell reception up here, right?"

"Right," he confirmed, pulling off his beanie to run his hand through his hair. "I'll have to go down to get the medics, but I don't want to leave you here alone."

"I can go." They both turned to the girl. "I'll go down and let the medics know. It's the least I can do."

"Thank you," Seth said. "I really appreciate that."

"Yeah, thank you," Tara echoed, surprisingly relieved that he could stay with her.

"I'll go down as fast as I can," she said with determination on her face.

"No," Seth and Tara yelled at once.

"No. Take your time and be safe." Tara spoke calmly, hoping it would dampen the girl's postcrash adrenaline. "We don't want you to fall again."

"Okay," the girl said, deflating a little. "Bye. Don't freeze to death or anything."

With those reassuring words, the teenager shoved off on her snowboard and disappeared down the slope. Tara shifted her seat on the snow, then winced in pain.

"Dammit," Seth growled as he shrugged off his backpack. "We need to get you more comfortable. Well, as comfortable as you can be sitting on the freezing snow with a possibly broken ankle."

"Seth, look at me." And when he did, she said, "I'll be okay. It's probably just a sprain. It's not a big deal."

"You wouldn't have gotten hurt if I hadn't dragged you up here."

"What?" She rounded on him. "You didn't *drag* me anywhere. I chose to come up here. The Ego has many sides, doesn't it? This isn't about you. It was just a freak accident."

He stayed stubbornly mute as he lined up their skis perpendicular to the slope and gently shifted her so she sat on the skis. She was proud of herself for not making a peep while he moved her even though it hurt like hell. But she had to say something when he zipped off his jacket, and put in around her shoulders.

"What do you think you're doing? You're going to freeze." She tried to shrug it off but he planted his hands firmly on her shoulders.

"I have an extra thermal shirt in my backpack. I'll be fine." His expression told her that he wasn't going to change his mind, so she let him wrap his jacket around her. Once he put on his extra layer, Seth carefully placed his backpack under her injured leg to elevate it. The throbbing became slightly more bearable.

"Thank you."

"You don't have to thank me," he said glumly.

"Stop beating yourself up. My ankle hurts pretty bad and I don't have the strength to argue with you right now."

"Shit. I'm sorry, Tara." He knelt beside her and brushed her hair away from her face with cold fingers. *Geez.* He'd taken his gloves off to get her situated. The sweet—and unnecessary—gesture squeezed her heart.

"If you're sorry, stop fussing. And put your gloves back on. Okay?"

"Okay." He sat facing down the hill, so his back was supporting her side. "Lean on me."

She leaned into his broad back and sighed. She was in pain and cold, but having him beside her made things not suck as bad. She might go as far as to say it bordered on nice. "This is kind of nice."

"What?" He swiveled his head toward her, but she was hidden behind his back. "Did you hit your head, too?"

"No, I'm serious. This is the longest stretch of time we've ever spent together, and I haven't killed you, yet. I say it bodes well for our remaining two dates."

She felt his back tense against her, but his tone was light when he responded, "That really must be some sort of a record. Admit it. I'm growing on you, aren't I?"

"Don't try to sabotage the game. You know the rules. I'm not allowed to fall in love with you, so I can't let you grow on me. I'm not taking any chances." She was messing around with him, but it was also a good reminder not to let herself get too attached to him. With a mental shrug, she snuggled closer to his back. "I've just gotten more skilled at tolerating you."

"You sweet talker," he said dryly. "I tolerate you, too."

He was proud of himself for not losing his shit at the emergency room. Every hospital staff member was working hard and doing their best to take care of all the patients, but they were just bombarded. After giving her some ibuprofen, they had Tara wait three hours to be x-rayed. She was in pain and tired, and it made him feel utterly helpless and furious that there wasn't more he could do.

Once they got back to the hotel, they were both exhausted and hungry.

"I'm so relieved it isn't broken," Tara said, settling into the wheelchair he'd rented from the hotel. "Now all I want is some room service and a hot bath."

Shit. He hadn't mentioned to her that they'd be sharing a room tonight. It seemed like a sound plan when he booked the room, but now he wasn't so sure.

"Tara, when you suggested an overnight trip, I had assumed—hoped—that we'd stay in the same room." He paused to clear his throat. "Before you say anything, I wasn't being completely presumptuous. There's a sofa bed, if you'd rather have me sleep there."

"I don't think you're presumptuous. That's what I wanted, too," she said with an adorable blush.

"Good. I'm glad." He sighed with relief that Tara wasn't offended, but at the same time, his body heated up at her words. *Get yourself under control.* With her injury, nothing was happening tonight. Which was a goddamn shame, but he wasn't going to risk hurting her.

After checking in, he pulled Tara into their room, then stopped for a moment to orient himself. How could he make her more comfortable? "Do you want to sit in front of the fireplace, while I make you some tea?"

"Tea? I'm not sick, Seth. I just have a sprained ankle. Let's have some coffee with Bailey's. There must be some in the mini bar."

He chuckled as some of the tension left his body. Since she didn't voice any objections to sitting in front of the fire, he maneuvered the wheelchair to a plush chair by the fireplace and gently placed Tara on it. Then he pulled its twin chair close and lifted her injured leg onto it, placing a cushion under her foot.

"Comfy?" he asked.

"Yes. Thank you," she said with her smiling face upturned toward him. He kissed her lightly because he couldn't help himself, and stepped away.

"Coffee with Bailey's coming right up."

Once he finished making their drinks, he brought the steaming mugs to her and handed both to her. "Don't get any ideas. One of them is mine."

"Spoilsport." She pouted.

He gingerly lifted her leg and sat down in the chair across from her and replaced her foot on his thigh. Reaching to retrieve his drink, he said, "Tsk-tsk. If you're not good, I might not share the whiskey and hot chocolate."

She grinned and took a sip of her drink. "Mmm. This hits the spot."

"How does your ankle feel?" He placed his mug down by the fireplace and slowly peeled off her fuzzy hospital sock. Her ankle was still swollen to the size of her calf, and he frowned.

"The Motrin is really helping. I barely notice the throbbing," she said cheerily, taking another sip of her adult beverage. "After this drink, I think I'll be a happy camper."

"You should have your bath once you're finished. The front desk is sending up our bags, so you could change into something more comfortable after that."

"Are you suggesting I slip into my lingerie for you?" Tara wiggled her eyebrows.

"Please try not to torture me. Put on the most modest, figure-obscuring clothing you have."

"Party pooper." She stuck out her tongue at him.

"There will be no parties tonight," he said like a true party pooper, and wistfully stared at the tip of her red tongue. "You can't even shift in your seat without wincing."

"You can't be serious." Her eyes widened with disbelief. "I can handle it."

"Oh, no you can't, sweetheart," he growled, letting his half-hooded eyes travel down her body.

Tara's jaws went slack as she stared at him, her cheeks glowing pink. He bared his teeth in a wicked smile, quite pleased with himself. It was his turn to torment her a little. But before they could tease each other into a frenzy, they were interrupted by the arrival of their bags. Seth tipped the bellhop and closed the door behind him. Then he brought Tara's duffel bag for her to sort through.

"I'll get the water going for your bath." He walked into the luxurious marbled bathroom with its Jacuzzi tub and separate shower. He raised his voice to be heard over the water. "You're in luck. It's a Jacuzzi tub. Do you want a bubble bath?"

"Ooh, that sounds heavenly," she purred.

When Seth came out of the bathroom to get her, Tara was already standing on one foot, holding on to the back of the chair for balance. She hugged her change of clothes to her chest with her free arm.

"Can you help me get to the bathroom?" she asked.

"No, I'm just going to stand here and watch you army crawl over there." She let go of the chair for a second to punch him in the arm. "Ow."

"And I don't want you carrying me there, either. Just let me lean on you and I'll hop the few steps to the bathroom."

"Sure, if you want the people below us to call the front desk for making a ruckus." Ignoring her protests, Seth scooped her into his arms and carried her to the bathroom. Then he described the game plan as though it were a simple matter. "There's a vanity stool you can use to . . . um . . . undress, but the tub is pretty high, so you're going to need help getting in there."

"I can manage," Tara said quickly, blushing to the roots of her hair. Was she embarrassed or majorly turned on by the thought of being carried by him with only a towel between them? He was hoping for the latter.

"You're going to break your neck trying to hop around on one foot. Just put a towel around yourself when you're ready, and I'll perch you on the side of the tub." And he wouldn't be tempted to rip the towel off of her. Not at all. He settled her on the stool, and scowled when she gave him a narrow-eyed glare. His intentions were honorable. He couldn't help the odd lustful thoughts here and there. He wasn't dead after all. "I'm not trying to get you naked. I have some self-preservation instincts. Besides, I've already seen you naked, re-member?"

"Now I do," she groaned, planting her palm on her forehead. "Fine, fine. Go away. I'll call you when I'm ready."

He went outside and stood a couple feet from the door, so he didn't feel like a lecherous creep but was still close enough to get to her in one bound if she needed help. There was some grunting and shuf-fling on the other side of the door, so Seth focused his mind on nam-ing the capital cities of all the states, not her undressing progress.

"Ow, ow, ow," she whimpered.

Shit. He was at the door in an instant with his hand on the handle. "Tara? Are you okay? Do you want me to come in?"

"No! It just hurt a little to pull my foot out of my ski pants. I'm fine now. Give me two more minutes before you burst in here."

He growled with frustration. If he'd helped her, she wouldn't have hurt herself getting her foot out of her pants. Seth wished they were already at the point in their relationship where he could help her un-dress and get her in the bath without all these obstacles. But they only had two dates left then he would be leaving for Paris. Rather than the usual excitement and anticipation, he felt something akin to regret at the thought. Why did he have to leave for Paris so soon? Because he had an incredible job he couldn't pass up, and a promis-ing future ahead of him.

With an impatient sigh, he raked his fingers through his hair. They weren't in a real relationship. They were playing a game. But was he just playing a game with her? *Shit.* Acid filled his stomach at the unavoidable truth. He wanted more. More time. More than a game. More Tara.

"Okay. I'm ready," she said quietly from the other side of the door.

Pushing aside his troubling thoughts, Seth took a deep, steadying breath and let himself into the bathroom. The hair she'd braided for skiing now fell in waves down her naked shoulders. The towel covered her from her chest to her knees, but so much glorious skin was laid bare for his perusal. *Fuck.* She wasn't displaying her nakedness for him to admire. She was waiting to be carried to her bath.

He cautiously lifted her into his arms, making sure he didn't jostle her injured foot. "You all right?"

"Mm-hmm," she said, not meeting his eyes.

That was a wise decision. Their faces were only inches apart, and if she turned toward him, he didn't know if he had the willpower to resist kissing her. He set her down on the tiles that surrounded the whirlpool tub. Now all she had to do was pivot on her bottom and slide into the tub.

"Okay. You're all set." Seth took a step back and then another to put distance between them, because she looked criminally beautiful perched on the corner of the tub. "I would offer to bring you another drink, but I don't want you drowning in the bubbles."

"Haha. I'll be fine." When his worried gaze lingered on her, she continued, "Seriously, shoo. You don't need to stand guard."

"Don't try to get out on your own," he warned again, terrified that she might slip and smash her head somewhere. "Call me when you're done."

"All right. All right. Stop with the fussing," she said, but there was a smile behind her voice.

Seth closed the door, tempted to lock it behind him. But he wouldn't be able to get inside again to help her, so he was just going to have to rely on his self-control not to bust in there and jump into the tub with her. He paced the small expanse of their one-bedroom suite like a caged predator to work off some of his restless energy. Even in his teenage years, he'd never felt this kind of suffocating sexual frustration before. His skin felt stretched so tight around him that he could imagine himself bursting out of his body like a fucking werewolf.

He stomped to the kitchen and poured himself a tall glass of ice water to cool himself off. He chugged it down all at once and was rewarded with a brain freeze, but at least he didn't feel quite as overheated.

"Seth?" Her lovely voice reached his ears from far away.

Muttering to himself while pacing back and forth sure made time fly. A good twenty minutes had passed. "Yeah, I'm coming."

In front of the bathroom door, he shook out his arms while he shuffled his feet like a boxer. When he was somewhat in control of himself, he entered the bathroom and promptly wanted to walk back out. She was up to her neck in bubbles with her wet hair piled on top of her head and cheeks rosy from the warm water. She looked like a fucking cupcake, and—God—he wanted to eat her up. How the hell was he going to keep his hands off of her tonight?

"Can you come stand here and hold your arms out for me?" she asked in a tiny voice. "And please close your eyes."

He rolled up his sleeves as he walked to her, and stood with his eyes closed as wet, slippery hands gripped his arms and pulled. Her arms slid against his forearm as she pulled herself up higher. *Just a little longer. You can't possibly die from a hard-on.*

"Eek!" she squeaked and wobbled with a splash.

Seth's hands wrapped around her instinctively to steady her. By some miracle, his eyes were still shut. "Are you okay?"

"Yeah." She sounded breathless.

Only after confirming that she was okay did Seth realize the placement of his hands. He'd hooked his hands under her arms, and the edge of his palms were grazing the sides of her breasts. *Fuuuck.* In a low growl worthy of a werewolf, he said, "Can you grab your towel?"

"Yeah. Got it."

"Can you wrap it around yourself?"

"Done."

He finally opened his eyes and glared at her. She stared back at him with giant eyes. He unceremoniously lifted her out of the tub and set her down on the vanity chair. After handing her an extra towel, he walked out of the bathroom without another word. He was a fucking stone Buddha for resisting the temptation known as Tara.

CHAPTER TEN

Well, fuck.

Tara was so turned on she was practically panting. She never knew that one smoldering look could push her to the point of trembling need. She squeezed her thighs together and tilted her head back, running her hand down her neck.

When she finally felt a bit less frenzied, Tara used the extra towel Seth left her and briskly dried herself off. She'd thankfully packed a loose, oversized T-shirt and a pair of yoga pants to wear when they were inside. Her real nighttime wear consisted of a black silk chemise and lace underwear, but since they were going to be good and chaste tonight, she kept the chemise in her overnight bag. There was nothing she could do about her minimalist underwear.

And there was no way she was going to tug on her yoga pants over her grapefruit-sized ankle. It would hurt like hell. So she was left with her gray Totoro T-shirt that barely hit her mid-thigh and her lacy black panties. She hoped the shirt was thick enough to obscure her nipples, because she refused to wear a bra to bed.

Once she was dressed, she sat still for a moment, making sure she was ready to call Seth back in. The man was too sexy for her sanity, and she had to prepare herself for the visceral impact of his gorgeousness. *Deep breaths.*

"Um, Seth? I'm ready to come out." Her voice came out an octave higher than usual.

"I'm here," he immediately replied, making her jump a little. It sounded as though he was right outside the bathroom door. *Oh, Lord.* She hoped he didn't overhear her heavy breathing.

He opened the door slowly, as though he couldn't trust that she was decent. Finally, he walked in and found her sitting demurely on the stool. His eyes didn't have wildfire burning in them anymore, so she was saved from yanking her shirt off and offering herself to him. *Thank goodness for small mercies.* Since there was no point in arguing with him, she wrapped her arms around his neck when he lifted her off the stool as though she didn't weigh close to her healthy 137 pounds.

"I'm going to put you down on the bed, so you can lie down."

"I don't need to lie down," she protested as he laid her down on top of the covers, resting her head on the fluffy pillows.

"Yes, you do. We need to elevate your foot above heart level," he said, lifting her injured foot and layering pillows underneath it. He studied her for a second, then added one more pillow. "It can't be helped. I'm keeping you on your back all night."

She gasped, happily scandalized, the same time Seth cringed.

"I didn't mean . . ." Were his ears red? Yup, he was definitely blushing.

"I knew what you meant." She did, but she'd been hoping he meant other, dirtier options.

"And you'll get to sit up when room service comes," he said, rubbing the back of his neck.

Ooh, room service. But wait. "Did you already order?"

"Of course not. You haven't even looked at the menu yet. I wasn't going to pick your food for you."

"Oh, good." She nodded in approval, and eagerly grabbed the menu he handed her. "I was starting to worry that you might be a caveman with all the carrying me around you've been doing."

Tara reached for the phone on her nightstand when she made her decision. A chicken club with steak fries. "You know what you want, right?"

"I'll have the bacon cheeseburger with a side of shoestring fries. Thanks."

"Ooh, perfect." Her mouth watered with all this talk of food and fries. "I'm getting steak fries. Can we share?"

"Hell, yeah." He grinned happily at her.

"Yay," she said, smiling back at him. Nothing was sexier than a man who shared his fries. "I'm going to order."

"Go right ahead." He walked away from her and rummaged around the plastic bag they'd brought back from the ER.

After she ordered, she leaned back on her pillow. "I hope they hurry. I'm starving."

"I'll make you some hot chocolate to hold you over once I've bandaged your ankle," he said, coming to sit by her feet with a fresh roll of elastic bandages.

"I can do that." She pushed herself up on her elbows. He'd been taking care of her all day.

"Lay back down, Tara. I want to do this, okay? I still feel like shit that you got hurt."

"Okay. If it makes you feel better," she said, holding back a smile.

If she were honest with herself, she quite enjoyed having him take care of her like this. It felt like a big warm hug, and made her heart ache a little. She liked it a lot. *Hmm.* This should worry her. Warm and fuzzy feelings had no part in the dating dare. Well, she was hurt, dammit. She deserved to be pampered a little, and she might as well enjoy it. Just for tonight.

"See. That wasn't so hard." He'd bandaged her ankle, not too loose, not too tight, and it felt worlds better.

"Thank you." Her smile felt more than a little sappy.

"Now, I'll get you that hot chocolate with whiskey, then I'm going to jump in the shower."

She nodded happily, excited for her hot chocolate and imagining him wet and naked. Humming to himself, Seth set about making her drink, then placed it on her nightstand. He stacked her pillow behind her so she could sit up halfway.

"I won't be long. And I'll leave the door ajar in case you need me." He handed her the mug and placed a kiss on her forehead. "Enjoy your drink."

What she wanted to enjoy was a peek at him in the shower. Tara laughed quietly, shaking her head. She'd had no idea she was so lascivious. She must've been looking forward to their weekend getaway and first night together more than she'd thought. But thanks to her sprained ankle, she was relegated to bed rest.

When she was halfway done with her spiked cocoa, there was a knock at the door.

"Room service," a voice said from the hallway.

"Hold on please," she yelled, pushing herself up into a sitting position.

"Stay in bed. I got it." The shower turned off, and Seth hurried out of the bathroom with a towel tied around his waist.

She might've swallowed her tongue. Wet, nearly naked Seth was something to behold. How were his abs so defined when he ate truckloads of food? And as she'd suspected, his pecs were sculpted masterpieces. Her mouth was suddenly dry, so she gulped down the rest of her hot chocolate as her eyes followed her date.

Once their dinner was rolled into the sitting area, Seth turned to her. "Give me a second to dry off and put some clothes on."

Boo clothes. Tara managed not to pout. "Sure. Take your time."

By the time Seth returned in a soft, worn T-shirt and a pair of basketball shorts, Tara's stomach was growling impatiently. The smell of greasy fried food was enough to make her drool.

He maneuvered the rolling tray to rest flush against her side of the bed and brought himself a chair to sit across from her. When he removed the silver lids, she couldn't help but squeal with delight.

"Oh, my gosh. That's heaven on a plate," she said, taking a huge bite out of her chicken club. The chicken was soft and juicy, and the bacon was crispy without being overcooked. With the cool crunch of the lettuce, the sweet tartness of the tomato, and the buttery avocado, she couldn't have asked for a more perfect bite.

She proceeded to demolish her sandwich and didn't come up for air until she'd finished the first half. Seth had already wolfed down his juicy bacon cheeseburger and sat munching on his fries. She picked up a steak fry and held it out to him. "Trade."

He plucked a small handful of his shoestring fries and placed it on her plate. "Here you go."

"Aww, Seth. You really know how to woo a girl." She fluttered her eyelashes at him for his generosity. She should offer him more, but her steak fries were thicker than his skinny ones. Still, she placed two more fries on his plate.

"So french fries are what does it for you?"

"I'm a woman of many facets." She stuck her nose up in the air. "Don't try to figure me out."

"I'll take that as a challenge." Seth grinned, all cocky confidence.

Tara hid her answering smile by starting on the second half of her sandwich. She tried to munch and swallow like she normally did, but Seth was staring at her with a quiet intensity that made her self-conscious. *Should I take smaller bites so it doesn't look like my cheeks are bursting? Nah.* This was the gluttonous facet of Tara. *Take it or leave it.*

When they'd cleaned off their plates, they had a debate about whether or not he should carry her to the bathroom to wash her greasy hands. They came to a compromise. He brought her a hot wet towel to wipe her hands on. She felt like a pampered airline passenger in the first-class section.

"Please don't tell me to lie down," Tara said when Seth came to perch beside her on the bed. "I'm so full, I need the help of gravity to keep my food down."

Chuckling softly, he piled two extra pillows underneath her foot. "Do you want to watch something?"

"Sure. What's on?"

He handed her the remote. "You pick."

She scrolled through the menu. Reruns, cartoons . . . *ooh,* Twilight. *After all he's done for me, I shouldn't force that one on him.* He would probably sit through it and pretend to enjoy it for her sake. He was just sweet like that. Oh, there was a Marvel Universe movie. Something they could both enjoy. Well, she really didn't know what kind of movies Seth liked, but it was a safe bet.

"Does this one work?"

"Awesome." He slid onto the other side of bed and rested his back against the headboard with his long legs stretched out.

It was surprisingly hard to concentrate on the blockbuster film. There was a good foot and a half of empty bed separating them, but

Tara could swear she felt his heat against her skin. She snuck a peek at him to find him absorbed in the movie, so she gave herself permission to stare at him, reveling in his hotness.

"See anything you like?" he asked casually with his eyes still glued to the TV.

Dammit. He must have excellent peripheral vision. She had to think fast, and a question she'd been meaning to ask him popped into her head. "Did you always know you wanted to pursue photography?"

"No." For a moment, she didn't think he would continue, but he sighed and glanced at her. "Not until my junior year in college."

"Oh? What did you major in before then?"

Another longish pause. "Mixed-media art."

He wasn't being very forthcoming with his answers and she wondered if she should stop prying. But now she was dying to know what had caused him to change his path. She felt as if she was missing an essential part of his story, and this was it. What was making her confident, easygoing Seth falter?

"Why did you change majors?" she asked gently.

"I'm getting a beer. Do you want one?" Without waiting for her answer, he shot out of bed and strode to the minifridge. "I think they have a couple bottles from Mammoth Brewery."

"Sure, I'll have one of those. They make good beer." Tara let him take his time with answering. But he acted as though the conversation was over and stood studying the fridge with great interest. It seemed hard for him to talk about. Maybe it wasn't fair of her to expect him to open up to her without making herself vulnerable first.

"I changed my major in the middle of college, too," she volunteered after taking a fortifying breath.

"You did?" That caught his interest and he hurried back to the bed with their beer. "What happened?"

She wasn't sure if he was really that interested in her change of major or he was just happy he wouldn't have to talk about himself. It was probably a bit of both. "When I went to college, I had no idea what I wanted to do with my life. I just thought I wanted to get out of Weldon and I wasn't the least bit interested in working at Weldon Brewery. I thought beer was gross in my teens."

Seth laughed. "So what was your major initially?"

"My school had one of the best viticulture and enology programs, so I thought I'd give it a go."

"This is getting better and better. You were studying to become a winemaker?"

"Yes, yes. The irony runs deep." Tara smiled at Seth, who was much more relaxed than he was a few minutes ago. "But I realized pretty quickly that what I wanted to do was become a master sommelier, so I shifted the focus of my courses to follow that path. I loved it."

"When did you realize that viticulture and enology wasn't the right major for you?" He was sitting crossed-legged on his side of the bed facing her, eager to hear the rest of her story.

"My college boyfriend decided that for me," she said quietly, nagging shame digging its claws into her. She'd let him decide for her.

"What?" he said in a measured voice.

"Jason said I was wasting my time because it was almost impossible for women to become master sommeliers. He implied I certainly wouldn't be able to become one." *How dare he?* she roared inside her head, still blindingly angry after all these years. Some of that anger was directed at herself for being too afraid to stand up to him. "He chastised me for not thinking of my immigrant parents, who worked so hard to give me a good life, and told me to choose a nice, stable career for them. He convinced me that graphic design was a fitting job for someone like me."

"Tara," Seth said, a wealth of empathy resonating in the single word.

"I was so much in love, and so damn young. I believed everything he said was because he loved me and wanted the best for me. I suddenly felt guilty about not thinking about my parents. I felt foolish for pursuing a pipe dream when I had them to think of."

"God, Tara. I'm so sorry that happened to you. I know you loved him, but your ex was an arrogant, misogynistic asshole. He had no right to say any of that belittling shit to you. They were all lies." He reached out and smoothed her hair behind her ear. "Never doubt that you're a good person, and you can do whatever you set out to do."

Emotion choked her, and the back of her eyes prickled with impending tears. "Well, my adventures in enology weren't a complete waste. The lessons on body, scent, and flavor apply to beer as well. I think my background in wine has given me a leg up for brewing and aging beer to give it different nuances and layers."

He seemed conflicted for a moment, as though he wanted to ask more about her relationship with Jason, but also to let her move on to safer topics. To her relief, he chose the latter. "I can see that. Your brews are amazing."

"See. Everything in life has meaning. You just need to find out what it is."

Seth muttered under his breath. She couldn't quite catch it. Something about breaking someone's jaw. She tucked her chin to hide her smile, appreciating his anger on her behalf. It was sweet.

She thought that a lot. That Seth was sweet. It happened so gradually that she had no idea how much her opinion of him had changed. She would never have thought that the cocky, superficial playboy could be so sweet. Maybe it was because he wasn't who she'd thought he was. He was more. Her heart picked up speed, and her mind asked too many questions at once. *No.* She didn't want to think about that.

He was looking at her with an inscrutable expression, and she decided she didn't want to know what he was thinking either.

"So are you really going to be a Boy Scout and just sleep tonight?" she blurted.

"The last couple weeks of being near you but not having you was more than I can handle. I want you so much, I don't think I could be gentle. I don't want to risk hurting your ankle more." The heat in his eyes and the rough regret in his voice shot straight to her vagina.

"You can't say sexy things like that and not put out." She flopped back onto her pillows and grabbed the front of her shirt, fanning herself briskly. "Why is it so fucking hot in here?"

Seth lay down next to her, chuckling low in his chest. The vibrations reverberated in her stomach, making all the butterflies take flight. He leaned in close and ran the back of his fingers down her bare leg. "Are you feeling frustrated?"

"Yes, dammit. I'm unbearably frustrated, and I want you to make love to me *now*."

"May I suggest a compromise that we both will be happy with?" His clever hand traveled toward her inner thigh. "Let me elevate your leg for you."

"It's already elevated to high hell." Then her eyes widened as Seth lifted her injured leg by her calf and methodically removed a pillow at a time. Her breath came in small puffs. "What are you doing?"

"Elevating your leg," he cooed as he hiked her leg over his shoulder, crouching low near the bottom of the bed. "Are you comfortable?"

"Yes," she squeaked. "Very."

He turned his head and kissed the inside of her thigh, one side then the next. He'd shaved his accidental beard, and she appreciated the smoothness of his cheeks. "I'm going to make you feel good now. Okay?"

"Okay." Then she added, "Thank you."

"You're welcome." His voice was a gruff rumble, and the heat of his breath licked at her center.

She let her head flop back onto her pillow, hot and cold at once. He was going to kill her. She was going to die. *But, hey. There are worse ways to go.*

S eth leaned back in the office chair and stared blankly at the ceiling. The lighting in the small office at the back of the restaurant was rather dim. Maybe he should've had some extra recessed lighting put in yesterday when the electricians were installing them in the dining hall. *Nah.* That probably would've been overkill. He should just let the interior decorator know the office needed a desk lamp.

As his brain prattled away, he realized how exhausted he was. He hadn't slept in four days. In Mammoth, sleep proved elusive after watching Tara fall apart like a goddess against his mouth. And since they got back, it had been torturous not to see her while she rested her ankle at home. Three days of their disappearing time together was spent apart, and he felt the loss acutely. Maybe he should've snuck in through her bedroom window to see her. *Ha!* But he wanted to see her so desperately that he wasn't above playing the role of a lovesick teenager.

Thankfully, she was finally back on her feet and working, but he was fast losing it. The temptation to snatch her and lock them in his bedroom for their last two weeks was growing stronger by the minute.

Not for the first time, he resented the time stamp on their relationship. Was moving to Paris that important? *Of course, it is. Stop letting your dick steer the ship.* He'd worked hard for the opportunity and couldn't give it up lightly. Besides, Tara had made it clear that she didn't want anything lasting.

His eyebrows burrowed together at the thought, his anger surfacing again. That douchebag ex of hers must've done a number on her. Her luck with love and relationships wasn't much better than his. He knew there had to be more to the story to have made her so insistent that he was a playboy and all they deserved were four dates. To have made her determined not to give him anything more than that. He didn't like it.

Sure, he'd cultivated his playboy image and never dissuaded anyone from believing it. And hadn't he been the one to suggest they have four dates? Yes, but he was damn sure she was keeping him at arm's length for reasons of her own.

Whatever the case, he wanted to convince her otherwise. He didn't care if he was contradicting himself. And he definitely wasn't ready to analyze why he wanted more. But he wanted more of her than their half-joking dare and one-month expiration date. They only had two damn weeks left.

But all that mattered right now was that he had to see her. He didn't have a third date planned yet, so he needed to come up with a good reason for another nondate. They'd made good progress on the website and it was nearly finished, so that wasn't going to cut it.

He righted his chair and ran his fingers through his hair, frustrated in every sense of the word. This was getting ridiculous. He should just call her and ask her to come to the house for a sleepover. His cell phone vibrated just in time to save him from grabbing his keys to go barge into the brewery.

"Hey, Aria," he said, his frustration dropping a few notches. It was always great to hear from her. "How are you?"

"Awesome as usual. How are you doing with the restaurant and housesitting gig?"

"It's going a bit too smoothly. I'm getting a little bored over here," he drawled.

Which was a complete lie. Being with Tara was far from boring. He had no idea why he said that. Maybe it was because Aria was like a bloodhound when it came to sniffing out romance. He had to keep his relationship with Tara a secret from her.

"That's perfect, because Lucien and I are coming for a visit," she announced.

"Today?"

"No time like the present. If you're free, that is."

"My evening is wide open." He was thrilled about Aria and Lucien's sudden visit even as his suspicions grew.

"I am absolutely not coming over to check up on you," she said as though she'd read his mind. "Landon would never ask me to do something like that. He trusts you because you're a big grown-up now."

Seth rolled his eyes. Landon couldn't help himself. He would hover and fuss over him until they were both old men with walkers. "Do what you gotta do, Aria. Landon's an asshole, but this will just go to show him that he could finally lay off. The restaurant is coming along incredibly well."

"I think Landon wanted to make sure you were doing okay with such a big change coming up in your life. He wouldn't have trusted you with overseeing the completion of the restaurant if he didn't trust you with his life," she said, loyally defending her friend. "Besides, I want to get my fill of you before you abandon all of us for Paris."

"I can't wait to see you guys." Seth chuckled. He adored Aria, and he definitely wanted to spend time with her and Lucien before he moved. "Is it safe to assume that you're covering dinner as usual? Because all I could manage for a dinner party is takeout."

"Don't you dare ruin my fun. I'm just going to throw some things together for us."

Which translated into a gourmet feast. Tara loved Aria's cooking. *That's it.* He could invite her over for a dinner with their friends. He was actually surprised that Aria hadn't suggested it yet. And it was definitely nondate territory. "And by us, you're including Tara, right?"

"Of course. How could I forget Tara? I would love to invite her gorgeous twin brothers, too, but I don't think they can shut down the brewery for the night to come play with us."

Seth heard Lucien's muted voice in the background say, "The gorgeous twins can't come? That's a damn shame."

"Don't be jealous, baby," Aria told her husband. "You're handsomer than the two of them combined. I was just saying. You know, objectively speaking."

"Stop with your lovers' spat," Seth cut in. "So should I ask Tara to join us around seven?"

"Yes, we'll be there by four to prepare dinner, but we can eat around seven."

"Should I get the wine?"

"Are you trying to insult Lucien?" Aria made a good show of sounding horrified. "We'll be bringing a box of his vineyard's finest wines. But do ask Tara to bring a few growlers of her best ales. I'll make some beer-friendly appetizers to pair with them."

"Got it. I'll see you guys soon," Seth said.

"We can't wait, sweetie." Sometimes she seemed to forget that he wasn't the gawky teenager he was when they'd first met.

And like the sap that he was, the first thing he did when he got off the phone was to text Tara.

SETH: Can you get tonight off?

TARA: Why? I already took too many days off for my sprained ankle. I should be working extra days.

SETH: Aria and Lucien are coming and want to invite you over for dinner.

It wasn't his idea at all.

TARA: Ugh. How can I resist Aria and Lucien?

SETH: Hey . . . and you can resist me?

There was a pause before she responded.

TARA: You know I can't resist you.

Her breathless cries as she fell apart in his arms echoed in his mind. *No, she can't resist me.* A lazy smile curved his lips at the thought.

SETH: Just making sure. So can you come over? Around seven?

TARA: I'll prevail upon the kindness of my brothers' hearts. Again.

"Yes." Seth pumped his fist, extraordinarily proud of his accomplishment.

Then he heard a small cough behind him. He spun around to find the interior designer standing at the door of the restaurant's office. *Ah, yes.* He hadn't closed the door.

"The chairs are here," the designer said with the slightest arch of his brow. "Do you want to check them out before we accept delivery?"

"Sure. I'll come with you," Seth said, keeping his expression bland.

He stood back and let the interior designer take charge of inspecting the chairs since it was his area of expertise. Once the chairs were accepted and lined up in one corner of the dining hall, Seth called it a day and headed back to the house.

He was used to coming home to an empty house, but his place was a minimalist two-bedroom condo. It seemed happy to be empty. But Aubrey and Landon's house seemed lonely and sad without its family. Suddenly missing his brother and his new family, Seth climbed the staircase and headed to his room. It hit him that he would be moving across the sea in a couple weeks, and he would rarely get to see them. And he would miss and worry about his mom.

I'll miss Tara like hell.

The thought stopped him midstep. He could barely stand not seeing her for a few days. Would he be able to turn around and leave her in two weeks? *Fuck.* It wasn't a matter of what he could or could not do. He didn't have a choice. He resumed his trek up the stairs. There was no point in torturing himself about the future. He had her for now, and he would make the most of their remaining time together.

When he reached his room, he headed straight for the shower. He bowed his head under the hot spray and let the water stream down his face and the rest of his body. He washed away his sudden punch-in-the-gut panic and focused on the evening ahead with Tara and his friends. After drying off, he pulled on a pair of jeans and a charcoal pullover and jogged down the stairs. Just as he reached the bottom of the stairs the doorbell rang, announcing the arrival of guests.

Seth swung the front door open with a big grin on his face, only to witness a makeout session in progress. He immediately proceeded to close it shut, but Lucien slapped his hand against it, his laughter floating into the house through the narrow gap. Seth opened the door again but stood blocking their path with his arms crossed over his chest.

"Hey, is this the way you treat your friends?" Aria said, bending down to pick up the lemons that had spilled out of a shopping bag—the bag she'd obviously dropped on the ground to wrap her arms around her husband's neck.

"It only took me a few seconds to open the door. How do you end up shoving your tongues into each other's mouths in that short amount of a time?" Seth said with almost convincing indignation. "Have some control, guys."

Lucien kissed Aria again for good measure, and smiled happily. "Your time will come."

"Now you're quoting a fortune cookie." Seth threw his hands up in the air. "I give up."

He stepped aside to let his friends come in, giving them belated hugs. It was a good thing Lucien hadn't dropped his bags, because he seemed to be carrying the bulk of the groceries that was destined to become their dinner.

"So how have you been doing out here all on your own?" Aria said teasingly, while rummaging through the groceries. "You must miss your social life."

"Not to mention your tall, leggy friends." Lucien joined in the fun.

"I've been doing great. Early nights and celibacy do wonders for one's health," he said wryly. Aria and Lucien burst into laughter. Like most people in his life, they were firm believers in his playboy persona.

He'd been partly serious, though. Slowing down his hectic life and enjoying the calm of Weldon had unknotted some of his tension. He'd been running too fast to take in the blurry images of his life. Everything was quieter, slower here.

Then there was Tara. Being with her made everything around him too clear, too bright. It was bringing into focus his deliberately hazy life. He was having trouble ignoring his increasing need to reassess his life. His mind was clamoring to conjure up what-ifs that would include Tara. But he wasn't going there. The shortcut to heartbreak lay that way.

Wiping her eyes, Aria continued to arrange the ingredients on the kitchen island, while sticking others in the fridge. "So how's Tara doing?"

"She misses Aubrey." He cleared his throat. He didn't know if he could sound casual talking about Tara. He wanted to shout to the world how amazing she was. "But otherwise, it's business as usual. She mentioned something about getting started on a new seasonal brew."

"So you guys keep in touch?" Lucien asked, handing Seth a glass of red he'd just poured.

Seth cleared his throat again. When that didn't work, he took a sip of his wine. "Well, she is the only person I know in Weldon. Besides, she's been helping me with the restaurant's website. Did you know she has a BA in graphic design?"

Now he was just blabbering. *Shit*. If Tara saw him bumbling around like this, she'd probably kill him. She was absolutely adamant about keeping their dating a secret.

"Really? So she didn't always want to be a brewer?" Aria said, cocking her head to one side. "She seems like she was born for the job."

Seth was this close to blurting that she'd originally started out as a viticulture and enology major, but that had been a private story that Tara had shared with him. And it didn't seem like a lot people knew about her asshole ex.

He was acting like a nervous wreck just talking about her. How was he going to be when she showed up? Could he make it any less obvious that he was interested in Tara? But the truth was, he was more than interested. He was downright infatuated with her.

That was not good. Not good at all.

CHAPTER ELEVEN

Thank you so much, oppa." Tara kissed Jack on the cheek for covering for her. Sometimes the perks of being the baby sister came in handy.

She couldn't wait to hang out with Aria and Lucien, but she was dying to see Seth. She felt a bit shy about spending time with him after that night in Mammoth, but then again, maybe that was why her heart was racing to see him again. *Good gracious, that was hot.*

Her mind flooded with heated thoughts as she slid into her car and pulled out of the parking lot. Her phone dinged with a text from Roger, and she impatiently deleted it. There was only one man she hungered for right now.

Tara got to Aubrey and Landon's house in record time and sprinted up the porch steps, unable to tame her desperation to be with Seth. Before she could knock, the front door swung open, and she was wrapped in a pair of strong arms.

"You've stayed away too long," Seth growled before his lips crushed against hers.

Tara welcomed his hard, hungry kiss, because she was starving, too. She pushed him back against the door and proceeded to show him how much she'd missed him. He moaned against her sensual onslaught, and she growled like a wild thing, rejoicing in her conquest. She actually wanted to laugh triumphantly when she felt the evidence of his desire pushing persistently into her stomach. The validation that he wanted her as much as she wanted him was heady, and she didn't want the kiss to end.

"Tara, wait." Seth tried to avert her next kiss by turning his head but she grabbed his hair in her fists and turned him to face her again. "Baby, we really need to stop."

"Not going to happen," she said against his lips.

"If you kiss me one more time, I'm going to throw you over my shoulder, take you upstairs to my room, and make love to you until you can't see straight," Seth warned in a low, sexy voice. "Aria and Lucien might think it very strange that we're not coming out of the room to join them for dinner."

"Shit. I completely forgot that Aria and Lucien are here. I'm a horrible friend."

"Not a horrible friend but maybe a horny one."

"Shut up," she said, punching him lightly on his shoulder. With her breathing slowing down to a semi-pant, she waved her hands in the general direction of his nether region. "Do you have all that under control?"

"Give me a minute." He walked to one end of the porch and took deep breaths. They sounded unsteady at first, but slowly evened out. After a few more breaths, he returned to her side. "All right. Let's see how long it takes for Aria to figure out what's happening between us."

"No, no. We can't let her figure anything out. Quite honestly, even I don't have us figured out. We need to be very careful. Don't smile at me too much. And *do not* give me that look."

"What look?"

"That look you're giving me right now. Like you want to throw me down on your bed and have your way with me."

"I can't help it because that's exactly what I want to do."

"Well, stop it for just a few hours. Okay?" Her whole body flushed with desire, but they had to hold it together. "You promised to keep our dating a secret."

"All right. I'll do my best. I'll undress you with my eyes at a later, more convenient time."

"At a later, more convenient time, you can undress me with your hands and teeth," she said in a husky voice.

"You're so cruel. Do you know that?"

"Maybe a little, but I so enjoy watching your eyes turn nearly black when you're turned on."

"If you do anything remotely close to this, I'll kiss you senseless with Aria and Lucien watching."

"Sorry, sorry. I'll behave. Okay?"

Seth mumbled something under his breath and opened the front door to let her through. As soon as she walked into the open kitchen, Tara realized she'd forgotten the beer in her frenzy to see Seth.

"Shit," she said, covering her face with her hand.

"Well, hello. Nice to see you, too," Aria teased, pulling Tara into a nice, tight hug. "What's going on?"

"Hi, Aria. It is so great to see you, and your hubs. Hey, Lucien." She waved at him. "But it just hit me that I forgot to bring the beer."

"That's a shame. We do love your beer. But it isn't a catastrophe," Lucien said, coming to stand beside Aria, tugging her close. "I brought plenty of wine to get all of us happily drunk."

"Well, thank heavens for that." Tara smiled at the couple. "I promise to visit you guys soon and bring over a keg of beer."

"We'll take that." Aria high-fived her husband.

They were just so gosh darn cute. An invisible thumb pushed down on a pressure point in her heart, making it ache just so. The point where she felt her loneliness the keenest. But having Seth by her side eased the ache.

"It smells like foodie heaven in here." Tara walked toward the kitchen island. "What do you have going?"

"Oh, a little of this and a little of that," Aria said with a shrug.

"Well, madam." Seth appeared at her side and twirled an imaginary mustache. "First, let me lead you to our table, where the antipasti have already been set out for us. It's a charcuterie board large enough for a party of twenty with all the meats and cheeses you can imagine."

Tara's eyes widened at the beautiful sight. There were prosciutto and iberico in the mix, and myriad arrays of hard to soft cheeses. When she spotted both crumbly and creamy blue cheese, she nearly swooned. With the honey, preserves, and a variety of fruits and crackers, she could make dinner out of the charcuterie board alone. But alas, Aria had other nefarious plans to fatten her up.

"The primo will be bucatini all'Amatriciana. She's generous with the chili flakes, so expect a robust kick," Seth continued. *Mmm. Bacon-y, tomato-y, spicy pasta.* Tara had already been salivating at the salumi and cheeses, but she was all but drooling now. "The secondo will be osso buco with a side of roasted seasonal vegetables."

"Don't tell me. She even made dessert, right?"

"Why, of course. The dinner won't be complete without the dolce." Seth did a decent job of looking mildly outraged. "The dessert will be Limoncello mousse cake."

"Oh, my goose bumps, Aria. So you threw this together just like that?"

"Well, I wouldn't say just like that." Aria laughed. "Good food takes time. I've been in the kitchen for nearly three hours."

"And you still look like you walked out of a fashion magazine. Oh, I give up." Tara threw up her hands.

"Ha! Says the hottie who turns heads everywhere she goes," Aria retorted, shaking her head.

"Yes, yes. Both of you are ridiculously gorgeous," Seth jumped in. "But Lucien and I helped, too. I set out that spectacular charcuterie board, and Lucien poured the wine to keep our chef happy."

"That's awesome. Thank you, everyone." Tara was actually impressed. The meat and cheese board was beautifully laid out. He really did have an artist's eye. "Whereas I had one job to do . . ."

Seth chuckled and tousled her hair. He'd become increasingly affectionate toward her, and it felt normal for them to constantly touch, nudge, and bump each other. But to Aria's keen eyes, it was a new development. And her raised eyebrow told Tara that it was noted with interest. Seth awkwardly stepped aside from Tara, and she busied herself rearranging random items on the island.

"So when do we eat?" Tara blurted a little louder than necessary.

"Right now," Aria announced, clapping her hands together. Tara was grateful she didn't say anything about Seth and her unintentional PDA. "Let's enjoy the charcuterie that our host set out like an artist's palette."

"I know. I almost feel bad messing it up," Tara said, popping a chunk of blue cheese into her mouth. "Almost."

Everyone started out taking a small slice here and there to maintain the gorgeous layout as long as possible, but once the wine was poured, they all dug in properly. Tara had to remind herself to savor each bite instead of wolfing down the whole board. She didn't want to miss out on the feast to come. But cheese.

"The pasta water's boiling," Aria said, stretching her neck to get a good look at the stove. "Tara, do you want to keep me company while I put together the pasta?"

"I would love to." Tara stood and piled her plate with more meat and cheese to hold her over.

"Hey, leave some for us," Seth teased.

"I'm in a generous mood. Knock yourselves out." Despite all their efforts, they'd hardly made a dent in the charcuterie board. She went to stand next to Aria and watched her add the bucatini into the salted boiling water. "Need any help?"

"Sure. Just stir the pot once in a while so the noodles don't stick together."

"Yes, ma'am." Tara saluted Aria with a wooden spoon. She'd really missed her friends, and being with them along with Seth almost made her giddy with happiness.

"So you must be spending a lot of time with Seth?" Aria said casually, putting chopped garlic into the tomato-based sauce.

"I wouldn't say a lot." Tara reined back her giddiness to formulate a neutral answer. Aubrey had told her about Aria's dead-on instinct for sniffing out budding relationships. "We do meet up to work on the website occasionally, but I can usually work on my part at home."

"I see," Aria said as though she really saw all. Tara gulped. "I was just thinking it must be nice for Seth to have someone he knows here. He must feel like he's in limbo, living in a new town for a month while his old home is packed up and his new home is waiting for him. I think your presence might be anchoring him."

"I'm hardly his anchor. We barely know each other." Tara gave the pot a good stir, avoiding her friend's eyes. She and Seth had gotten to know each other too well in the last couple weeks.

"Still, don't you think you'll miss him when he's an ocean away?" Aria salted the sauce, which was bubbling away happily on the stove. The pancetta and the garlic smelled mouthwatering.

"Maybe . . ." Tara trailed off, her heart suddenly constricting. Seth was leaving soon, which was exactly what she'd thought she wanted, but her twisting heart strongly disagreed. She would miss him. So much.

She unconsciously sought him out across the kitchen, and he immediately met her eyes as though he felt her gaze on him. He grinned lazily at her, sexy and warm, and she mustered a small smile for him. But inside, she was free-falling. He was leaving. The thought of the empty spot he would leave hit her viscerally. And it hurt like a bitch.

Tara couldn't let herself wallow in this pain-ridden panic. She stirred the pasta more vigorously than necessary, earning a searching glance from Aria. *Shit.* Had her friend been trying to gauge her reaction with her comment? She sighed. It didn't matter. She had no time to spare for worrying.

She would make the most out of her time left with Seth. To build memories that she could pull out on those achingly lonely days. Tara finally allowed herself to admit that she cared about him. It couldn't be helped. She wanted him. He was nothing like Jason. He was sweet, kind, and considerate, and he made her feel safe and cherished. She didn't want to hold back anymore. Besides, she didn't need to be afraid of giving him too much power over her. They only had two more weeks together.

Only two weeks. *Well, fuck.* She had better stop dragging her feet, and take him to bed tonight.

I f Tara was the cat, then he was definitely the cream. She'd been staring at him with hungry eyes all night, and he was dizzy with want. He didn't know what happened, but something had shifted. And he was very eager to find out what had changed to bring about this cat-and-cream situation.

Lucien switched to sparkling water long before the night drew to a close for the long drive to Bosque Verde. He was charming the ladies with his anecdotes despite the lack of alcohol. He was proof that designated drivers could have just as much fun.

Although he'd had a fantastic time, Seth was eager to see his guests off. He was an ungrateful bastard after Aria and Lucien had driven three hours to treat him to dinner. But this bastard didn't exist on bread alone.

"I'm literally a bite away from exploding," Seth said, taking another bite of the Limoncello cake.

"Boom." Tara made a mushroom cloud with her hands—all the while looking at him like he was something she couldn't wait to devour.

Holy Mother of God.

"Should I open another bottle of wine?" he asked like a good host, hoping his friends would take the sensible route.

"Oh, no. It's getting late." Aria put down her napkin on the table. "We have to get going. Lucien has a morning meeting tomorrow."

"Aww, already?" Tara said with genuine regret. She was a much better friend than he was.

"I'm afraid so," Lucien replied, standing up with his plate in his hands. "You'll understand when you're as old as me."

"Yes, of course. Early fifties is so ancient." His wife rolled her eyes and reached for the plates as well.

"Stop that," Seth said, waving away their hands. "You guys did the shopping and the cooking. At least let me clean up."

"Yeah, you have a long drive back." Tara backed him up. "I'll stay and help him clean up. It's the least I can do."

"Are you sure?" Aria covered a yawn with her hand.

"Yes, I'm sure." Seth gave Aria a tight hug before she could fuss anymore. She was truly an excellent human being, and he was going to miss her. Then he turned to Lucien. "It was good seeing you."

"We had to see you before you left for my old home." He squeezed Seth's shoulder.

It hit him that this was really goodbye for a while, and emotion clogged his throat. "I should've taken some French lessons from you. I'm going to be that uncouth American when I get to Paris with my awful French."

"Landon said it was better than your Korean," Aria said teasingly, grabbing him for another hug. "Take care of yourself. We'll miss you."

"I'll miss you guys, too," Seth said into her hair.

He and Tara walked their friends to their car and watched until the taillights disappeared into the night. She placed a warm hand on his shoulder, sensing his distress.

"Dammit. It's not like I'm never going to see them again." Seth pulled Tara into his arms and buried his face in her neck.

"Saying goodbye is tough. Don't be so hard on yourself," she whispered, drawing soothing circles on his back.

"God, Tara. It's going to wreck me to say goodbye to you." His voice was a husky rasp, saturated with fear.

Tonight made real to him that he had to leave her soon, and the thought was unbearable. Holding her in his arms felt like home. How the hell was he supposed to walk away from this?

"Don't say that. We'll make the best of the two weeks we have left together." She spoke with quiet determination.

"And how do you suppose we do that? Our first two dates were interrupted by a bunch of rascally kids and a speed-hungry teenager. It's like the world wants to throw in a monkey wrench before we get too cozy."

"Don't worry. I'll body block any and all monkey wrenches. Our last two dates will be all about us, but we'll talk about that later. First, we need to talk about the nondates."

"I want nondates with you every day," he said. "Please don't say no."

"I want to see you every day, too," she said, her face buried in his chest. He pressed her closer to him. "When we first started the dating dare, one month seemed like forever. But now two weeks seem far too short. So I'm changing some of the rules."

"Like what?" he asked with half trepidation and half curiosity.

Tara tilted her head to meet his eyes. Her expression held secrets and promises, bold and captivating. "The first rule I hereby ban is the keep-your-pants-on during nondates rule."

He dragged in a breath with great difficulty. "I second that."

"Do you now?" She got that cat look again, and Seth swallowed hard.

"Yes?" Why the hell did that come out like a question? He was all for taking his pants off during nondates. Like tonight. To show her how much he wanted to take his pants off, he made his voice low and growly and repeated, "Yes."

"Good," she said. "That's very good."

Then she buried her fingers in his hair and tugged his head down. Her kiss was fire and sugarplum, delicious and multifaceted like she was. She licked, nipped, and dropped butterfly kisses on the corners of his mouth. Her greedy hands traveled down to his back and clung tight.

He held back and let her lead the kiss as long as he could, but when she nibbled on his bottom lip and mewled, his control snapped. With a long groan, he tipped her head back and drove his tongue into her sweet, sweet mouth.

"You're my undoing," he rasped, trailing kisses along her jaw until he reached her ear. He sucked her earlobe into his mouth and was rewarded with her moan.

"Good," she said breathlessly, pressing herself against him until not a single molecule could get between them. "I spin out of control when you touch me, but I don't care as long as I can have you."

"God, yes."

She could have him as many times as she wanted. Tonight and every night for the next two weeks. His heart froze remembering he had to leave soon, and he shoved the thought far, far away. Making love to her was not just another hookup. She was special. She was Tara. And he wasn't going to continue groping her in the driveway. He lifted her into his arms and walked toward the front entrance.

"I'm taking you inside." *To my bedroom. To my bed.*

Tara nodded vigorously while clinging to his neck. He burned everywhere she touched him, and his hands were on fire where he held her. It was almost too much to bear, his need for her. He took the stairs two at a time to reach his bedroom.

When he lowered her onto his bed, she kept her arms around his neck so he couldn't go far. "Confession. I've fantasized about being carried to bed like this."

"That's what I'm here for." He grinned down at her as he climbed into bed next to her. "Making your fantasies come true."

"Oh, goodie," Tara said, cupping his cheek in her hand.

"We're going to be so good together," he promised. They were going to fit perfectly.

He slipped his hand under her shirt and caressed her silky skin from the bend of her waist to her back, traveling up until he reached the clasp of her bra. He undid it with a single flick of his wrist.

"Wow. Did you just do that with one hand? On the first try?" She giggled nervously. "I'm pretty sure I'm far less experienced than you. I might not be as good at this as you."

"That's impossible," he said fervently. And her lack of experience appealed to the caveman in him. He much preferred to show her the many ways they could enjoy each other himself. "A kiss from you can bring me to my knees. No one else has ever affected me that way before."

As though she wanted to test what he said, she rose on her elbow and brought her lips to his. With a groan, he pulled her on top of him, and spread her legs to straddle his hips.

"Take your shirt off," he said.

Tara grasped the bottom of her shirt and pulled it over her head in a single, fluid move, throwing it on the floor. Her unclasped bra quickly followed suit. He lay frozen because it hit him that Tara was sitting topless on him. She was fucking spectacular. His hands twitched at his side but he was too much in awe to touch her right away.

"How are you so beautiful?" he whispered, suddenly unnerved by how much he wanted her.

"If I'm so beautiful, why aren't you touching me?" Tara grabbed his hands and planted them firmly on her breasts, and both of them moaned loudly.

It was as though she was custom-made to fit his hands. Her firm, small breasts were perfectly round and crowned with pinkish-beige tips, which turned hard as he swirled his thumbs around them. Tara's head titled back as she thrust her breasts into his hands. Unable to hold himself back any longer, he raised himself into a sitting position with his hands firmly grasping her ass.

He bent his head and teased her breasts with his mouth. Drunk on the small, whimpering sounds she made, it took him a moment to realize that her hands were tugging impatiently at his shirt.

"Sorry," he said, and whipped it off to give her the access she sought. When he tried to return to what he was doing, Tara planted her hands on his chest and held him off.

"I want to look at you." Her eyes roamed his torso hungrily until she laughed incredulously, shaking her head. "How do you even look like this?"

"Why? Do you like it?" he asked, shamelessly fishing for compliments. He hissed when Tara's soft fingers traced the grooves of his abs.

"What do you think?" She pressed her breasts against his chest and sighed deeply. "I can look at you all day. But I'll save that part for after we give each other earth-shattering orgasms."

"You first," he growled, and flipped her onto her back. He finished undressing her and threw his own clothes on the floor. Then he positioned himself on top of her, naked skin against naked skin. *God, it feels so good.* "Is this okay?"

"A hell of a lot better than okay," she said breathlessly.

With a satisfied smile, he traced kisses down her torso, making sure to give her lovely breasts the attention they deserved. He paused when he reached her hips to trace a tattoo of a vibrant iris. The royal purple, rich burgundy, and a splash of deep yellow of the tattoo made the flower almost look real.

"I like this. The iris reminds me of you. Sensual and passionate," he said with his mouth brushing kisses over the tattoo.

"Thank you." She shivered against his touch.

He moved down to kiss the junction between her thighs. "I like this, too. You're just pretty everywhere, baby."

Then, because he wanted to taste her and have her fall apart against his tongue, he kissed, teased, and licked her until her hands fisted in her hair and she screamed his name.

"Good girl." He slid up to kiss her firmly on her lips. He had to be inside her. He couldn't wait another minute. She protested when he broke the kiss. He placed another quick kiss on her lips to settle her. "Condom."

"Here. Let me," she said, once he pulled one out of the nightstand.

She reached over and took the condom package from his hand and ripped it open. *Fuck.* When she reached over to roll the rubber over him, he had to keep a tight rein on himself so he wouldn't come before he even got inside her. But it was a close call with her warm, firm hand gripping him.

"Are you sure you want this?" he asked, holding himself still at her entrance.

"I want this very, very much," she said, pulling his hips closer to her.

"Good."

They came together with a sigh, and he worshiped her with his trembling body until the world splintered and fell around them.

ood morning, baby." Seth's voice was husky with sleep on the other end of the line. Tara could almost see him lying in his bed with his sheets low on his waist, revealing his glorious chest and abs.

"Good morning," she replied, suddenly wide awake.

"I wanted to wake up with you beside me," he said softly, sending a shiver down her back.

"Me, too. Sorry I had to come home." She lay flat on her bed and stared up at her ceiling. She would so much rather look up at Seth's face as he held himself over her.

Last night had blown her mind. Seth hadn't been kidding when he said he was there to make her fantasies come true. So. Many. Orgasms. She was still limp from them.

"When will I see you?" he asked, impatience lining his tone.

"When do you want to see me?"

"Right now works."

"It's barely past seven." She laughed, delighted at his urgency. She felt the same way.

"I make some mean scrambled eggs, and Landon's toaster does a decent job of popping out toast."

"Coffee?"

"French-pressed," he said smugly.

"I'll be there in forty-five minutes. Bye."

Tara jumped out of bed and dived into the shower stall. She had to leave in twenty minutes if she wanted to get to Seth in time. It was a good thing she was so low-maintenance. After a quick shower, she brushed out her damp hair and put on some tinted lip balm, and headed out the door.

She reached his place on autopilot, busy thinking about what she wanted to do with him, and parked in a cloud of dust. She ran up the steps to the front entrance, dismissing self-control and dignity. He opened the door before she even rang the doorbell. "How do you always do that? Do you look out the window waiting for me?"

"Yes," he said, smiling happily.

It made her happy, too, so she threw herself into his arms with enough force to make him widen his stance for balance.

"Whoa." Seth laughed, his warm breath against her neck.

"This is good," she sighed.

"Yeah, it is." His voice was muffled because he was busy placing soft kisses along her jawline.

Just as she melted against him, her stomach protested loudly. *Food now. Sex later.* The rest of her lust-infused body thought otherwise. *How barbaric to think of food at a time like this. The glory of sex awaits us.* When her stomach growled again, Tara buried her face in Seth's chest and mumbled, "About that breakfast . . ."

"I did tempt you over here with the promise of breakfast." He lifted his head after one last kiss behind her ear. "Sorry, I got side-tracked."

"Lead the way," she said, linking her arm through his. "I'm assuming you'll be stripping down to your boxers to cook for me?"

"What? You know I'm shy." His eyes twinkled with mischief. "But if you join me, I might take my shirt off."

"Are you sure you can take it?" She employed her medium eyebrow arch to express mild cynicism.

"Actually, no. I don't want to feed you burnt eggs. But I could still take my shirt off." He grasped the hem of his shirt with a cocky grin, giving her a tantalizing view of a strip of abs.

"Wait," she said, reaching out to stay his hands. She swallowed, literally salivating after him. "Don't. I can't take it either."

"You'll be fine." Her hands dropped to her side without resistance when he proceeded to pull his shirt above his head.

Once he tossed his shirt onto the back of a kitchen chair, she stepped up to him because she had to get her hands on him. She smoothed her palms around his broad chest, then moved on to explore his abs. Seth groaned. She wanted to drizzle maple syrup into the ridges of his six-pack and lick it all off.

"You don't understand, Seth." Her hands didn't cease moving over his naked torso. "I can't stop touching you . . . but I need to stop so you can cook. Please put your shirt back on. I'm starving."

"I . . ." He cleared his throat and reached for his shirt with her greedy hands still roaming his body. "I see your point."

Even when his T-shirt fell over her hands, Tara was reluctant to take them off of him. *Listen, hands. You need to disengage. That's an order.* Trailing her fingers down his stomach, she slowly let her hands drop to her sides, then took a step back for good measure.

"Okay." She flapped her hands to send him off. He was still too close. "Go make us breakfast so we'll have energy for our after-breakfast activities."

With a smug smile curling his lips, Seth walked to the fridge and pulled out some butter, eggs, and milk.

"Ooh, I didn't know you were making fancy scrambled eggs." Tara went to stand by the island so she could watch him cook. It was so sexy.

"Fancy scrambled eggs? Don't all scrambled eggs have these ingredients?"

"Milk maybe, but butter is a definite level up."

Seth chuckled. "These are the only eggs I know how to cook. Aria taught me before I went to college, saying that I won't starve as long as I know how to cook some eggs."

"It's Aria's recipe? Well, then. They're fancy eggs for sure." She rubbed her hands together. "Can I help?"

"Do you want to slice some bread for toast?" he said, pointing at half a loaf of country bread.

"Sure. We get crusty bread with the eggs? This is totally gourmet." She sliced three pieces of bread and cut them in half so they would fit in the toaster. "Do you want olive oil on the bread?"

"No, thanks. I think of bread as a conduit for the butter." He smiled at her and returned his attention to whisking the eggs quicksilver fast.

He placed a generous pat of butter onto the heated pan, then added beaten eggs when it was just melted. He stirred the pan until fluffy morsels formed and took it off the heat. The toaster dinged as soon as Seth plated their decadent scrambled eggs, so she joined him at the kitchen table with a plate of toast. He went back into the kitchen, but returned quickly with French-pressed coffee.

"Ah, a man of his word," she said appreciatively.

"Always. Now let's eat," he said, as he poured her a small glass of orange juice from the carafe on the table.

Tara needed no more encouragement. The first bite of the creamy, fluffy eggs had her lashes fluttering. "Oh, my googly eyes. This is incredible."

"Thank you. I've had years of practice." He laughed, shaking his head. "*Googly eyes?*"

"Shush. Things pop out of my mouth before my brain registers it. But really, this is so great."

As Tara shoveled the eggs into her mouth, something niggled at the back of her mind. He'd learned how to make this before he went to college, and had a lot of practice since then. Did he make scrambled eggs for every woman he slept with? *Whoa.* Where did that come from? *I can't be jealous. Especially over his past.*

She stopped tasting the eggs, remembering how he'd changed the subject when she asked him why he switched majors in junior year. Did it have something to do with a college girlfriend? It was none of her business, but she wanted to know what had happened. She was probably just projecting her experience with Jason on Seth.

"Hey, where are you?" Seth asked softly.

Tara looked down at the plate to find it cleaned off. "I like to give delicious food my complete and undivided attention."

"Hmm . . ." He didn't buy it, but he didn't push it either. "More coffee?"

"No, thanks. I'm good," she said, shaking off the last vestiges of her mulling. "I'll do the dishes."

"The dishes can wait," he said, gazing at her with sudden intensity. "Take your shirt off."

"Oh."

"Should I come do it for you?"

"Sure." She seemed incapable of uttering more than single-word responses.

Seth came around to her side and lifted her up from her chair. He leaned down to kiss her neck and spread his hands under her shirt, caressing her back. When he tugged at her shirt, Tara lifted her arms to help him with the disrobing.

"I would love to have you in the kitchen, but I don't think we should desecrate Landon and Aubrey's sacred place."

"The bed. Now." Tara began pulling Seth by his hand, but he lifted her in his arms.

"Quicker this way."

"Good idea." She hummed happily and nibbled on his ear.

With a curse, he adjusted his hold on her and ran to his room. He plopped her down on the middle of the bed and immediately jumped on top of her. She giggled and squirmed under him. He easily caught her hands and held them over her head.

"Hello, Tara," he said in a low, rumbling voice.

"Hi," she replied in a breathless whisper, and gave a miniwave with one of her captive hands.

"I like having sex with you." Growly. Sexy. *Gah.*

"I like it, too." So much so that she was growing impatient with all the talking. "Kiss me already."

"I really like *you*." His eyes roamed her face with such tenderness, she nearly melted into goo. It frightened her how happy she felt about it.

"Thank you," she said, but couldn't admit to him that she really liked him, too.

It was too much . . . sharing. They weren't supposed to get attached to each other. Making the best of the rest of their time together was one thing, but letting her emotions get sucked in too far was something else entirely. Yes, she was really into him, but that was for her to know and protect. Seth wasn't Jason, but there was no reason to hand him a weapon he could wield against her some day.

"You're welcome." Seth smiled a bit wistfully and said, "Now I'm going to kiss you."

Before she could tell him it was about time, he swooped down and captured her lips, and all she managed was a soft moan of approval.

S eth held his breath, wanting the moment to last forever. Waking up with Tara in his arms felt so right, he could hardly believe it.

He glanced at the clock. It was almost eleven. He must've worn her out. That made him grin like the smug bastard he was. He would hate to wake her from her catnap, but she might have plans before she went into work. Seth placed a gentle kiss on her shoulder and ran his hand down the silky skin of her arm.

"Do you have the early shift today?" he asked when her lashes fluttered as though she was considering waking up.

"No." She stretched luxuriously with her arms above her head, then went limp with a happy sigh. Finally opening her eyes, she turned onto her side to face him. "How about you? Do you have to go into the restaurant?"

"Not for another couple hours, but I've been neglecting the website lately. I should get that finished."

"Perfect. Since I'm here and all, I will lend you my expertise."

"Thank you kindly," Seth said, tucking her hair behind her ear.

"Before we do that, I have something to confess." Her cheeks were flushed, but she had a look of fierce determination on her face. "It doesn't feel right keeping this from you."

"You sound so serious. Are you a spy or something?" Seth laughed nervously. What could she possibly have to confess to him?

"Aubrey never asked me to help you with the website," she nearly yelled in a rush of breath.

"What? Why would you lie about Aubrey asking you to help me?" He was thoroughly confused. Why would she . . . Then it hit him. And Tara's expression—the one that said she wanted to hide behind the dresser—confirmed his suspicions. She'd come up with the lie to spend more time with him. He smiled so widely that his cheeks cramped. "Why you sly little fox."

"Look. I'm sorry I lied to you, but no harm done, right?" She pulled the covers over her head. "Can we just never talk about this again?"

"I went to Comfort Zone that day hoping to find you there," he said softly, tugging away the sheet from her face. "In fact, I was going to stake out there for hours, waiting for you."

"You were?" Tara's eyes were wide and shining. "You wanted to spend more time with me, too?"

"Yes, and you provided the perfect excuse." Seth tapped the tip of her nose. "We make quite a pair, don't we?"

"Yeah. A pair of cowards. Why didn't one of us just say, 'Hey, let's hang out more'?"

"It was the beginning of the dating dare, and we had game rules to follow. And I think neither of us wanted to scare the other off."

She cupped his cheek and asked, "Have I scared you off now?"

"No, you can't scare me off. I'm going to spend every day I have with you like it's the last day of the world."

She leaned over and gave him a kiss as sweet as honey. But he really needed to get out of bed before he was tempted to make love to her again. He gave her a quick kiss in return, and reluctantly rolled out of bed.

"Nice ass," Tara said appreciatively as he picked up his clothes off the floor. "You sure you need to cover that up?"

"Are we having that conversation again?" he said, pulling on his boxer briefs. "We won't get anything done without clothes on."

"Boo," she said with an adorable pout. "We would totally get things done. Dirty, fun things."

He pulled on his shirt to another resounding *boo* and reached to get her clothes off the floor. She was all covered up in the bedsheets, but he knew she was naked under there. If she didn't get dressed now, he was going to fail adulting today. But he couldn't let Landon down.

"Please put some clothes on before I jump you. I really need to work on that website before I go to the restaurant."

"Oh, fine," she said, picking up her panties from the top of the pile. "Well, don't just stand there. Go away so I can get dressed."

"What? You let me undress you but you're not going to let me watch you get dressed?"

"That was different. Now we're trying to unsex things." She nibbled her lower lip. "Go. I'm feeling shy, okay?"

"Boo," he said as he closed the bedroom door behind him.

The coffee had gone cold so he made another carafe and poured it into two mugs. Tara drank her coffee black, but he added a teaspoon of sugar and a splash of half and half into his. The Parisians would probably laugh at him, but he didn't plan on changing his ways. He had a sweet tooth and he was a sucker for all things creamy.

He took the steaming mugs, set them out on the living room coffee table, and brought out some oatmeal cookies from Comfort Zone to earn brownie points with Tara. His laptop had fallen asleep on the sofa, so he plopped down next to it and woke it up. A picture of Tara filled his screen. He'd been going through the pictures he took of her in the hills to select a few to show her. But the one on the screen . . . His heart was bare on that one. She looked like an angel in a dream, radiant but untouchable. The yearning that exuded from the photo was not something he was ready to share with Tara.

"Seth?" Her voice came from right behind him. "Is that me?"

Shit. Would she be spooked by how much he longed for her? He hoped she saw it as just another picture of herself, where she studied her smile and the angle of her face with overly critical eyes like everyone did. He coughed into his fist. "Um . . . yeah."

"Is that . . . is that how you see me?" She spoke in a soft whisper as though she might break the spell.

The awe in her voice made something flare in his heart. A small spark of happiness that she saw it as more than just a picture. Like the soaring joy he used to feel when someone appreciated a piece of his art.

"Yes." There was no use lying. The picture was taken through the lens of his soul. Something he hadn't done since college.

"I don't know what to say." She came around the sofa to sit beside him. "The picture is breathtaking. It feels funny saying that about a picture of me, but it's more than that. Something about it just grips me, and its beauty touches me viscerally. It's as though I'm seeing a glimpse of your dream. The intimacy of it . . . I feel like I should look away, but I can't."

Seth cleared his throat for the tenth time. She saw him, but she wasn't spooked. She was enthralled. Blood pounded loudly in his ears. "Do you want to see some more?"

Tara looked at the pictures he showed her with gasps of delight and whispers of praise. When they were done, she had tears in her eyes. "Thank you for sharing that with me. I'm honored."

"It was my pleasure," he said, realizing he'd really enjoyed showing her the pictures. He shifted on the sofa to see her face clearly. She didn't look upset. She probably didn't catch that those pictures of her were infused with his feelings for her.

"Why did you stop pursuing art?" She trailed the back of her hand down his cheek. "Your fashion photos are spectacular and artistic, but what you just showed me felt like your *art*. Something you love. I don't understand."

He put aside his laptop and cradled his coffee in his hands. "It's something I put aside a long time ago, and don't intend to resume."

"But why?" She wasn't going to let it slide this time. She'd shared an important part of her past with him. He should offer her the same consideration and explain what happened.

"Art was my first love." His voice broke on the word *love*. "I started out sketching as a kid, then my mom taught me how to paint. When I was in high school, I discovered mixed-media art, and it was as though a whole new world had opened up to me. Of course, I chose to major in it in college."

Tara nodded and gently squeezed his forearm.

"I was a shy, quiet kid. I went to my high school prom with my friends because I was too scared to ask my yearlong crush to go with me." He laughed softly through his nose. He found his words coming easier with Tara's warmth beside him. "My sophomore year in college, I met Jessica. She was beautiful and outgoing, always surrounded by people clamoring for her attention. I fell hard for her. She was so far out of my league. I expected another bout of unreciprocated love. I was more terrified than flattered when she started pursuing me. The first few times she asked me out, I actually refused."

"You were in love with the woman and you refused to go out with her?" Tara half-smiled, shaking her head.

"I know. I was that shy and naive. I'd never had a girlfriend or even been on a date back then. I thought I was going to make a fool of myself if I accepted. But she was relentless. She would wait for me in front of my classes and show up at my art studio. And finally I thought, what the hell?"

"Way to go, young Seth." She mock punched him on his shoulder.

"It was wonderful the first few months. She was intelligent and genuinely interested in my art. I thought she was the one. Someone I could spend the rest of my life with." Seth put his mug back on the coffee table and raked his hair with his fingers. "But things changed. I guess the novelty of having an introverted artist for a boyfriend wore off quickly, and she started complaining that it was boring when it was just the two of us. I tried to change for her. I even went to frat parties and dealt with the drunken crowd and noise. I spent more time trying to please her, and less time on my art. She made me feel as though I had to pick between the two of them."

"No," Tara whispered, and took ahold of his hand.

"But when it came time to prepare for my first open exhibit, I begged Jessica for her understanding. She grudgingly gave me some space. I was so grateful that I planned an elaborate romantic dinner for us after the exhibit." He stopped and took a deep breath through his nose. He wasn't sure he could continue. He'd never told anyone about the next part.

"Oh, Seth. You don't have to tell me any more if it's hard for you. I understand."

Tara's soft reassurance fueled him on. "The night of the exhibit, she showed up with her entourage. I think they were all a little drunk. I smelled alcohol on them. They were rude to the other student artists with their rowdiness and absolute disrespect for their work. But they were outright cruel to me when they came to my wall. They laughed and insulted my work, saying they looked like a five-year-old's finger painting, and Jessica laughed right along beside them. Then she launched a lance through my heart. She said I would never make it in the real world with my third-rate talent, and should look into drawing caricatures at amusement parks. She and her friends cackled like a pack of hyenas, and I couldn't take it. She sullied something sacred to me. I ran out of the exhibit and never turned back."

"That's when you changed your major?"

"The very next day, I went and changed it to photography. I felt like I didn't have to bare my soul when it came to photography, especially if I wanted to go commercial. And thanks to my mixed-media major, I had taken a great many photography classes already, so I was even able to graduate on time." Seth tried to shrug nonchalantly. "In the end, it all worked out. I have a successful career and I got past my shy stage."

"There's no doubt that you're a talented photographer. Your magazine spreads are so full of life and dazzling. But these pictures of me . . . they feel different. Your soul is in it. I think somewhere inside, your love of art is clamoring to get out."

"You're reading too much into those pictures. I photographed a woman I admire and desire on a perfect day in the sun. That's just the way I see you—beyond beautiful—and my lens captured that."

Tara gazed at him with sad eyes, but she just cozied up beside him on the couch and kissed him lightly on the lips. "Flatterer."

"Hey, I'm only telling the truth." He kissed her back, then pulled away quickly. Kissing her was addicting, and he really needed to get some work done. Besides, he could use something to pour his attention into. The past was threatening to encroach on the present with its dark claws. "Now stop kissing me, so I can get to work."

"Aw, man. Do I have to?" She grinned cheekily and scooted away from him, leaving a respectable distance between them.

"And quit being so adorable," he said with feigned irritation.

"You're such a dork." She crinkled her nose at him, holding back a laugh.

And just like that the darkness receded into the past.

CHAPTER THIRTEEN

Tara had the 5 p.m. to 2 a.m. shift tonight, but her mind was hardly at the brewery. She couldn't stop thinking about what Seth had told her earlier today. Her heart broke at hearing his story. It was such a damn shame that he was letting his true talent waste away because a cruel little bitch stomped on his heart until it became a stain on the sidewalk. No one should experience something like that. Especially not someone as kind and gentle as Seth.

But at the same time, she felt intensely jealous. Was Jessica the love of his life? He'd said something about spending the rest of his life with her. Did life lose meaning for him when he let her go? Is that why he chose to give up art? Was he was still pining for her even after what she did to him?

The customer jumped a little when she slammed down his blond ale a bit harder than necessary, making it slosh onto the table.

"Oh, my gosh. I'm so sorry. It must've slipped my hand," Tara said, picking up his glass again. "Let me refill it for you. It'll just be a second."

Fuckity hell. She was losing it. No matter how frustrated or angry she was, Tara never let her mood affect her work. But the green monster was on a rampage through the brewery.

If anyone so much as looked at her wrong, they got her glare from hell. The kind where actual fire flickered in her eyes. Or at least it did in her mind.

"Here you go. Sorry about that again." Tara deliberately set down the cup with care and forced a smile for the customer.

"No problem," he said nicely enough, then speed walked away from her like rabid raccoons were on his ass, glancing over his shoulder once.

"What did you do to him?" Jack asked, watching the customer retreat.

"Nothing . . ." she hedged. "I just slammed down his glass on the counter like a bartender does to strangers in spaghetti westerns."

"Right." Her brother studied her face, and said blandly, "Should I avoid you tonight? I don't want you jumping down my throat."

"So you're just going to avoid me? Don't you even care why I'm feeling down?" Righteous indignation burned in her voice.

"You're not feeling down. You are mightily pissed off about something, which means you can't be reasoned with tonight," he said matter-of-factly. "I'll give you a big hug and pat your back when you're a little less scary."

"I am *not* scary," she growled. She might have shown some teeth.

"Of course, you're not." Jack backed away from her step by step. "I'll go take some orders now."

Traitor. And he was the nice one. If Alex were out front, he'd be pressing every button to raise her blood pressure even higher. He thought she was hilarious when she was cranky. She did come up with some creative curse words when pushed just right, and those could be pretty entertaining.

Jack took off in a jog once he was out of arm's reach. Tara muttered unkind things about her brothers under her breath. Not really deserved, but she was in a black mood. And the fact that she was in a black mood put her in a worse mood. *What is wrong with you?*

Tara gasped. What was wrong with her was that she wanted to fix him. She wanted to mend Seth's heart, so he could start his art again. She was going out of her fucking mind. Who was she to fix anyone? She had enough baggage to last her a lifetime without adding someone else's to the load. All she would probably do was break him even more.

She was getting in too deep. It was time she admitted that Seth was different from her other flings. There was a connection between them that couldn't be ignored, and being in his arms felt so right. She already missed him, even though she saw him earlier that day. What had she gotten herself into? How had she allowed him to get so close? Tara knew what would happen if she opened her heart to someone again. She couldn't. Never again.

He's leaving. She wanted to sob out loud. The mantra that had kept her feeling safe all this time now felt like a thousand needles in her heart. When he left, she would be safe again, but did she want to be safe if it meant Seth would be out of her life? She put down the glass she'd been drying after nearly dropping it. *Do not answer that question.*

"What's wrong, baby?" Her mom came out from the kitchen wiping her hands on her apron. "Jack said that you were being scary."

"It's nothing, Mom." But Tara ruined the reassurance by sobbing in the middle of it.

"It's okay. Everything will be okay."

Without further question, her mom enveloped her in a hug and did what moms do best—make everything better somehow. But they were out in the hall, so Tara backed out of her embrace. "Thank you. I . . . I just miss Aubrey a lot today."

It was true. She needed to talk to her best friend, and figure out what was happening to her. At this point, keeping her dating dare with Seth a secret seemed foolish. Aubrey would never judge her. She knew how emotionally abusive Jason had been, and would understand Tara's fears and tangled thoughts.

"Are you still struggling with your best friend being married?" Her mom squeezed her hand. "Your time will come soon."

"Ha!" She clamped her hand over her mouth, but it was too late. She'd already spit in her mom's face. Literally.

Her mom lightly slapped her arm. "I'm serious. Why do you make jokes out of everything? You're twenty-eight years old. It's time you started thinking about things like marriage."

"Oh, Mom. Please don't tell me to find a nice young man and settle down. I always brag to my friends that you are the coolest mom because you never ask me when I'm going to get married. At least not directly."

"Just because I try my best to mind my own business doesn't mean I don't worry about you. And I don't need to be a cool mom. I just want to be a good mom."

Tara couldn't help it. She gave her a quick, tight hug. "You *are* a good mom. The best mom."

"Oh, my baby girl." She tapped her cheek gently. "Remember I'm always here if you want to talk to me."

"I know," Tara said. "Now let me get back to work. I think Jack secretly dropped off a bunch of orders to avoid direct contact with me."

With her laughter lingering in the air, her mom returned to the kitchen. Although nothing was answered, Tara felt more like herself. She checked the counter, and her cowardly brother had indeed left a stack of orders for her. Laughing softly under her breath, she returned to doing what she loved best. Sharing her brew with her customers and seeing happiness bloom on their faces.

She shouldn't lose sight of her goals. She had new brews to perfect, rivals to beat, and the World Beer Cup to win. And two more dates with a lovely man before he walked off into the sunset.

Seth got out of bed and paced the floor. He was restless and couldn't sleep. Maybe it was because the bed still smelled like Tara and he missed her. It hadn't been more than twelve hours since he'd seen her. Had he ever yearned for somebody so much? No. Not even with Jessica. When she was off somewhere, he'd enjoyed the quiet, solitary time with his art.

Was it the lack of art in his life that made him so focused on Tara? His days were busy—the finishing touches on the restaurant were turning out to be quite time-consuming—but he still noticed her absence keenly. Opening up to her earlier in the day had been difficult but cathartic in a way. Her warm sympathy and respect for his space had touched him deeply, and he felt that much closer to her. And . . . it felt as though something had awakened in him.

He reached for the nightstand and opened the single drawer. It held his never-used but ever-present sketchbook and the pencil he kept sharpened to a point. He pulled both out and sat down on the bed with his back against the headboard. The restlessness seemed to settle into his hands and made them tremble . . . until he drew the first line. Then they became as steady as a surgeon's and whirred across the paper in a storm of sketching.

A deep sigh resonated inside him as though a long-held breath had been released, and a painful constriction in his chest eased. He hadn't even known the pain existed until it was gone. The next breath he took felt as if it was the first full breath he'd taken in years.

Seth ripped out pages after pages of finished sketches until they nearly covered the entire bed, and still he couldn't stop. He didn't want this to end. His yearning for Tara hadn't diminished since she was the subject of every one of his drawings, and he felt somehow connected to her.

The sketches were a reimagination of the photos he'd taken of her. In one drawing, a side of her face filled the page with the surrounding beauty reflected in the iris of her eye. In another, she was but a wisp of wind on the hills, an apparition on the verge of appearing or disappearing. Once a sketch was melded with one of the actual photos, he would have a finished piece. Then an image that existed only in his mind—which mirrored his thoughts, dreams, and hopes—could be shared with the world.

His hand stilled. What was he doing? He'd vowed never to make himself vulnerable again—bearing his heart and soul for people to stomp on—because his heart wasn't strong enough to be shattered a second time. But his art still hummed its alluring melody in his veins. After being silenced for so long, it demanded to be heard. And Tara . . . she could never be pushed aside. She had been ever present in his mind since the wedding.

He was scared shitless. The foundation he'd built his adult life on was being throttled, and his head was shaking from the force of it. Art and love were a part of his past, but so was his heartbreak. Was he going to allow something that happened years ago to continue impacting his life? His future?

I don't know.

Seth gathered the sketches on the bed and hid them away in the nightstand with hands that shook again. He couldn't look at them anymore. Look at her anymore. He lay down with his arm thrown over his eyes. He didn't expect sleep to come, but sweet oblivion overtook his turmoil with dawn just peeking over the mountains.

He woke up a few hours later in a foul mood with bleary eyes and the first thrums of a headache. His sketching fever felt like a dream, but his cowardice felt unbearably real. But being a coward, he didn't want to figure out *why* he was being so cowardly, so he shoved his messy thoughts into a dusty corner of his mind. After a quick shower, Seth headed out for Weldon. He wasn't enjoying his company very much, and would rather be buried in the bustle of strangers.

Pancake Hut was busting at the seams as usual, and the sight lifted his spirits. A tall stack of hot, fluffy pancakes would be a great way to turn around his morning. Simple and satisfying. The way his life had been before the dating dare. Now a prickling sense of dissatisfaction shadowed his day unless Tara was with him. *This has to stop.* He had less than two weeks left to start a new chapter in his life. All this disquiet, yearning, and soul-searching wasn't going to do him any good. His path was set. His time in Weldon was only a layover.

Seth got himself on the waiting list, and went out to stand on the sidewalk with the long line of hungry customers. Everything moved a little slower in Weldon, but he was starting to like it that way. He walked with his head down toward the end of the line when a familiar voice said, "Hey, Seth."

He stopped a second too late and had to backtrack a couple steps. It was Jack, Alex, and . . . Tara. *Shit.* It took superhero strengths to keep his eyes from devouring Tara. The woman he'd been thinking and dreaming of all night. He still felt exposed and vulnerable after his remarkable night, and he wasn't sure how well he would be able to hide his feelings for Tara from her older brothers.

"Good to see you guys. How are you doing?" Seth shook hands with Jack and Alex, and gave Tara a jerky nod in his best attempt to be casual.

"Jack and I are doing swell, but our baby sister is in a black mood," Alex said over Tara's muffled moan. She had her face buried in her hands. It was difficult to make out, but she seemed to be muttering *kill me now* on repeat. "So we brought her here to cheer her up, and make Scary Tara go far, far away."

"Thanks for that, Alex," Tara said with a touch of acid, and took a peek at Seth through her fingers. With a defeated sigh, she lifted her head and met his eyes, looking adorably flustered. "So what brings you here?"

"Pancakes," Seth said with a smile that soon disappeared at Tara's not-so-amused glare. "I needed a pick-me-up as well."

"Don't let her scare you." Jack placed a supportive hand on his shoulder. "She'll be all better after pancakes. A full Tara is a happy Tara."

"Why don't you join us?" Alex said, waving him closer.

"I don't want to cut in line." Weak excuse. But he couldn't figure out how to act normal in this situation.

Tara coughed to cover her snort. She seemed to find his discomfort amusing despite her black mood. Why was she in a bad mood? He would ask her later. For now, he was glad he could make her laugh at his expense.

"You're joining our party of three, so you'll just be taking our empty fourth seat," Jack reassured him. "No harm done."

Seth shot her a panicked glance and she lifted her shoulder in the world's subtlest shrug. Her faintly amused expression told him she was resigned to the awkward breakfast.

"In that case, I'd be happy to have the company," Seth said, joining their huddle.

They were seated within thirty minutes in a cozy booth, and oversized laminated menus with way too many options were handed to them. Seth already knew what he wanted, and the Park siblings seemed to have the menu memorized, so the orders were taken quickly.

"So you guys are working together on Landon's website?" Jack asked, taking a sip of his coffee.

"Yeah, we've made a lot of progress," Seth responded, then realized Tara would have no excuse to see him without suspicion if the website was finished. "But there are still some details to tweak."

"Those little things are the time-consuming ones," Tara chimed in, nodding repeatedly for emphasis.

"Well, you better hurry and finish that," Alex said, accepting his skillet-sized western omelet from the server with a wide grin. "You're leaving for Paris at the end of next week, right?"

"Right." Seth choked on his answer so he repeated himself. "Right."

He and Tara never talked about it. About his leaving. Without meaning to, he had been avoiding the topic entirely. But she never brought it up either. Was she planning to wave him off when the time came? Sudden frustration clogged his chest. No mess, no fuss. Why did she want that so badly? Did her relationship with her ex still hold so much power over her?

Seth caught his rising anger and relaxed his clenched jaws. What was his problem? No mess, no fuss was exactly what he wanted, too. *Liar.* His conscience was exhausting him this morning. Despite the tall piping-hot stack of pancakes in front of him, his hunger deserted him.

"You must be excited to start a new life in a new country," Jack said, sounding a little wistful.

"Yeah." Seth cleared his throat. "Sure."

But he wasn't sure how he felt anymore. When he'd made the decision to take the job, he was excited for a new chapter in his life to begin—the move would propel his career forward and take him away from his comfort zone. He'd hoped the change would fill up the nagging hollowness he felt in his current life. Yet in the last few weeks, he'd hardly thought about Paris.

"I love Paris," Tara piped up, saving him from more questions. "When I was still studying wine, I went and lived there for six weeks on a summer program. Honestly, I love California wine more than French wine, but the baguette and cheese . . ."

"You wouldn't stop talking about it when you came home." Jack smiled affectionately at his little sister. "I still don't get why you changed your major, though. Not that I'm complaining. You were meant to be a brewer. But graphic design was so out of the blue."

"I was barely twenty." Tara shrugged, cutting out a perfect triangle from her stack of pancakes. "It's really too young for anyone to decide what they want to do with their lives."

So even her family didn't know about her douchebag ex. Not wanting Tara to get uncomfortable with where the conversation was heading, Seth brought it back to Paris. Besides, he wanted to know more about Tara's love of Paris. Why hadn't she brought it up before?

"You know what I love about Paris? Berthillon ice cream," Seth said.

"Berthillon? That ice cream store near Notre Dame?" Her eyes got as big as Alex's omelet.

"Yup. That one."

"Best ice cream in the world," she said with hushed reverence.

"No truer words," Seth said, high-fiving Tara. "I'm going there for a triple scoop as soon as I land in Paris."

Tara smiled at him, but there was a hint of sadness in her eyes. Perhaps she wasn't quite as indifferent to his leaving as she acted. His grin broadened.

"I like being home in Weldon just fine," Alex said between gigantic bites of food. "We travel often for beer festivals and contests, which is fun. But living somewhere else is a whole other story. I don't want to know what homesickness feels like."

"Me, too," Tara said in a near whisper, staring at her hands wrapped around her mug. "Traveling is fun and exciting, but nowhere in the world is worth leaving home for. I know what homesickness feels like, and I don't want to feel that way again."

Seth's eyes shot toward Tara, but she continued studying her coffee. It was black as usual. What had she meant by that? She hadn't just been talking about being away from home for college. Homesickness seemed to be a loaded word, and his stomach lurched for reasons he didn't understand.

Not knowing what to say, Seth stuffed pancake into his mouth, washing it down with gulps of coffee.

"Your place is here." Alex tapped her nose. "Weldon Brewery needs you. Our family needs you."

"And I need you guys," she said with love written plainly on her face.

Seth's heart constricted painfully. They were right. Tara's place was in Weldon. It was her dream to become a champion brewer and to grow Weldon Brewery into an institution. Everything she wanted was here.

An inexplicable sense of hopelessness weighed him down, like gravity wanted to hug him tight. But why? He knew going in that she belonged in Weldon, and their time together was limited. He doggedly shook off the despair that threatened to overtake him.

His place was in Paris. A new chapter of his life awaited him. Even if he wanted things to be different—and he didn't—there was going to be an ocean between them soon.

CHAPTER FOURTEEN

Seth and Alex did the usual Korean tug-of-war over the bill, and Tara watched with avid attention. They were both so stubborn, she wondered who would get the honor of paying for their meal. It was a win-win situation for her. She got free breakfast either way.

"You're a guest in our town," Alex insisted, tugging the bill toward him.

"And I'm grateful for you welcoming me here. It wouldn't be right for me to let you pay," Seth countered with a tug toward his direction.

"We've been inconsiderate in not inviting you to a meal sooner. Let us make it up to you." Tug.

"This might be our last meal together. It'll be my farewell treat." Tug.

Then her big brother brought out his ace card. "I'm the oldest one at this table. It's my prerogative to treat everyone to breakfast."

"I . . . fine." Not having anything to trump the age argument, Seth grudgingly released his hold on the check. "But you have to let me treat you next time."

"Sure. Of course," Alex answered disingenuously. There would always be a who-gets-to-pay tug-of-war. Her brother handed their server his credit card, wearing the high of his victory on his face. "Here you go."

Seth sighed ponderously. "Thank you for breakfast. It hit the spot."

"Anytime," Alex said.

Once their food was paid for, they shuffled out onto the sidewalk and said their goodbyes. Except for Seth and Tara. He caught her gaze and lifted his eyebrow a couple millimeters, and she gave a tiny nod. They were going to spend the rest of the day together.

When Tara didn't follow her brothers down the street, they turned to look back at her. Jack cocked his head to the side. "Coming?"

"Alex was right about us needing to hustle on the website. I have the late shift today so I might as well lend Seth a hand," Tara said, stepping closer to him. "You guys, go ahead. I'm sure he'll give me a ride back after."

"All right then. We'll see you later," Jack said, and Alex waved them goodbye.

Once her brothers were out of sight, Seth placed a possessive hand low on her back, sending a delicious shiver through her body. His breath was warm against her cheek when he growled, "Eager to get to work?"

"If by work you mean hot, sweaty sex, then yes," Tara whispered, leaning closer to him.

"Dammit, woman." His laughter sounded both amused and pained. "You can't turn me on like this in the middle of the street."

"Oops, sorry. But you started it." Her sympathetic smile matched the sincerity of her apology. "Maybe you can walk it off."

He raised his eyebrows. "Walk it off?"

"Yeah. We'll take a stroll to Comfort Zone as an excuse, and pick up some dessert for after lunch."

"You have to promise to be on your best behavior. I'm a little trigger-happy right now. I couldn't stop thinking about you last night."

It was Tara's turn to flush. She'd been in such a jealous craze last night that his words were a balm to her soul. He wanted her. Even if it was only for now. He wanted her badly. And her primal instincts told her to make him hers. *Now.* But alas, they were in the middle of the street, as Seth pointed out. She needed to walk it off herself.

"We are mature adults who are fully capable of not tearing each other's clothes off in public. We'll be fine," she said primly, more to convince herself than him.

They walked along the sidewalk with their hands grazing against each other's. Each barely there touch sent a shiver down her back. It was the most contact they could have since they couldn't hold hands in public, but it was more than enough to keep her heart racing.

It was a lovely sunny day with a cool morning breeze. They walked in silence for a few blocks enjoying their surroundings and allowing their desire to simmer down.

"How come you never told me about living in Paris?" Seth glanced at her, then looked forward again.

Why? He was leaving soon. She didn't want to be reminded of it by mentioning Paris. "I don't know. It never came up, I guess."

"I see." His brows were still furrowed. It was obvious he didn't see.

She sighed. There was no use burying her head in the sand anymore. "It was the summer after my freshman year. I was so in love with wines that I wanted to learn more about it during vacation. But I didn't want to do something boring like summer school, so I signed up for a summer wine program in Paris. It was such a place of romance and history. Learning about their wine and winemaking process seemed like a treat."

"And was it?" Seth asked.

"It really was. I loved it there and made some great friends. I don't think I'll ever forget it."

"You should look me up if you decide to visit Paris again," he said lightly.

Her heart fell to her stomach, then lodged itself in her solar plexus. *What is that supposed to mean?* Was he suggesting a vacation fling after this one? He was so casual about reminding her that he would be gone soon. Was it going to be that easy for him to say goodbye to her? She couldn't even think about him leaving without anxiety squeezing at her heart. But that was her. It wasn't fair for her to expect more from Seth.

"Yeah, sure." She hoped her tone matched his nonchalance. "If you promise to buy me a triple cone from Berthillon."

"It's a deal," Seth said with a crooked smile.

"I wasn't finished," she admonished. "I also want a sugar and butter crepe from a street vendor, and to eat it sitting on the grassy hill at Sacré-Cœur."

"Demanding, aren't you?"

"Only because I'm worth it." She arched her brow and dared him to contradict her.

"You certainly are," he said, his appreciative glance traveling over her body. "Anything else? Do you want to ride on the carousel at Trocadéro?"

"Oh, please no. That carousel is ridiculously fast. I hung on for dear life the one time I rode it. The view of the Eiffel Tower became a giant blur." She hugged her stomach. "I couldn't look at the Eiffel Tower without getting nauseous for weeks."

"You know what? Your demands will make a wonderful date." Seth linked his pinky with hers. It was the most innocuous of touches, and it made her toes curl. "Except for the carousel. We won't do the carousel."

"Definitely," she said.

Tara felt sadness wash over her again. It was a wonderful date that would never happen. Because she knew that when Seth left, that would be the end. Sure, they could see each other at get-togethers if he came to visit Landon and Aubrey, but it couldn't go further than that. She wasn't sure if she had the strength to only have him for bits of time and let him go again and again.

He wasn't like her other friends with benefits. The feelings he brought out of her . . . they weren't the sort she would feel for a friend. It really was all or nothing with him. So she had to go with nothing. Because *all* was not an option.

Their conversation dwindled again, and they continued strolling down the street until Comfort Zone came into view. She reluctantly withdrew her finger from his touch. He glanced sideways at her with a wistful expression that reflected her own. She felt the loss of connection keenly. When it came to Seth, she seemed to feel everything keenly.

The bakery was full of customers. It was a good thing they planned on doing takeout. They greeted the server and peered at the goodies in the display case. Even with Seth's help, she had trouble making her choices. Everything looked so scrumptious.

"Tara?" a familiar voice said behind her.

When she straightened and turned, Roger leaned down to kiss her on the cheek. She shot a panicked glance at Seth and evaded the kiss, giving her friend an awkward hug instead. Her friend with benefits.

"Roger, I didn't know you were in town," she said, then vaguely remembered receiving a text from him about coming to Weldon sometime. *Sometime must be now.*

"You must've missed my texts," he said with a winning smile.

"Oh? Sorry about that. How . . ."

She forgot what she was about to say when Seth straightened beside her. "Hi, I'm Seth Kim."

"Roger Stephens. Nice to meet you."

The two men shook hands, and she looked at them with bewildered eyes. This was so weird. Her former lover meeting her current lover. *Wait. Is Roger my* former *lover?* She realized the answer was yes. After Seth, she couldn't imagine being with him again. She couldn't imagine being with anyone else. No one else but Seth.

She was on the verge of freaking out in front of the two men when Justine walked out from the kitchen. "Tara? Perfect timing. I swear you have the best luck when it comes to food."

Grateful for the interruption, Tara went around the counter and enveloped the sous-chef in a tight hug. "Hey, you. How are things going? Are you enjoying your freedom?"

"Oh, God, no. I miss Aubrey so much. I can't wait till she comes home."

"Me, too. She'll be back in less than a week, so we won't have to wait long."

"In the meantime, I need you to be my test subject. I made two new desserts I want Aubrey to consider adding to the menu. I'd love your thoughts on them."

"Ooh. New desserts?" Forgetting about her predicament with the men standing behind her, Tara rubbed her hands together in anticipation. "When can I taste them?"

"They just came out of the oven. Come on back," Justine said, leading her by the arm. "Sorry, Seth. I'm going to borrow Tara for a bit."

"No problem," he replied, giving Roger a speculative glance.

Tara wasn't at all sure if it would be a good idea to leave the two of them together, but she so badly wanted to escape that she let Justine lead her away. She hoped she didn't regret this later.

So . . . you're from out of town?" Adonis also known as Roger asked, flicking back his golden bangs to better reveal the turquoise blue of his eyes. *Is this guy for real?*

"Yeah." Seth narrowed his eyes. "How did you know?"

"I'm guessing you two are together?" The other man sized him up with a sideways glance.

"Yes, we are." Even if it was meant to end next week, they sure as hell were together now.

"Well, as far as I know, Tara only dates out-of-towners." Roger let that hang between them.

"Is that so?"

Seth felt a hot tingling at the base of his neck. So this guy was one of Tara's former lovers? From the way he tried to greet her, maybe Roger wasn't exactly her *former* lover. She might be planning to get back with him once Seth was out of the picture.

"And never for long." Roger's smirk made Seth's hands curl into fists. "I tried to convince her to make what we have more permanent, but she balked at the idea and threatened to break things off completely."

"Why exactly are you telling me this?"

"Because I saw the way you looked at her. You've got it bad for her." He stopped to observe Seth's reaction. When he got nothing, he shrugged. "But you won't be able to hold on to her."

"You know nothing about me and Tara," Seth said through clenched teeth.

"No offense, man." His expression told a different story. "Just offering you some free advice."

"I appreciate your concern, but I don't intend to lose her." Blood pounded in Seth's ears. He meant every word. He wasn't going to lose her. He couldn't.

"Well, good luck with that," Roger said with a humorless laugh and walked out of Comfort Zone empty-handed.

Seth's head was spinning. He wanted to keep her. Although he had shoved aside his bubbling questions this morning, his subconscious seemed to have already chosen what he wanted. He wanted Tara. He didn't want their relationship to end when he left for Paris. The realization was too new, too bright to put under the microscope, but he was certain they had something that was worth keeping. His heart shook off its bindings and pumped with renewed life, and bliss spread through him as bright and warm as the first light of day.

It had been so long since he had wanted something. Really wanted it. He'd been content with safe. With superficial success and satisfaction. But the thought of going back to that life made him feel hollow. The happiness he'd felt in the last few weeks with Tara ruined him for anything less than real.

He had let something that happened during college impact his life choices for the last seven years. Because of one broken heart, he'd sworn off love. And he'd let the pain of that heartbreak lead him to give up his art. His dream. How could he not have realized how foolish that was? Sure, he'd worn his heart on his sleeve and allowed himself to love Jessica with all his loneliness and desperation. But had it even really been love? Or had he been so desperate for someone to belong to that he'd glommed onto her like she was his lifeline?

He was nineteen back then. He knew nothing. The last few years should've been spent on figuring out what he wanted out of life instead of closing himself off to it. Well, that was going to change, starting now. There was so much to explore and learn about himself and who he wanted to be. But he was already certain of one thing. He didn't want to live the rest of his life without Tara in it.

Seth didn't fully understand what was happening between them, but he wanted to explore it further. She made him feel so alive, and he hadn't known happiness greater than when he made her laugh. He wanted to make her happy. He wanted her to know that she was an amazing person and she could do anything she wanted with her life. She was the most confident and driven person he knew, but there was a vulnerability to her that he ached to protect.

The bustle of the busy bakery receded into the background, and an acute stillness overcame him. Sunlight seemed to bloom inside him and hope filled him to the brim. He was going to reclaim his life, and allow himself to live to the fullest. The thought of returning to art still frightened him, but if his soul commanded him to create again, he wouldn't fight it. He would throw himself in headfirst as he used to. Art wasn't about being safe and secure. It was about taking risks and facing the fear of uncertainty. It was life and it was beautiful. And maybe he would allow himself to love again. He wasn't sure he had the choice anymore. He was already halfway in love with Tara. The realization shocked him, and fear—fierce and overwhelming—rose inside him again.

Like an unforeseen thunderstorm, dark clouds blew in to hide the light and hope inside him. Knowing that he wanted her didn't mean Tara felt the same way. What would she think of his epiphany? Could he be just another out-of-towner to her? Someone briefly passing through her life? That didn't ring true. She cared about him. But Tara wouldn't sleep with someone she didn't care about. Maybe she cared about all her hookup buddies.

Seth knew Tara. She wouldn't just pick up any guy off the street. Whoever these passersby were, she would choose them carefully. Maybe she'd accepted his dare because he happened to meet her criteria. A vicious claw tore at his heart. Anger, jealousy, and pain. He wanted to be more than a temporary fix. He could be so much more for her.

His pain fueled his anger, and soon he allowed fury to overtake him because it was more bearable than anguish. He didn't know how long he sat at the counter fuming, seeing nothing. All logic lost to him.

"Hey, look at what I have." Tara appeared beside him and held up a bagged box. "Justine hooked us up. Her new desserts are so delicious."

"Are you ready to leave?" he asked without emotion.

She blinked in surprise then shrugged. "We have what we came for."

"Let's go." Seth stood abruptly from his seat and headed straight for the door.

"Hold on. You're like a runaway train. I can't keep up." Tara gave him a sideways glance. "What's going on?"

"Nothing," he said curtly.

Apprehension dawned in her eyes, and she stayed silent and stiff beside him as they walked back to his car. Once they were seated and speeding through the streets, Tara finally spoke.

"What happened with Roger?"

"What could possibly have happened between Roger and me?

It was a pleasure meeting one of your hookup buddies." He stared straight ahead as the vicious words cut the air between them.

"Seth . . ."

"So you only date out-of-towners, do you?"

"Who I've dated before you and who I'll date after you is none of your business."

Seth stayed silent because she was right. He was being an utter asshole. But he wanted to roar with pain.

"Stop the car," Tara said in a cutting tone.

"What?" He turned to her in shock. This wasn't what he'd wanted.

"I said stop the fucking car. Right now."

He slowed the car down to a stop near the park where they'd had their first date. She unbuckled her seat belt and his heart stopped beating, thinking she was getting out before they had a chance to talk this through. Instead, she spun in her seat to face him.

"What the hell are you getting at?" she hissed.

"Well, your movie-star-handsome boy toy guessed right away that I was from out of town. When I asked him how he knew, he mentioned that you only dated out-of-towners who passed through town." He needed to stop himself before he took it too far, but the words continued to pour out of him like lava overflowing from a volcano. "Adonis supposedly wanted something more permanent with you, and you freaked out and threatened to break off your convenient arrangement with him."

"Roger should've kept his big mouth shut. None of this is any of your business."

"So did you say yes to my dare because you knew I'll be out of your hair in a month?"

Tara hesitated for a moment then lifted her chin. "Yes."

"Am I one of them? Just passing through your life? Will I get to see you again for a meaningless hookup every year or two when I visit Weldon?"

"I . . ." She drew back from him as though he'd struck her. "Are you judging my lifestyle? You suggested the dating dare because you wanted the same thing. You wanted something fun and uncomplicated to entertain you before you left for Paris. Don't you dare deny it."

"We're not talking about what I want right now, because you have no idea what I want."

"Isn't that convenient for you?" She huffed a humorless laugh. "Since we're talking about me, let me make one thing crystal clear for you. When this is over—which obviously is now—you will be out of my life. Permanently. You will never be one of my fuck boys, so don't concern your pretty little head over it."

Seth listened to her with rising panic. *This is over? Now?* No. That was not what he wanted. That was the last thing he wanted. "Tara . . ."

Before he could do anything to salvage the mess he'd instigated, Tara swiftly opened the passenger door and got out of the car. She was half a block away by the time he managed to catch up with her.

"Where are you going?" Seth asked with a tremor in his voice.

"Home." She didn't bother turning to look at him.

"I'm sorry. I'm so sorry. Let me take you home. We could talk later."

"No, and no."

"Tara." He took a gentle hold of her arm and she shook him off violently.

"Don't touch me. Don't ever touch me again." She finally spun to face him, and the anger and hurt in her eyes tore at his heart. "I'm going to walk home, and we won't be talking again. This would've ended in less than two weeks anyway. It's not worth the trouble."

Tara walked off and Seth let her go. Maybe there was nothing left to talk about. He knew everything he needed to know now. He wasn't worth the trouble.

CHAPTER FIFTEEN

Too focused on holding back her tears, Tara didn't notice that Seth wasn't following her anymore. By the time she turned around to look for him, she'd come too far from the park to spot him. Maybe he was there, staring at the direction that she'd disappeared to.

She stomped down on the urge to run back to the park to find him. She'd done nothing wrong, but she felt guilty when he questioned her life choices. When she felt anxious to appease him, she'd lost it. Tara refused to be that needy, sniveling girl again. She would not be ashamed of who she was. This was her life, and she could do with it as she desired. No one dictated what she did. Not anymore.

But she hadn't meant what she said. Even as the words were coming out of her mouth, she knew they were lies, but she had been too angry and scared to stop them. She didn't want this to be the end of them. Not like this.

Roger was a good guy and she'd been happy with the arrangement they had. They spent time together when he was in town, and lived their separate lives when they were apart. They liked and respected each other, and had great chemistry. Or so she'd thought until she met Seth. What she had with Roger was like a tame kiddy ride compared to the breakneck-speed roller coaster of desire that she shared with Seth.

And there had only been Roger for a very long time. Tara didn't have a black book of out-of-town fuck boys like Seth implied. She was perfectly proficient at meeting her own needs when necessary. She just sometimes missed the human connection.

But she shouldn't have to explain her past to Seth. Why should she have to tell him about the men she'd been with before him? Then she thought about how she would react if they ran into one of his ex-lovers, a gorgeous model. She would go mad with jealousy. Just imagining it made her stomach twist. And she would feel insecure. She would wonder if she was just one of the women in his long line of casual lovers.

Had that been it? Was Seth seeking reassurance that he meant more to her than a casual fling? Despite their agreement to keep their relationship a fun, simple fling, did he wish it was more than that? Just as she did?

It was too much to think about right now. She was angry and hurt, and too worked up to properly engage in "what if I were in his shoes" exercises. Tara let herself into her house and kicked off her shoes, letting them land wherever they fell. She didn't know if anyone was home and she didn't care. She headed straight for her room and fell facedown on top of her bed. Might as well be comfortable while she mulled over her fight with Seth. But even though it wasn't yet noon, she fell into an exhausted, dreamless slumber.

There was an urgent buzzing sound coming from the purse she dropped on the floor. *What the hell is that?* As she slowly surfaced from the depth of sleep, she realized it was the text alert on her phone. A glance at the clock told her that she'd been out for more than an hour, and she knew who was texting her.

The buzzing had grown increasingly closer together. After taking a deep breath, she reached her hand into her purse and rummaged around till her fingers wrapped around her cell. She pulled it out and saw that she had twenty-seven text messages.

SETH: I'm a monumental asshole.

She wouldn't go so far as monumental, but he had been an asshole. As his text messages continued, his insults at himself grew increasingly amusing.

SETH: I'm a piece of chewed gum stuck on the bottom of a second grader's desk with black pock marks made by a freshly sharpened pencil.

Then the humor slowly leeched out of his texts.

SETH: Tara? Can you say something please?
SETH: I'm trying to apologize. I guess I'm not doing a very good job of it.
SETH: God, Tara. I am so very sorry. I shouldn't have said what I did. It was none of my business.

The tightness in Tara's chest eased a little at his apology. But her lack of response increased the desperation in his pleas.

SETH: Please forgive me. I will never act like a jealous fool again.

So he had been jealous. A small smile lifted one corner of her mouth. Although she had every right to feel a bit vengeful after the things he'd said, she shouldn't enjoy her power over him this much. But it felt good that it wasn't just her who was tortured by the green beast.

SETH: Did you mean it? Are you done with me?

SETH: Please tell me you didn't mean it.

SETH: Tara? Are you going to ignore me forever?

SETH: Well, I sure as hell am not done with us.

SETH: Goddammit just say something. Anything.

Tara gasped and sat up on the bed. *Oh, no.* He was suffering, and she was here gloating over his messages.

TARA: Anything.

The ellipses began scrolling immediately on the screen.

SETH: Just one second. I'm going to collapse on the couch from relief.

TARA: Oh. Take your time.

SETH: Were you torturing me with your silence for fun?

TARA: Maybe . . .

SETH: I can't say I blame you.

TARA: You wouldn't dare after the dick move you pulled.

SETH: No, I wouldn't. Tell me. What was going on with you? Are you okay?

She loved that he was worried about her despite the ordeal she'd unintentionally put him through.

TARA: I fell asleep. It seems having a fight with you sucks away all my energy.

There was a short pause.

SETH: I'm so sorry, Tara.

TARA: You should be.

SETH: I am.

TARA: Good.

SETH: Will you forgive me?

Not wanting to put him through more unnecessary torment, she replied succinctly.

TARA: Yes.

There was another pause. A bit longer this time.

SETH: Thank God. You scared the shit out of me.

TARA: I'm sorry, too. I didn't mean to hurt you.

SETH: That's fine. I deserved it.

TARA: It's not fine. I shouldn't say things like that lightly.

SETH: I have to see you. Right now. I need to hold you.

She wrote her next message with her heart beating double time.

TARA: Leaving now.

She rose to her feet, picking up the purse she'd thrown on the ground, and rushed out of her room. She found one of her shoes at the start of the hallway and the other one by the front door. Slipping them on, she rushed to the driveway and hopped into her car.

An odd urgency filled her, and her foot grew heavy on the gas pedal. She couldn't believe that they wasted precious time fighting.

Not wanting to be pulled over—and to waste more time before she could see Seth—she constantly checked herself and slowed down, but she got to Aubrey's house much sooner than the speed limits would've allowed.

As usual, the front door swung open before she even reached it. She didn't know who jumped whom first, but they clung to each other without an inch of space between their bodies.

"Tara," Seth sighed into her hair, embracing her even more tightly.

"I didn't mean it." She couldn't breathe, but it didn't matter. She was in his arms . . . she was home. "We're worth fighting for. I want to be with you every minute we have left."

"I believed you for a split second, but I couldn't give you up that easily." He inhaled deeply. "I know you care about me. Just as I care about you."

"I do." She pulled back far enough to caress his cheek. "I care about you, Seth. More than you know."

Seth opened his mouth on the verge of saying something then closed it. Tara held her breath searching his face. What was she hoping for?

In the end, he just said, "Let's go inside."

He led her inside with his arm wrapped around her waist as if he couldn't stand being apart from her. Without stopping, they walked to his bedroom and closed the door behind them. Seth glanced at her with a question in his eyes.

"Yes. I need you," she answered.

He turned to her and held her face in his hands, and looked and looked at her as though he couldn't get enough. He smoothed his thumbs over her lips, then leaned down to touch his lips on hers—feather-light and tentative. She kissed him back, letting him know

they were okay. And they kissed like that—sweetly and tenderly—
for as long as they could before passion swelled over them.

When his hand fisted in her hair and he tilted her head back, she
parted her lips with a long sigh. His tongue swept the inside of her
mouth, lapping up the sound like a prize he was claiming. She could
go on kissing him like this forever. Making out with him was better
than sex. Well, the sex she knew before she met him. Sex with him
was actually even better than making out with him.

So she decided to move things along toward that end. She leaned
back despite his growly protest and pulled off her shirt. Then her bra.
The protests stopped instantly.

"If you're trying to kill me, you might be succeeding," he said with
a groan.

"You're such a boob man," she teased, biting her lip when he
cupped her breasts and slowly massaged them.

"Aren't you glad I am?" He brushed his thumbs across the peaks,
making her head fall back.

"Yes," she hissed when he gave one a hard pinch. "That hurts so
good."

"God, Tara. What are you doing to me?"

"Making you desperate for me." She grabbed him by the hair and
brought his lips a breath away from hers, caressing him with each
whispered word. "Because I want you completely out of control—your
soul bared and naked—when I take you."

He kissed her hard.
Not only because he wanted to . . . needed to. He kissed her
to stop the flow of words that were bringing him to his knees. He

couldn't bare his soul to her because he didn't know what he would reveal. Would he reveal his new resolve to keep her, and his yet-unidentified feelings for her? He wasn't ready, and he had no idea if she was.

All he could show her was that he wanted her. Wanted her like he had never wanted another woman. He wanted her to know, so she could never doubt that she was special to him. Someone he cherished.

Seth lifted her off the ground and carried her to the bed. Before he lay down beside her, he stripped off the rest of her clothes and did the same with his. Finally, as he held her in his arms, skin to skin and limbs tangled, he had enough control to ask her.

"Aren't you afraid of what you would find?" he asked, smoothing the back of his hand from the side of her breast to the curve of her hips. A shiver ran through her and he smiled.

"I am." Her hand roamed his chest until it came to rest just above his heart. "But I want to see you. I want to make you mine even for a short while."

"For a smart woman, you are astoundingly dense." She drew back in surprise but he pulled her back into his arms. "Didn't you know I was yours ever since you said, 'You need to stop staring at my ass'?"

"You can't be serious," she whispered.

"I haven't looked at or thought of another woman since then. You are all I see. Awake or dreaming."

"Me, too. You're all I see."

Seth sucked in a sharp breath. "Say it again."

"You're all I see. You're all I want."

And that was all it took. He was falling down a cliff without a safety net. Falling for her. Deeper. Endlessly. Maybe he had a chance of keeping her. Forever. He gazed at Tara wordlessly. Shallow lines were forming between her brows. He probably looked a little frenzied.

"I'm gonna make you feel good, okay?" he growled.

"Okay." Then a naughty smile lit up her face. "And I'm gonna rock your world."

He laugh-groaned. She was so funny and so fucking sexy. "I'd like that very much."

But when he touched her, it was with breath-catching tenderness and reverence. His Tara. She was too much. So special. So spectacular. And she responded in kind, smoothing her hand down his jaw. Kissing his cheeks, his eyes, behind his ears. They made love with such intimacy that Seth knew he would be changed irrevocably. He was scared, but he didn't let his mind shy away once. Every second was precious, something to be shored up inside of him.

When they came back to the present, they were both shaking, and holding tightly onto each other. He never really knew what earth-shattering sex meant until now. He felt as though his entire life had crumbled down and rebuilt itself around him. And he looked down at the woman in his arms, knowing that he was forever hers.

Seth loved her. With all his heart and stunted soul. He couldn't hold anything back or keep a corner of his heart safely to himself, because he'd already given everything to her. He was terrified, but he wouldn't have it any other way. Tara deserved nothing less than all of him.

"Hey." He pulled the tangled sheets over them, because she was still shivering. "You okay?"

"Yeah . . . I think so." Her voice was thick with emotion, and tears filled her eyes.

His stomach dropped out. "What's wrong, baby? Talk to me."

"I don't know." She covered her mouth to stop a sob from escaping. "That was wonderful and I'm so happy. I don't know why I'm crying."

He pulled her head against his chest and smoothed his hand over her hair again and again. She felt it. His unspoken words. His love for her. And she was crying happy tears. It was a very good sign. Even so, seeing her tears made his chest ache and the back of his throat prickle.

"Cry as long as you need," he said, his voice rough with emotion. "I'll be right here."

She smiled through her tears. "Good. Stay right here."

His heart screeched to a halt, or so it seemed, until it began pumping at triple speed. She probably meant for now, but could she have been implying that she wanted him to stay after the month was up? Just thinking about the possibility made him float in air.

Her tears soon stopped falling, but the smile she offered him still wasn't quite steady.

"What should we do now?"

"I brought in the dessert you left in my car," he said, kissing away the last tears lingering on her cheeks. "Should I brew some coffee? We could have dessert in bed while we think about what to do for the rest of the day."

"Your plan sounds like you want to spend the rest of the day in bed." Tara laughed. "Why don't we have some coffee and dessert and get that website finally finished?"

"My idea is more fun." He leaned down to kiss her on her neck. She considerately tilted her head to give him better access.

"We could always come back to bed after we're done with the website. It could be our incentive to focus on the work." Contrary to her words, she grasped one of his hands and placed it on her ass. She moaned when he squeezed it.

God, he loved her ass. It was so round and soft. He also loved her breasts and how perfectly they fit in the cup of his hands. To make sure they still fit, he cupped both of them. *Perfect.* He licked and suckled the tips until she was writhing under him.

"I think we need to finish this first. Otherwise, we'll never get any work done," he said in a choked voice when she ground her hips against him.

"What work? Stop talking nonsense and make love to me."

"Right." He stopped talking altogether and kissed her like she was the only woman on earth and he'd searched a lifetime for her.

It was true. She was the only woman in the world for him. And now that he'd found her, he would hold on to her with all his strength.

CHAPTER SIXTEEN

S eth was an exceptionally persuasive man, and he'd made leaving his arms very difficult this afternoon. Tara barely made it into work on time. Then only an hour into her shift, she stepped out to the brewery's parking lot to give him a call. He picked up before the first ring.

"Dude, I'm trying to work here," she said in mock anger, wearing a wide grin on her face. "Can't you be apart from me for one hour without texting me incessantly?"

"It's important." He was wearing an equally goofy smile on his face from the sound of his voice. "I need to know if you're available for our third date this Thursday. I figured the weekend would be packed at the brewery, so Thursday will be easier for you to change shifts with Jack or Alex."

"Why do you have to know right now?"

"I have to make reservations for this date," he said, not very forthcoming.

"What kind of reservations?"

There was a pause before he replied. "Secretive kind of reservations."

"Hmm . . . I don't like secrets."

"Do you like surprises?"

"Maybe. If they're the good kind."

"Oh, this will be good." He sounded positively gleeful. "So are you free Thursday? Around six o'clock?"

"Yes, I'll make sure to be free." Tara smiled as his excitement spread to her. "Can you give me a hint about what I should wear? Is there a dress code where we're going?"

"Yeah, but it's not strict. Just wear one of your formal dresses."

"A formal dress?" Her jaws went slack at the same time her mind automatically went through the few formal dresses she had hanging in her closet. "What are you wearing?"

"A tux."

"Holy Toledo." The thought of Seth in a tux made her knees go weak, and she had to lean against the lamppost she was standing next to.

Seth's low, sexy chuckle told her he knew exactly how she was reacting to that tidbit. It had been awhile since she'd seen The Ego. She'd kind of missed it. It was so hot when he got all cocky.

"You have to tell me where we're going," she demanded.

"Not a chance."

"What if I tell you I won't come unless you tell me?"

"I don't think you'll do that."

Dammit. He was right. She wouldn't miss date number 3 for the world. She was *dying* to know what the surprise was.

"The Ego is clouding your judgment. The only thing predictable about me is that I'm unpredictable." She didn't know what the hell she was saying. She was trying to salvage some pride here.

"Just come. Okay? Please? I promise you'll be happy. I only want to make you happy."

"Oh," she sighed. Well, if he put it that way, how could she resist?

"Okay. I'll be ready. I just have to figure out a convincing tale to tell my family why I'm going out in a formal dress. Maybe I'll tell them I'm having a very belated prom night."

"You've never been to prom?"

"No one asked me, and I was too shy to ask someone."

"I find that hard to believe."

"I'm a woman shrouded in mystery."

"Then allow me to peel off every layer."

"Man, you're a master of making everything suggestive. How are you turning my awkward high school years into something sexy?"

"It's a gift."

"You're such a dork."

"That's a gift, too."

Her laughter trilled through the night air, and sang in her ears. Even though her cheeks ached, her smile held strong. She couldn't help it. "I should be getting back. Since I've answered your question, will you stop bothering me at work?"

"Only if you promise to text me when you get home."

"It'll be past midnight."

"I'll wait up for you. I want to say good night."

He wanted to wait up for her just to say good night? Her heart turned into pink goo. "Okay. I promise."

"I can't wait."

Good gracious. He was killing her with sweetness. It was officially now her favorite way to die. "Stop being corny. I'm gonna go."

"Bye," he said with laughter in his voice.

She loved hearing laughter in his voice. She loved hearing his voice, period. Before she made herself sad thinking about not hearing his voice again, she burst into the dining hall and took up position behind the bar. The phone call had taken less than five minutes, but there were new orders for her to fill. Just as she finished pouring the last batch, Justine walked up to the bar.

"Hi, Tara."

"Hey, girlfriend." Tara extended a fist across the counter, and Justine bumped it as she settled into a stool. "It's so nice to see you here. You should come by more often."

"I'm usually in bed by nine like a granny." She shrugged a graceful shoulder. The woman seemed to do everything gracefully.

"It's not easy keeping the hours you do. What time does Aubrey usually get in? Four in the morning?"

"Yeah. She told me I could come in at six and she'll do the prep work on her own, but you know I can't do that. I'm not letting my boss do all the hard work while I'm snoring away."

"Aubrey honestly won't mind," Tara reassured her.

"I know she won't. More the reason I want to be there with her. She's an inspiration."

"She feels the same way about you. You guys are like baker soul mates."

"I like the sound of that." Justine sighed a little dreamily. She was too cute.

"So what do you want to drink?" she asked while filling new drink orders Alex dropped off.

"Aren't you going to card me?" the sous-chef said with the confidence of a twenty-one-year-old.

"We don't card people who look over thirty-five," Tara deadpanned.

"Harsh." Justine attempted to glare at her.

"Not at all since you look closer to eighteen."

"Hey . . . that's not much nicer. I'm a grown woman." She turned in her seat and gazed at Alex. "I wish people could see that."

Wait, Alex? Well, well, well. Wasn't that an interesting development? "I was just teasing. You're a beautiful woman with a stunning figure. No one could miss the fact that you're all grown up."

"Thanks." She smiled, erasing the brief note of sullenness.

"Why don't you try Good Beer?"

"All your beers are good." Justine's eyebrows burrowed in confusion.

"No, that's the name of the beer." Tara cracked up every time she told the story. "My dad rarely gets to name the brews since Jack, Alex, and I are always trying to one up each other. But our new summer pilsner turned out so good that we decided to have Dad do the honors. And Good Beer is the brilliant name he came up with."

Justine laughed delightedly. "Your dad is so cute."

"Cute? That's one adjective I've never thought of in conjunction with my father. Goofy? Yes. Cute? No." Tara wrinkled her nose. "But I'll be sure to pass that on."

"Well, where is my Good Beer, woman? Time's a ticking. It'll be my bedtime soon."

Bedtime. Tara served up a tall cold one for her friend, her thoughts wandering to a certain someone waiting up for her. Her special someone.

"Don't do it, Tara." Justine's voice broke through her lovely daydream.

Blinking rapidly, she brought herself back to the present. What was she talking about? Did she miss something? "Don't do what?"

"You had the *exact* same expression that Disney princesses wear right before they belt out a song about their prince."

Tara had so many thoughts about that statement that she blurted out the first thing that came to her. "What's wrong with Disney princess songs?"

"Well, there's nothing wrong with the songs. I love a good Disney medley myself, but I was afraid you'd climb on top of the counter and start twirling around."

"Oh, my goodness." Tara snorted. "Can you imagine the whole pub jumping up and dancing at the chorus?"

"I totally can, and it's scary how much I'd enjoy it." Justine chortled, clapping her hands.

"Me, too. Why is this so freaking funny?" Tara wiped at her eyes.

"I think both of us have been working a bit too hard," Justine gasped, holding her side.

The seriousness of the situation didn't hit Tara until their friendly neighborhood baker left soon after finishing her Good Beer.

Seth Kim made her want to burst into Disney love songs. That was bad. Really bad.

Tara had never been to prom? Well, that changed everything.

Seth had spent days planning their third date. He wanted to pamper Tara and make her happy, because nothing made him happier. But his plans hadn't felt quite right. A helicopter ride to San Francisco to watch a musical. It sounded like a night to remember . . . until he realized he'd unconsciously stolen the idea from Richard Gere's character in *Pretty Woman*.

But a long-awaited prom night tailored specifically for Tara? Finally, something special enough for her. And he got to be her date. He would make it a night neither of them could forget. Which meant he had a shitload of work to do before Thursday.

Since he only had a vague notion of what prom night entails, Seth conducted thorough research on the topic. What the hell was prom proposal? *Wow*. Kids these days went all out. Well, he would go all out, too. He'd grown a thick skin over the last few years. He wasn't afraid to humiliate himself a little—or a lot—for the right woman.

Seth moved his tux to the office so Tara could use his room to get ready. She should be coming any minute now. He ambled to his room, then returned to the office shaking his head. He couldn't remember why he'd walked there in the first place. Then he paced around the oversized desk until he caught himself. *Oh, for God's sake.* He was walking around in circles. *Calm the hell down, Kim.*

He loved Tara. He loved her so much that he needed a bag to breathe into whenever he thought about it. But he wasn't sure if tonight was the night that he confessed his feelings to her. He had to tell her. There was no question about that. The question was, what comes after that?

Would she be open to a long-distance relationship? Could they take turns visiting each other every couple months? How long would they be able to keep that up? It sounded exhausting. And only getting snippets of her throughout the year wasn't enough for him. He couldn't even imagine being far apart from her for months at a time. His soul balked at the idea of leaving her here.

But he couldn't ask her to come with him. Her life—her dreams— was here in Weldon. No matter how much he wanted to be with her, he would never ask her to give up her dreams for him. He couldn't ask her for such a great sacrifice, because that wasn't love. That was possessiveness. He couldn't bear the idea of asking her to change in any way for him. She was too perfect for that.

What about him? Was going to Paris worth leaving Tara for? Was it his dream? He didn't know anymore. There was no doubt that it was the chance of a lifetime for a fashion photographer. *Fuck*. He couldn't see a way to make it work. But he sure as hell wasn't giving up on them. There had to be a way. A love this overwhelming could not have found him, only to stop him from having her because there would be an ocean between them.

Seth was pacing in circles again to match his circular thinking. He stopped himself from doing both. He wouldn't be able to give Tara her special night if he was a nervous wreck. *Deep breath*. He stomped to the kitchen, poured himself a tall glass of water, and chugged it down.

There was a knock at the door, and Seth rushed down the hall to open it. He swung the door open to find a perplexed Tara staring at him.

"Is everything okay?" Her concerned eyes searched his face.

"Everything's great." He cocked his head to the side, wondering if she could see the turmoil on his face. "Why do you ask?"

"I had to knock," she said, as though those four words should explain everything.

"Yes, I heard. That's why I came to open the door." The furrow between his eyebrows deepened.

"You weren't waiting for me this time?" She sounded a smidgen disappointed.

He understood now. He had always opened the door for her before she even reached it. Lost in his thoughts, he'd forgotten for a moment that she was coming soon. He pulled her into his arms. "Of course, I was waiting for you. I was counting the seconds. I just got distracted at the last minute."

"That's totally fine," she said wrapping her free arm around his waist. The other was holding a folded garment bag. "It was silly of me to be so surprised that I had to knock on the door. You've spoiled me."

"And I haven't stopped spoiling you. It was just a bleep. You don't know how desperate I am to see your face every time we're apart." Afraid that he'd revealed too much of his feelings, he swiftly changed the subject. "Come on in. We have to get ready for our date."

Tara came in after him, her laughter a thing of beauty. "How long do we have? I don't want to make us late for your secret reservations."

"About forty-five minutes. I know it's a bit tight since you have to do your hair and makeup, too."

"Most men have no idea how long it takes a woman to get ready for a special occasion."

"I *am* a fashion photographer. I know how much effort goes into all that. Men have it so much easier."

"You so do. How long do you need to get ready? Like ten minutes?"

"Tops," he said.

"Yup. Easy. Where should I change?"

"My room." He took the garment bag from her hand and led her to the guest bedroom. "Do I get to stay and watch you change?"

Tara laughed and planted her hands firmly on his chest and pushed him out the door. "Not a chance. You have to let me surprise you a little, too."

He pulled her to him for a fast, hard kiss before she closed the door on his face. He stood grinning for a minute before he jumped into action. God, he was actually nervous. Did he think she might say no?

Seth rushed to the office to change into the tuxedo he'd borrowed from Landon's closet. They were similar enough in size that it fit pretty well. At the hallway bathroom, he slicked his hair back from his forehead with a bit of hair wax. He studied himself in the mirror and shrugged. Not too shabby. Because he struggled a bit with the bow tie, it took him fifteen minutes to finish up.

He next went to the kitchen to make sure the butternut squash ravioli from Lola's Trattoria was staying warm in the oven. The salad and bread were ready to be served. The ivory corsage and boutonnière were looking fresh and lovely in the fridge. He would have to grab them once she said yes.

Right. He had to ask Tara to the prom. He took a deep breath and blew it out through his mouth. Was he sweating? *Shit.* He was sweating, for God's sake. Taking another calming breath, Seth went into the living room to grab the prom-proposal poster he'd made. He glanced over it. It really wasn't too bad. He'd put a picture of Tara in one corner and a picture of himself in the other corner, and wrote "Can you picture us at prom?" He'd shamelessly copied some kid's idea on Pinterest, but it seemed appropriate. He was going full corny. There were no halfways.

Oh, he almost forgot the cupcakes. He sped to the kitchen and grabbed the box of cupcakes. Like her brothers said, the way to Tara's heart was through her stomach. He checked his watch. He had about ten minutes to spare, but he couldn't stand waiting around.

Seth paced back and forth in front of his room, and finally caved and knocked on the door. "Are you ready?"

"You're early," she said through the closed door. "But yeah. I'm just about ready. Give me two minutes."

"Okay."

God, two minutes is going to feel like an eternity. He had his poster leaning against the wall next to him and he held the box of cupcakes in his hands. Seth cleared his dry throat. He had his work cut out for him not to sound like Kermit the Frog. Did he have enough time to run to the kitchen for a sip of water? No.

Just then, the door inched open to reveal a magnificent Tara in the burgundy maid-of-honor dress he hadn't been able to look away from. He was having the same trouble now. Lust, raw and searing, spread through him, and he wanted to have her right this moment.

A sultry smile spread across Tara's face, and she leaned against the doorframe with one arm stretched above her head. "You like what you see?"

"Yes. Please. Thank you," Seth said thickly.

She took a step toward him and was stopped by the outstretched box of cupcakes. She glanced down with a perplexed frown, and looked back up at him. "Seth?"

Shit. Get your act together. He had a prom proposal to make happen. "Here. This is for you."

"Mmm. Cupcakes. Thank you." She cocked her head, looking curiously at him. "What is it for? Did you want to have this later?"

"Yes. No. Just stand right there." He was the definition of smooth.

"O . . . kay?"

Seth retreated a couple steps and picked up his poster with the back facing her. After a deep breath, he spun it around so she could see it in all its glory. Tara covered her mouth as a half sob and a half laugh escaped her mouth.

"Can you picture us at prom?" She laughed, and a single tear rolled down her cheek. She quickly wiped it away before another one took its place. "I knew you were cheesy, but this one beats them all."

"I want to take you to prom." His voice was finally steady. All his ridiculous nerves were gone and he realized he meant what he said.

He wanted to take her to prom and fill that missing gap from her memories. "Will you let me?"

All attempts to laugh at the situation stopped, and Tara gazed at Seth with a tremulous smile. "Yes. I would love to go to prom with you."

His heart grew wings and flapped against his chest, demanding release. Seth wanted to kiss the daylights out of her, but once he started, he wouldn't be able to stop. That wouldn't do. He was taking his girl to prom.

"I'll be right back," he said. At the kitchen, he grabbed the corsage and boutonnière and ran back. He was gratified to see Tara standing exactly where he'd left her, staring down at the poster leaning against the wall. "This is for you."

"A corsage? Oh, my gosh. It's so pretty." She put the cupcakes aside, and held out her arm to him.

He put down the boxes on the floor and stood with her corsage in his hand. He slipped it onto her delicate wrist, and the flowers seemed to come alive and glow against her soft skin. "Do you like it?"

"I love it. I've always wanted to wear one." Her voice was husky again.

Seth took out his boutonnière and held it out to her. "Will you do the honors?"

"Of course." She took it from his hand and stepped close to him. God, she smelled so good. Carefully, she pinned the flower on his lapel and stepped back to examine her handiwork. "Perfect."

"Thanks." With a smile, he offered her his arm. "Let's get going before we're late for our dinner reservations."

"We're going out to dinner dressed like this?" She looked momentarily panicked until they rounded the corner to the kitchen where he'd set the table with a red-and-white-checkered tablecloth and two glowing candles. "What are you up to, Seth Kim?"

"Welcome to the fanciest Italian restaurant I know. Lola's Trattoria."

A delighted peal of laughter escaped her lovely lips, and she threw herself into his arms. "Oh, my goose bumps. This is so perfect. All of my friends went to Lola's for their prom-night dinner."

"Perfect is good." Seth's chest expanded with pride. "I want tonight to be perfect for you."

When Tara walked over to the table and reached to pull out her chair, Seth was by her side in a flash, clicking his tongue.

"Oh, geez," she huffed.

"Come on. Let me do this." He moved to stand close behind her, covering her hand with his own. "Let me pamper you, baby."

"Well, if you put it that way . . ." She let go of the chair with splashes of pink staining her cheeks.

Once she was seated, Seth returned with their pear, candied walnut, and Gorgonzola salad. Reaching for the sauvignon blanc chilling on the table, he said, "Wine?"

"Are we allowed to drink? I mean, we're only high schoolers." With eyes bright with anticipation, she held out her glass to him. "Screw it. It's prom night."

"That's right." Seth filled their glasses, then lifted his in salute. "Anything goes on prom night."

CHAPTER SEVENTEEN

When he sat down across from her, Tara paused with her fork of salad halfway to her mouth. "Did you have a wild prom night?"

"Nope. I went with a handful of my friends and we left early because we got tired of standing against the wall all night."

"Oh, my dandelions. You were a wallflower," she said, hugging her hands to her chest. "But seriously, I can't believe you never took a date to prom."

"I told you I was painfully shy until . . . after." He coughed and changed the subject. The brilliant words that popped out were "How do you like the salad?"

"It's delicious. This is my favorite salad from Lola's." She took another bite and chewed thoughtfully. "You and I have a lot in common. I wouldn't have believed it if someone told me that a month ago."

"How do you figure?"

"Well, we now know that neither of us had a date to the prom because we were both too shy in high school. We both changed majors in college because of our unfortunate relationship choices. And we both have quite a bit of emotional baggage."

"You're making us sound like sad, unlucky souls."

"No, I disagree. I say we're warriors for charging forward and making a great life for ourselves despite a rocky start to our adult lives."

Seth raised his glass. "To warriors."

"Damn right to warriors." Tara clinked her glass against his.

They ate their sweet and savory salad in silence for a few bites. This evening felt surreal. She couldn't believe the effort Seth put into it. She glanced down at her corsage and smiled. This was her prom night.

"This is so weird and wonderful. I feel like we've traveled back in time," she said, smiling across the table at him. "I seriously have butterflies in my stomach."

"Me, too." Seth chuckled, shaking his head. "I was sweating when I promposed to you. I was nervous as hell."

"Aww, that is so adorable." She reached across the table and linked her fingers through his. "Thank you for this. Really."

"It's my absolute pleasure. Really."

He gently untangled his fingers from hers, and stood from the table, reaching for her empty salad plate. "Let me bring our main course. We're on a schedule tonight."

"A schedule?" Her eyebrows rose up. "There's more?"

Seth shot her a quick, indignant glance. "Of course, there's more. I told you I'm taking you to prom tonight."

"Sorry. This is already more than I could've imagined."

"Well, prepare yourself." He wiggled his eyebrows, incandescent in his glee.

"For the best night of my life?"

"You overshot a bit there. I was thinking more of a prom night you won't forget."

"That works, too." Her cheeks ached from smiling so much tonight. It seemed to happen often when Seth was around. Maybe she would develop chipmunk cheeks by the time he left. *Shit.* Sad thoughts were *not* allowed tonight.

Seth placed their pasta dishes on the table. "Butternut squash ravioli with fresh sage butter sauce."

"No way. Is this a parade of my favorite dishes?" Tara couldn't resist and took a bite of ravioli dipped in buttery goodness. "I can't believe you're doing this to me. Do you realize how tight this dress is? The zipper is going to burst in the back."

"I. Love. That. Dress," he said, looking almost feverish with desire. It was a good look on him.

"I figured that out when you ogled me for hours at the wedding."

"Again, I wasn't ogling that night. I was gawking." His heated gaze traveled to her breasts, and he bit his lip. *Damn.* He was so sexy. "But now I'm definitely ogling."

"Stop that," she whispered, ogling him back. Seeing him in a tuxedo felt like being body-slammed by lust. *Must. Have. Friction.* Her body demanded satisfaction, but they were going to have to wait. She had a prom to attend. "If you keep making those sexy faces, I'll lunge across the table at you. You said we're on a schedule."

"Right." He stared furiously at his remaining raviolis. When he looked up at her, his eyes only held a hint of heat. "Let's finish eating and we'll be on our way."

"On our way?" He kept surprising her tonight.

"Yeah, so eat up," he said, digging into his ravioli.

After a moment, she followed suit. The sage in the butter married perfectly with the creamy butternut squash in the handmade ravioli. With all the butter and carbs, the dish couldn't be good for her, but having butternut squash in it gave it the illusion of being healthy, so she tucked it all away without guilt.

"Do we have time for cupcakes?" Tara asked hopefully, getting up to clear the table with Seth.

"There is *always* time for cupcakes. Besides, it only takes—like what?—two bites to finish? Let's each have one . . . or two."

"Who said I'm sharing my cupcakes," she teased.

"If you make me just watch you eat a cupcake, I'll end up carrying you to bed."

"Hmm. Tempting idea." Seth lunged for her, and she shrieked and ran to put the counter between them. "I'm kidding. Mostly. I'm mostly kidding. Here. Have a cupcake. I'll give you the chocolate-chocolate one since I'm nice."

She waved the cupcake in front of his face until he snatched it out of her hand.

"You are nice. Very nice," he said with a seductive smile that made her heart trip.

They each had a cupcake standing up and washed their hands together at the kitchen sink. Seth reached for her soapy hands and they played handsy for a bit, but they stopped before it progressed into more scintillating activities. A makeout session was inevitable, but the waiting would make it all the more satisfying.

Seth looked down at his watch. "Do you need to freshen up before we leave?"

"Sure. I'll only be a minute."

Tara went into the bathroom and reapplied her lipstick, dabbing it with a tissue. Then, after a moment's hesitation, she reached in and pulled her boobs up for Seth's ogling pleasure. The high quality of the dress prevented her from looking too promiscuous. She was just the right amount of promiscuous.

Seth was waiting by the front door when she returned from the bathroom. He was grinning like a little boy. He was so adorable, yet he never stopped being sexy as hell.

"Ready?" he said, offering her his arm.

"As I'll ever be." She hooked her arm through his and held her breath as he opened the door. What had him so excited?

A limo? He got us a freaking limo!

When they stepped outside, the chauffeur jumped out of his seat, and came around to open the rear door for them.

"Seth," she whispered, tugging on his arm. "There's a limo here."

"I know," he whispered back. "It's for us."

Tara shrieked and locked her arms around his neck, hugging him close. "Prom night is so much fun."

"It really is. When I was preparing all of this, I was just thinking of you, but I might be enjoying this more than you." Seth gently pulled down her arms and grabbed one of her hands. "Let's go. Our chauffeur is waiting."

They ran the rest of the way to the limousine and got inside. If she was expecting a tacky interior with white leather and disco lights, she would've been way off. The black leather was as soft as Morgan's cheeks, and the mahogany trim gave the car old-time elegance.

"Would you like some champagne?" Seth reached for the bar in the side compartment. "Or a martini?"

"No, thank you." She sat close beside Seth, shoulders and legs touching. "I would rather live out another one of my fantasies. Having a hot makeout session in the back of a limo."

"I think that can be arranged," he growled as he kissed her neck, and smoothed his hand down the side of her torso until he had a firm grip on her hip.

He quickly made his way down to her cleavage, and kissed the tops of her breasts almost reverently. "God, I wanted to kiss you like this that night. You're so beautiful."

"Are you talking to me? Or my boobs?" she said, tangling her hands through his hair and holding him in place.

"Your boobs. Definitely your boobs." His muffled laughter made her want to slap his arm, but when his tongue dipped under her dress and bra, she forgot everything.

"They like you, too. Very much." She moaned deeply, writhing against him. "Stay a while longer."

"With pleasure."

When she didn't think she could stand any more, he finally lifted his head and captured her lips in a kiss so sweet and so passionate that she pulled her dress up to her hips and straddled him to better enjoy it. He growled his approval and deepened the kiss, digging his fingers into her hair. It had taken her nearly half an hour to get her hair into an updo, but she didn't give a damn. He could dishevel the hell out of her until she looked thoroughly ravished. On second thought, he should go ahead and ravish her.

Seth was doing a fine job of it so far. His hands were moving all over her body as though he didn't want any part of her to feel left out. It burned her up. When his hand traveled up her thigh, lifting her dress higher, she whimpered, impatient for him to touch her hypersensitive center.

But instead, his hand stopped its upward trajectory and quickly pulled her dress down to cover her hips again. To her utter shock and indignation, he pushed her away from him.

"How dare you?" she seethed as she tried to tug his mouth back on her lips.

"Later. I promise you we'll resume later, but we're here." He sat her back on the seat and adjusted his pants and smoothed down his hair. "Our chauffeur's going to open the door any second now."

Tara quickly tugged down her dress and reached for her hair, which she was surprised to find still in good shape. Just as she noticed Seth's lips smeared with her bloodred lipstick, the door opened. To his credit, the chauffer didn't blink an eye at how disheveled the two of them must have appeared.

Her ears burning, she took his outstretched hand and accepted his help to get out of the limo. Seth climbed out of the car after her, and shared a grin with the chauffeur. She was surprised they didn't high-five each other. But it was adorable seeing how proud Seth was of himself.

He reached her side in two steps and offered her his arm again. "Shall we?"

Tara reached into her clutch and took out a tissue. Once she'd cleaned his mouth free of her lipstick, he took the tissue from her and cleaned around her lips.

"Now we shall," she said. When they turned around, she finally realized where they were. "Landon's restaurant? What are we doing here?"

"Come with me and you'll see." He was positively vibrating with excitement.

"What are you up to?" She narrowed her eyes at him suspiciously, but his excitement was proving contagious.

"The best kind of mischief."

She skipped a little to keep up with Seth's long, impatient strides. When they reached the entrance, he reached out and covered her eyes.

"Hey," she protested, tugging at his hand.

"Close your eyes. You can't look, yet."

"Okay. Fine. Just so you know, you're raising the expectations really high with all this fuss."

"I'm confident it'll meet your expectations," he said, sounding a smidgen smug. He led her by the arm into the restaurant and clicked on the lights. "Are you ready?"

"Just show me already. The suspense is killing me."

When he took his hand away, her mouth dropped open and no sound came out. He'd moved all the tables and chairs to one side of the dining hall and strung the entire room with lovely droplets of decorative light. And glittering star garlands hung from the ceiling as though the stars were spilling out of the night sky. At one corner, silver helium balloons happily spelled out the word PROM.

"Oh, my God," she gasped.

"Did you just say the Lord's name in vain?" Seth's eyebrows crept up to his hairline.

"An 'oh, my God' is warranted under such circumstances."

"Do you like it?" he asked hesitantly.

"I love it, Seth. All of it." She turned to him and caressed his cheek. "Thank you."

"You're welcome. You don't know how happy it makes me to see you happy." His voice broke at the end. "Okay. Before I become a slobbering mess . . . do you want to take our prom pictures?

"Prom pictures?" She laughed, super into the idea. "How? Where?"

Back at playing Mr. Mysterious, he said, "Please come with me."

She followed Seth as he made his way to a corner of the dining hall that was blocked off with a tall screen. He moved the screen to one side, revealing a setup with a gentle gray backdrop, lighting, and a camera on a tripod.

"I can't believe this," Tara breathed. "You've thought of everything, haven't you?"

"I hope so. There was no way I was going to disappoint you."

"I'm in awe. This is like Santa coming to your house on Christmas morning to open presents with you. It's wonderful."

"Good. You deserve it, and more," he said.

They shot their traditional prom pose picture, angled perfectly so her corsage and his boutonnière were in full view. Then they got creative. Seth stood behind her and pretended to bite her neck like a vampire. She jumped on his back in an impromptu piggyback ride, swinging her arm high in the air like an overzealous cowgirl. They stood ramrod straight side by side and wore their very best poker faces. Of course, they didn't forget the silly shot, where Tara pretended to pick Seth's nose while he wore his *duh* look.

By the time they finished their photo shoot, they were laughing so hard that Tara sank to the floor, hugging her aching ribs. Taking in sips of oxygen between bouts of laughter, she said, "Stop. Stop it. I can't breathe."

"What? I'm not doing anything. You stop it."

"Okay. I need to stop looking at you, because you keep getting that look on your face. I can tell you're trying not to laugh."

"Fine. I'll go hide behind the screen," he whizzed, and promptly did that.

That sent Tara into another bout of giggles. Then, slowly, very slowly—between random snorts—she finally stopped laughing and was able to take in a full breath.

Seth poked his head out from behind the screen, and asked, "Safe to come out?"

"I think so." She took another deep breath to make sure.

He reached her in two strides and helped her to her feet. He cradled both of her hands in his, and ducked his head to meet her eyes, wearing the most endearing smile. "May I have this dance?"

"Yes." Butterflies took flight from her stomach and fluttered around her racing heart.

Right on cue, music flowed through the room. Seth gathered her to him, and she wrapped her arms around his waist. They swayed together, song after song. Tara could hardly believe all this was happening. That he did all of it for her. It certainly was a prom night to remember.

"Now I'm sort of glad I never went to prom," she said quietly in his arms. "It never would've been this perfect with anyone else."

Seth held her even closer to him in response, and she melted against him. She never wanted the night to end.

He held her for a minute or an hour. He couldn't tell. Time didn't matter. Being with her like this—creating memories with her—felt so right. Seth couldn't let her go. He loved her. God, he loved her so much. If she couldn't leave with him, he would stay with her.

The pressure suffocating him lifted off his chest, and he knew that was the right thing to do. He didn't need to chase success. If it meant he could be with Tara, he would be happy opening a photography studio right here in Weldon. Fashion photography was a job he enjoyed, but it was only a job. Tara . . . she was everything.

He was confessing his love tonight. He couldn't contain it any longer.

"This is the last song, baby," he spoke into her hair, intoxicated by her scent.

"Mmm," she responded, snuggling deeper into his embrace.

God, she was so lovely. He spread his hands on her back and held her tighter against him. When the song ended, he placed a lingering kiss on her sweet lips.

"Thank you for this dance," he murmured, pressing his forehead against hers.

"You're welcome," she whispered.

He stepped back and got a firm hold of her hand, and didn't let go as he turned off the lights and locked up the restaurant. He couldn't bear to break the connection between them. Seth helped Tara into the limo and nodded at the chauffeur, who closed the door behind him.

Seth pulled her close and she laid her head against his shoulder. Playing absent-mindedly with his fingers, Tara stayed silent with her thoughts. Hopefully, she was basking in the warmth of a beautiful prom night. He certainly was. His body felt as though gravity didn't have as strong a hold on him as usual. This might be what it felt like to walk on clouds.

"Happy?" he asked, kissing the top of her head.

"Very," she said, lacing her fingers through his.

As the house came into view, Seth's anxiety overshadowed his happiness. Confessing his love to her could change everything, but change was what he wanted. No more of this spring fling nonsense. He wanted forever with her.

The chauffeur parked the car in the driveway, and came around to open their door. "I hope you guys had a great night."

"We did," Seth said, discreetly palming him his tip. "Thank you."

As the limo drove away, he opened the front door and led them inside the house. His blood pounded loudly in his ears as he headed for the kitchen.

"Do you want some coffee?" he asked, needing something to do.

"Sure." Tara cocked her head to the side for a second, then followed him. "That sounds nice."

Seth took out the French press and set the kettle on the stove. His

hands shook as he reached for the mugs. He hoped Tara didn't notice. Just to be safe, he stuck them into his pockets once he set the
coffee cups down on the counter.

"Is everything okay?" she asked, a slight frown marring her
smooth forehead.

"Yeah. Of course," he responded a bit took quickly. "I think I was
more nervous about tonight than I realized. I'm so relieved everything went as planned."

"It was perfect. I wouldn't change a thing about tonight." She came
to him and hugged him around the waist, resting her cheek on his
chest. Could she hear how hard it was beating? "Thank you, Seth."

He sighed and held her close, hoping the rest of the night went as
smoothly. She stepped away from him when the kettle began steaming, and allowed him to finish making their coffee. He carried two
piping-hot mugs to the kitchen table and set them down.

Tara sat down and held her mug between her hands, blowing on
the coffee. She still wore a dreamy expression. Seth allowed himself
to feel a moment of pride for putting that look on her face. But the
pride was soon overshadowed by good old-fashioned fear. Could he
really do this? Confess his feelings to her? Convince her to be his?

It wasn't the lingering shadow of his past relationship that made
him afraid. He realized he was finally over that. It happened a long
time ago, when he was just a kid. The love he felt for Tara couldn't
compare to what he thought was love back then. Perhaps that was
what paralyzed him with fear. Even the thought of losing Tara overshadowed his heartbreak from college. But if he didn't do this, he
wouldn't have a chance at keeping her.

Seth couldn't make himself sit down, so he stood across from
where she was sitting, gripping the back of a chair. She closed her
eyes as she took a sip of the coffee, then smiled warmly at him.

"You make the best coffee. The only problem is, it makes me crave something sweet."

"Not a problem. We still have some leftover cupcakes, remember?" He jumped at the chance to forestall the moment that would determine his entire future.

He forced himself to relax his grip on the chair and carefully let go. His fingers felt stiff from holding on to it like a lifeline. Walking slowly to the counter, he picked up the box of cupcakes and a plate for Tara to use.

When he set both of them in front of her, she glanced at her plate and frowned. "You aren't having any? That isn't like you."

"I'm still trying to get the butterflies to settle down in my stomach."

Looking unconvinced, she took a giant bite of her cupcake and got frosting on the corners of her mouth. Seth plucked a napkin from the stand and knelt in front of Tara. He tenderly wiped away the buttercream. And because he couldn't help himself, he kissed her softly on her lips.

"I love you, Tara," he whispered. "I love you so much."

She became motionless—as still as the moon mirrored on a midnight lake. And ice seeped into his veins and froze his cells. *Please say something. Say anything. Please.*

"No." She pushed away from him and shot to her feet.

"No?" His voice sounded as though he was hearing it from under water. He gradually stood from his crouching position.

Tara made a desperate sound and rushed into his arms. His arms automatically wrapped around her, and she kissed him, hard and demanding. He groaned deep in his chest and kissed her back, matching her raw heat. Then, she fumbled for his belt and unbuckled it, snapping him out of the fog of desire.

"Wait," he said, turning his face away. She pressed her lips against his to stop the words, and unzipped his pants. "Tara. Stop."

She whimpered, "No, no, no."

"Tara, look at me." He held her away with a firm hold on her arms. "We can't do this right now. We need to talk."

"But why?" she cried, her eyes desperate and wild.

"Baby, I need you to calm down." Of all the reactions, this wasn't what he'd expected. She was falling apart. *Oh, God.* Was he going to lose her? "I don't understand what's going on."

"Seth . . ." Her chin trembled, and she clamped her mouth shut and took a deep breath through her nose. "We have a dating dare. We have one more date left."

"Yes, we do have a dating dare, but it doesn't have to end with one last date," he said soothingly. She just needed time for the idea to sink in.

"But we promised not to fall in love with each other." Her voice rose, and she ripped her arms out of his hands and put the table between them. "You broke the rule."

"I did." A corner of his lips lifted in wry humor. "I completely broke the rule. I am so much in love with you."

"Please don't say that." She took another step back.

"Why, Tara? I'm only speaking the truth." Wanting to ease her worry, he buried his hands inside his pockets, despite his desperation to hold her tight in his arms. "Will you please hear me out?"

"This wasn't supposed to happen," she insisted, fire leaping into her eyes.

"It wasn't. I never imagined I would be able to love again. So deeply that my past relationship feels like child's play. This is real. It's mind-blowing and life-altering love." She stood still and silent, and Seth took that as a small victory. "I love you, and I want to be with you. I need to be with you."

"But you're leaving next week." She shook her head, and her fingers wrestled with each other. "You're going to be on the other side of the world."

"It doesn't have to be that way. I can stay." He smiled, and nodded encouragingly at her. She was freaking out because she was worried he would ask her to come with him. "I want to stay in Weldon with you."

"What?" Incredulity spread across her face, and the bottom dropped out of his stomach. "What the hell, Seth?"

"It's okay. It's what I want. I'll decline my Paris position and open a photography studio here." His words tripped over each other.

"You're going to turn down the chance of a lifetime to take small-town wedding photos and pregnancy shots?" she yelled, her hands curled into fists.

"Anything. I'll do anything to be able to stay here with you," Seth said, begging her to hear him. All that mattered to him was being with her. She just needed to understand that. "Fashion photography is only a job. I'm not trading a lifetime with you for it."

"I do not want to be that person who makes you give up your dreams. I cannot be the person that takes away your amazing chance." A sob escaped her, and she bit her lips to stop the trembling. "I once let a person use my love for him to manipulate and control me. I was so lost that I couldn't even remember who the real me was. I refuse to do that to you. Don't make me become that person."

"You could never be that person to me." A fine trembling started in his chest. This was about love. Once-in-a-lifetime, soul-mate love. It wasn't about manipulation or control. Why couldn't she see that? "Please, Tara. This is my choice. I'm in love with you, and I'm choosing to be with you."

"No," she said, unbending in her conviction.

He was beginning to hate that word. She kept saying it, but it wasn't the right answer. "I'm not asking you to tell me you love me right now. I'm not asking you to decide whether you want forever with me. I just want a chance to stick around and show you how much I love you."

"There will never be a forever for me." Her ferocity shot terror through his heart. "You know what's funny? It was never an issue—your caveat about not falling in love with you. I have nothing left in me to love another person. I'm incapable of loving you."

"I don't believe that. You are capable of more love than you can imagine. I've felt it. In the warmth of your touch, in the way you make me laugh, from the way your eyes linger on me, and in the way you make love to me. It's there. You just don't see it yet."

"I don't love you, Seth. I never will." Her eyes grew dull like she wasn't with him anymore. Like she'd already left. "Go to Paris. The dating dare is over."

Seth stood frozen to the spot while Tara moved around the house. When she returned to the kitchen, she was back in her street clothes with her hair loose around her shoulders, and she held the garment bag in her hand. But she was still wearing her corsage. That was the only fact he could focus on.

"Thank you for tonight. I'll never forget it. This month has been the most wonderful time of my life." She waited a second, as though she expected him to speak. The fact that he could still breathe surprised him. Speaking was beyond him. "Goodbye, Seth."

Once the front door clicked shut, the heartache he'd feared so much shattered him. He reached for the wall next to him, and slid down to the floor as the pain crashed into him again and again with undiminishing force.

CHAPTER EIGHTEEN

Tara functioned. She went to work, brewed her beer, tended the bar, and ate and slept. Well, she was being rather generous with the terms *ate* and *slept*. She tried to eat, but mostly pushed her food around the plate. And sleep only came to her in angry, dark snippets. But she was doing exceptionally well considering she'd forgotten how to *live*.

Aubrey was home, but wasn't due back at work until the following Monday. Other than a quick hello on the phone, Tara hadn't talked to her. And she couldn't visit her at her house because Seth was there. He was still close by. That small comfort kept her sane.

She spent most of her time trying to forget Seth's tender expression—so full of awe and gratitude—when he told her he loved her. No one had ever looked at her as though her existence was the greatest gift in the world. She had to forget all of it. If she let his love sink into her heart, there was no telling what she might do.

She also struggled to not obsess over their one remaining date. It made no sense since she was the one who called everything off, but she'd been greedily guarding the time she had left with him. Now she would never have her last date with him. The deal was to have *four* dates and to *not* fall in love, dammit. But what would having one more date accomplish anyway? It would only create more memories to haunt her when he was gone.

Then she would cry without pondering why she felt so wretched. Tara was petrified of thinking about the why. Why her heart burst into fireworks when Seth told her he loved her. Why she was so angry with him. She had broken the man's heart. He did nothing wrong but love her. But . . . that was it. Loving her was wrong. He promised he wouldn't fall in love with her.

Eventually, she would feel hollowed out enough for the tears to stop. And she could return to functioning. Brew, bartend, and pretend to eat and sleep. Her family was watching her with increasing concern, but she couldn't worry about that. She was holding tight to the string that was keeping the stitches of her life together. One slipup, and she would unravel and fall apart piece by piece.

She was doing the bartending part of functioning tonight. The place was crowded, and she welcomed the noise and bustle. It made forgetting a bit easier, and thinking a bit harder. The perfect combination.

For some reason, she was recommending Buzz Off to anyone who asked. *Buzz Off.* She liked how the words rolled off her tongue. "Buzz Off."

"Excuse me?" a customer she hadn't spotted asked from his seat at the bar.

"Oh, hello. How can I help you?"

"Did you just tell me to buzz off?"

Tara blinked. What the hell was this guy talking about? Why would she tell him to buzz off? Wait . . . "Oh, no. Not you. Buzz Off is one of our most popular brews, and I was just thinking that it was especially hot tonight."

"Well, then. I'll have a pint of that," the man said, thankfully appeased.

"Buzz Off. Coming right up."

Buzz buzz buzz. She served the customer his drink. *Buzz buzz buzz.* She had the wherewithal to be alarmed at how oddly she was behaving. Tara looked down at her hands, and spiraled into a panic. Where was it? Had she let go of the string that kept her life together? *The string is in your mind.* Right. She turned her mind inward and looked down at her figurative hands. The string had slipped some, but she was still holding on to it. It was a very small piece, and she held on to it with her thumb and index finger. It was such a perilous hold, she didn't know how much longer she could hang on.

With the last dredges of her will, Tara pulled herself together and went into the kitchen to look for Alex. "Oppa, could you cover the bar for me for a while? I feel weird."

"Weird how?" he asked, concern drawing his eyebrows down.

"I think I might be dizzy." She was. She also felt like throwing up. "And I feel a bit nauseous."

"That doesn't sound good. You should go home for the night." Alex reached out to feel her forehead. "You might have a stomach bug or something."

"No, I'll be fine soon. I just need some air." She pecked his cheek. "Thank you."

When she made it out to the parking lot, Tara headed straight for her car. She was hyperventilating and couldn't get much air in at all. She opened the door and sat leaning out with her head between her legs. The humiliating position was supposed to help with the hyperventilation.

Once she got her breath back, tears were streaming down her face again. *Shiiit.* She thought she'd pretty much cried herself out for the day. Now she was going to get dehydrated. Yes, hydration was what she was most worried about. She was losing it. This was an emergency. She fumbled for her phone and typed with shaking hands.

TARA: Code Fuck fuckity fuck.

AUBREY: I thought our emergency code was shit shit shit.

TARA: Aubrey!

AUBREY: Right. Sorry.

AUBREY: Where are you?

AUBREY: Do you need to talk ASAP?

AUBREY: Do you want me to come right now?

Before she could respond to her best friend's faster-than-a-speeding-bullet questions, her phone rang.

Without preamble, Tara said, "Yes."

"Okay. I'm leaving now." She heard Aubrey shuffling around on the other end. "Landon, I need to go out. Tara needs me."

"What's going on? Is she okay?" Landon's worried voice murmured.

"No, she's not okay. She used the emergency code."

"Oh, shit. Why are you still here? Go."

"Thanks, honey. You know the drill with Morgan, right?"

"Of course, I do. I *am* her dad."

"I love you," Aubrey said.

"I love you, too," Landon echoed in a soft voice.

Tara could almost see their tender kiss before Aubrey rushed out the door, which shut quite loudly behind her.

"I'm on my way," Aubrey said briskly. "Where are you?"

"I'm in my car at the brewery parking lot," Tara replied, suddenly limp with exhaustion. She pulled her legs into the car and shut the door.

"I'll be right there. Do you want me to stay with you on the phone?"

"No. You should focus on driving. I'll be fine."

"Okay. I'll see you soon. Call me back if you need to. I'm on hands-free mode."

"Drive safely." Tara hung up the phone and closed her eyes. She must've fallen asleep, because the next thing she remembered was a knock on her car window. She shot up from her seat and almost hit her head on the car ceiling before she got her bearings.

"Tara, are you okay?" Aubrey asked, trying to open the driver's-side door.

"No," she waved her friend over to the passenger seat and unlocked the doors. She must've locked them at some point. *Safety first!* The thought struck her as hilarious, and she was cackling like a witch when Aubrey got into the car.

Without a word, her best friend wrapped her up in a warm hug. The hysterical laughter quieted, and her breathing became steady. She hugged Aubrey back, and they sat like that for a few minutes. Tara had missed her while she was away, and now her world seemed normal again. Her life was still fucked up in the normal world, but it was nice to have some stability.

"So I did something while you were gone," Tara said, sitting back in her seat.

"I've been gone for nearly a month. I certainly hope you did something during that time," Aubrey said lightly, trying to put Tara at ease.

"I met someone . . ."

"What? Who? When?" Aubrey stopped herself and took a deep breath. "I'm sorry. So you met someone."

"I met someone wonderful."

Aubrey bit her lips, but managed to remain silent.

"We spent almost a month together and it was incredible. I'll never forget it."

"It *was*? What happened, Tara?"

"We agreed to go on four dates, and he dared me not to fall in love with him," Tara said, as tears streamed down her face like pouring rain against a windshield. "I laughed at him. He was ridiculously cocky, and I don't do love, as you know. I told him it won't be a problem, and made him agree not to fall in love with me either."

Aubrey nodded slowly as though she was processing every odd detail Tara revealed.

"I kept my end of the bargain. I cared for him more than I've cared for any other man, and I knew I would be heartbroken when he left, but I didn't allow myself to fall in love with him. He filled my world with life and color, but I still didn't fall in love with him." Tara's voice rose as she tried to convince herself with her words. "But he went and ruined everything. He fell in love with me. He wants forever with me. He said he would give up his dream to stay with me."

"Oh, my God, Tara. It sounds like he really loves you. I know you're afraid to love again, but Jason was a goddamn abusive asshole. You *know* not everyone is like that." Aubrey smoothed back Tara's hair from her clammy forehead, and squeezed her hand tightly. "Look at Landon. Look at your brothers. Look at Seth. There are *good* men out there. It sounds like your guy is one of them. You might've finally found someone who really deserves you."

"But what if I'm not good enough for him? If he gives up his dream to stay with me, how am I different from Jason? I would be demanding him to sacrifice who he is. I would be controlling his life, using his love against him. Sooner or later, he's going to hate me for it."

"Did you ever ask him to stay with you? To give up his dream?" Aubrey asked.

"No . . ."

"He's made his choice, and he chose you. You didn't *do* anything to him other than being yourself. You never tried to manipulate him or control him. Tara, it's his choice and he has every right to make his own decisions."

Tara heard Aubrey's words, but they failed to register. She was broken, and being with her was going to ruin Seth just as Jason had ruined her. She'd done the right thing. She gave him his freedom. Nothing was holding him back from following his dreams now.

"It's too late now anyways," Tara said hollowly. "I told him I didn't love him. That I will never love him."

"Oh, Tara. Did you mean that?"

"I don't know."

Then why did it feel like the world was crumbling down around her? Why did it feel as though she was being torn apart cell by cell? She broke his heart. She hurt him. And it hurt her even more. *But why?*

Because I love him.

Tara couldn't hide from it anymore. She was hurting because she hurt the man she loved. She couldn't stand to think that he was hurting as much as she was. *Oh, God.* She loved him, and when she broke his heart, she broke hers as well.

Seth."

"Yes," he said, turning toward the door. "What's up?"

"Is everything all right?" Landon asked. "I had to call you three times before you looked up."

"Sorry," he said, closing his laptop. He had just moved up his flight to the next morning. There was no point in staying here any longer. He was only torturing himself. "My mind was literally miles away."

"So how are you feeling about the move? Excited?" Landon walked farther into the guest bedroom.

Hating to lie to his brother, Seth shrugged his shoulders. "Did you have a chance to check out the website? What do you think?"

"It's better than I could've imagined. I like to just go there and stare at the pictures sometimes." Landon laughed. "I really appreciate all the effort you put into it. Thank you, little bro."

"You should thank Tara, too. She was a huge help. Did you know she majored in graphic design?"

"Yeah, Aubrey mentioned it." His older brother scratched his chin. "So you guys worked on the website together?"

"We did. She'll be happy you like it so much." The thought of Tara feeling happy brought a ghost of a smile to his face. "Don't forget to tell her."

"I won't." Landon's eyebrows furrowed together as he stared down at his feet. Seth knew him well enough to know what was coming. "You haven't been yourself the last couple days."

"No, I haven't." There was no denying it. Seth was heartbroken, and he did nothing to hide it.

"Do you want to talk about it?"

"Not really."

"Seth—"

"I'm kidding. I don't mind unloading some of it." Seth got up from his chair and paced the floor. There was no point sugarcoating it. "I got jilted."

"Jilted? Were you in a relationship I didn't know about?"

"Well, yes, but it's not what you think. I didn't purposely keep it from you. You just weren't around. I started dating her when you guys went on your honeymoon."

"You started something knowing you were leaving in a month? Did she—whoever she is—know about that?"

"Of course. We agreed to go out a few times while I was here, and end it when I left. It was supposed to be a fun distraction for both of us."

"Then how could you have been jilted?"

"Well, you see," Seth said with a wry smile, "I fell in love with her, and told her I wanted to stay with her."

"Holy shit." Landon plopped down onto the chair Seth had occupied a couple minutes ago. "You fell in love."

"Hopelessly so." Seth leaned against the opposite wall and crossed his arms over his chest. "I don't think I've ever been in love before. Not like this. I finally understand why you were such a wreck when Aubrey left you."

"I almost lost my mind," Landon agreed. "How . . . how are you doing?"

"I'm devastated. I hurt everywhere. Even my hair hurts, which is really weird." Seth laughed quietly. He just missed Tara so much.

"I know how that feels." Landon hesitated. "I can see how devastated you are, and I'm worried about you. But you don't seem like a man who just lost the woman he loves. In fact, you seem more like a person who's found himself. Am I making any sense?"

"You make so much sense that it's scary. If I believed I really lost her . . ." His breath caught in his throat and he clutched at his chest. "I can't even think about that possibility. I couldn't have lost her, because we belong together. I know she loves me, too, but she has to decide to choose me. I need to give her space and figure out a few things on my end."

"And then?"

"Once I have my life in order, I'm coming back to convince her that we're meant to be together."

"Good for you." Landon came up to him and folded him into a bear hug. "You're a better, stronger man than I was in the face of heartbreak."

"Thanks, hyung." He hugged his brother back tightly, then let go. "I wish it didn't hurt so much in the meantime. I miss her so much that I can't breathe sometimes. It's taking everything in me not to run to her right now."

"I'm so sorry, Seth." Landon sighed deeply. "So is she someone from around here? Would Aubrey know who she is?"

"Yes," he said, wondering how much he should tell Landon. But what was the point in keeping secrets? They were family and he needed all the support he could get. "Aubrey knows her exceptionally well. It's Tara."

"What?" Landon's voice rang in the room, and he cringed. The baby was asleep, and they listened to hear if she woke up. The house remained silent. With a sigh of relief, his brother said in a more moderate voice, "Tara? How did that happen?"

"It just did. I don't think anyone can plan who you fall in love with."

"Of course, kid. I was just surprised." His eyes suddenly widened. "Aubrey rushed out earlier to see Tara. She said it was an emergency. I wonder if it has anything to do with you."

"It has everything to do with him." They turned to the quiet voice in the doorway. Aubrey's wide eyes filled with tears, and she rushed to hug Seth. "It's you. You're Tara's guy. I'm so glad and so sorry that it's you."

"Did you . . . did you just see Tara?" Seth said, his voice breaking.

"I did. I put her in bed and stayed till she fell asleep." She searched his eyes. "She's hurting so much, Seth. She's so sorry she hurt you."

It felt as though fire engulfed his heart. He wanted to rush to her side and somehow ease her pain, but he was the source of her pain, wasn't he?

"She's hurting?" Landon asked incredulously. "She's the one who rejected him. How ever much she is hurting, it can't be a fraction of what Seth is going through."

"How could you say that?" Aubrey turned to her husband. "She didn't want to hurt Seth."

"Well, that certainly didn't go as she planned then," his brother mumbled.

Aubrey's chest rose as she prepared to blast some sense into Landon. Seth interrupted the needless argument. "Landon, relax. And Aubrey, I apologize on my big brother's behalf. You know he's always been protective of me. He's just rearing with guilt because I got hurt and there's no way for him to fix it."

"I know," she said quietly, and took ahold of Landon's hand. "And I'm just taking my frustration out on him. Sorry for being such asses."

"What can I do? You're family." Seth managed a smile.

Aubrey smiled, and Landon laughed sheepishly. He put his arm around his wife and pulled her close, as though they needed to share each other's strength. Seth pushed down the burst of envy he felt. He wasn't himself.

"So what are you going to do?" Landon asked Seth.

"For now? I'm leaving for Paris tomorrow morning."

"What?" Aubrey and Landon yelled in unison.

When Morgan's cry pierced through the walls, Aubrey sighed and shook her head. She turned to Landon. "I'll go. You stay and talk with Seth."

"Thank you," he said to his wife's already-retreating back.

"Sorry to drop that on you like that," Seth began. "It was an impulsive decision. I just couldn't stay here any longer . . . so close to her. But I'm only leaving a few days earlier. It isn't a big deal."

"But don't you want to talk to Tara before you leave?"

"I can't. I can't see her without begging her to have me. Neither of us is ready for that yet. We both need time." His entire being ached like an open wound, and his heart was too raw to risk rejection for a second time right now. He didn't know if he could survive it. No matter how much he longed to run to her, he needed time to heal. "It's going to be hell staying away from her, but the distance should help. She won't be twenty minutes away anymore. Too bad the distance won't help me miss her less."

"I understand. Do you need help with packing?"

"No, everything is packed and ready. I'm just going to roll out of bed tomorrow morning and leave. It's an early flight, so don't bother getting up for me."

"Don't worry. We'll already be up anyways. We're new parents, remember? Besides, there is no way I'm letting my brother leave the country without one last hug."

Seth nodded, too choked up to speak. His brother had his back if he couldn't make it through this one on his own. Because no matter what happened, he was going to get through this. He would find his way back to Tara.

CHAPTER NINETEEN

Tara was still in bed late the next morning when Aubrey texted her.

AUBREY: Tara, are you awake?
TARA: Define awake.
AUBREY: I have something to tell you.
TARA: Then tell me already.
AUBREY: Seth left this morning.

Her stomach dropped to her toes, shot back up, and rammed into her throat. She swallowed the bile, and sat up in bed.

TARA: Left? Left how? Did he go back to Santa Monica or his mom's house?
AUBREY: No, hon. He left for Paris.

She clicked on her calendar to make sure she had the date right. Yes, he wasn't supposed to leave for four days.

TARA: Why?

When Aubrey didn't respond right away, Tara realized how non-sensical her question was. It was because of her. He left because he couldn't stand being near her anymore. Did he hate her for her cruel words?

AUBREY: I thought I should let you know. You okay?
TARA: Thanks. Yes, I'm fine.

That was such a lie. She should take it back. She didn't want to ruin her relationship with Aubrey, too, by being dishonest with her.

TARA: I lied. I'm not fine at all.

With that confession, she ran to the bathroom and hurled in the toilet. Shivering and her teeth chattering, Tara sat on the cold floor for a moment to gather herself. Seth was gone. Really gone . . . It was worse. So much worse than what she'd imagined it would be like. She knew she would be heartbroken when he left, but she'd opened herself to him anyway. She'd thought being with him was worth the heartache. She was right on that count. She wouldn't trade the time she'd spent with Seth for the world, but damn it hurt.

When her butt started feeling numb from the cold, she pushed off the ground on shaking limbs and brushed her teeth. Her phone dinged.

AUBREY: Let me know if you want to talk. I'm here for you.

While she appreciated her friend's unwavering support, she needed to pull herself together first. The only sound that would escape her mouth if she opened it now would be sobs and wails.

Wait. A. Minute.

Why would Aubrey text her to tell her that Seth had left? Why would she ask if she was okay? *Oh, shit.* She knew. Aubrey knew that she'd had a thing with her brother-in-law and then stomped on his heart with construction-grade boots. Seth must've told Landon about them. Of course, he would. Who else would he lean on?

When she tried to keep it locked up inside, she nearly broke. She was so relieved that Seth had Landon and Aubrey for support. Well, not so much anymore. He'd left for Paris. Where he had no one. Would he be all right?

The tightness at the back of the throat told her she was on the verge of crying again, but she stopped herself. Crying was self-indulgence at this point. She'd broken Seth's heart in the harshest way possible and was trying to soothe her guilt and pain with tears. But she didn't deserve to have her guilt and pain soothed away. She let the full force of her pain wash over her, and she buckled under its weight. But she wouldn't turn away from it anymore. The least she could do was hurt with Seth.

The wallowing stopped now. She was a grown woman with responsibilities. She had to continue to function.

Pain was her constant companion now, but she'd learned how to function through it. And so she existed—day by agonizing day. She worked hard at the brewery and offered to help anybody, any way she could. She might as well do some good with her existence. Like putting in more hours at the brewery.

"Hey, Jack." She went and peered down at her brother. "Are the tables getting wobbly again?"

"Yeah, I spotted a few that are bugging me."

"Didn't you fix a bunch of them last month?" she asked. "It's so weird how they keep getting lopsided. Does the floor snack on some of the legs? The least they could do is eat them evenly."

He stopped fiddling with the legs of the troublesome table and looked up at her. "What's up?"

"What do you mean?"

"Why are you hanging around here? You usually couldn't care less about broken chairs and lopsided tables."

"Well, the past me used to be an inconsiderate creature. Now I've changed, and want to offer my help."

"You're being so *nice*." Jack got to his feet, dusting off his hands. "Why are you being so *nice*?"

"What are you talking about?" Tara clapped a hand to her chest, genuinely indignant. "I am nice."

"You're good and kind." Her brother's words appeased her a bit, but he kept talking. "But you aren't particularly nice. Not all the time."

"I take offense to that." She narrowed her eyes. It felt kind of good to be angry, so she let it burn.

"You're someone who knows your mind and aren't afraid to speak it. You never do something just for the sake of being nice." He lifted his hands as though to ward her off when she snarled at him. "For example, if I was struggling with these table legs, you would've offered your help without hesitation. But you know I enjoy fiddling with woodwork, so you usually leave me to it. You only offered to help this time because you were being *nice*."

"Fine. You could've just told me you don't need help. I don't know what the big deal is." Tara looked everywhere but at him. Something about this conversation was making her really nervous.

"Tell me what's going on, Tara. It's as though you've been trying to pay penance for something these last few weeks." Jack laid a big warm hand on her shoulder. "We know that there is something seriously wrong, but have no idea what. We're all worried—Mom, Dad . . . all of us. Please. Let us help you, or at least bear some of the burden with you."

Paying penance. Oh, God. He was right. Her guilt was making her find ways to make up for what she did to Seth by helping others. But how did that help Seth? She was such a mess.

"It's a long story, but here's the short version. I fell in love with Seth, but when he told me he loved me, I told him that I didn't love him and never would. So he flew away to Paris with a broken heart, thinking I don't love him."

"Why the hell would you tell him that when you love him?"

"I was afraid. I was afraid we would end up hurting each other in the end, and I didn't want to risk that."

"Seems to me you're suffering deeply right now, and I doubt Seth is in any better condition." Jack pulled her into a hug, and ran a gentle hand down her hair. She burrowed into him to soak up the solace he offered. "How is this any better than a hypothetical heartbreak in the future? Which might never happen? Why give up the chance for happiness when you have nothing to lose? Do you think it'll be harder than what you're going through now?"

"Jack, I broke his heart. How could I have broken his heart just because I was scared?"

"Because you were scared, Tara. People make foolish decisions when they're afraid."

Something that felt like life fluttered in Tara's chest. She'd chosen wrong because of her fears, but maybe she could change that. Maybe she deserved another chance. She stepped back from the hug and said, "Hey, are you calling me a fool?"

"If the shoe fits." Her lovely big brother grinned back at her. "So what are you going to do now?"

"Fix my monumental mistake, of course." Hope and fear were duking it out inside her. "What if he doesn't forgive me?"

"Are you going to let 'what if' make the decision for you again?"

"No." Tara shook her head resolutely. "Never again."

"There is the little sister I know and love." Jack tousled her head. "Now go and do whatever you need to do. I have you covered with the fam."

"Thanks, oppa."

She ran for the back office. There was no time to drive home right now. Tara needed to get to Paris as soon as possible. She woke the sleeping computer with a jiggle of the mouse, and jumped on the web. Heart pounding, she searched for the earliest flight to Charles de Gaulle. Luckily, there was a redeye to Paris tonight. It would take a chunk of her savings to buy a one-way ticket, but she would deplete her unborn child's future college savings to get to Seth. Without blinking an eye, she hit *buy*.

Tara didn't bother with a return ticket because she had no idea when she would be returning. She planned on staying there as long as necessary to win Seth back. She didn't want to leave her family in a lurch, but Weldon Brewery would be fine with the four of them for a while. With her decision made and her ticket bought, her urgency to go to him only grew. Almost a month had passed since Seth had left. Why the hurry now? *Who knows?* But every fiber in her being was telling her to go to him. Now.

"Jack," she yelled out to him. "I'm going home to pack."

"Okay," he said nonchalantly. "Bring me back some macarons."

The drive home was slow because she was shaking and had to pay extra attention to the road. She wouldn't be able to handle the long drive to the international airport.

"Call Aubrey."

Her car obediently dialed Aubrey, who picked up on the second ring.

"Hi, Tara." When she didn't respond right away, her friend asked in an alarmed voice, "What's wrong?"

"You've been asking me that every time I call you lately. Can't a girl call her best friend just to say hello?"

"Of course, you can. But are you?"

"No. To hell with hello," Tara said, suddenly impatient. "I need your help, Bree."

"Anything."

"I need a ride to the airport. I have a flight out at ten o'clock tonight."

"Oh, thank God," Aubrey said with feeling.

"I don't want you guys telling Seth anything. I have to do this on my own. Plus, I'm afraid he would run away if he knew I was coming."

"Don't be ridiculous. He would never run away from you."

"What do you call flying to Paris four days early?"

"Getting there a few days early for his new job?"

"Quit making sense. I feel inferior when you do that," Tara said wryly.

"You're in love. You're not supposed to make any sense when you're about to fly across the ocean to get your man back," Aubrey said. "Your flight's at ten o'clock? That doesn't give us much time. Getting to the airport alone will take us three hours with traffic. And you need to get there two hours before your flight time for international flights."

"Right. I'm almost home, and I'll be packed in ten minutes. What's the best outfit for groveling?"

"Tight jeans and a billowy top. The jeans will make you look good and the loose top will hide any anxiety sweat stains."

"Good call," Tara said, putting her car into park. "Okay. I'm home."

"Got it. I'm going to put Justine in charge here, ask my mom to watch Morgan for the rest of the evening, and have Landon pick up the baby after work." She was probably ticking them off her fingers. "I'll be at your house in half an hour."

"Sorry about putting you through so much trouble." She couldn't forget that her best friend now had a family of her own. Being a working mom was hard even without emergency chauffeur duties.

"Do not apologize. You would do the same for me in a heartbeat."

Tara couldn't argue with that. So she didn't. "I love you."

"I love you, too."

She pushed herself out of the car, her trembling somewhat better, and let herself inside. The house was quiet and she didn't run into anyone on her trot over to the garage. She quickly spotted her carry-on case and rolled it to her room.

Tight jeans and loose shirts. Right. Not allowing herself to think too hard, she packed as many of them as she could in her small suitcase, only leaving room for panties, bras, and toiletry. If she needed anything, she could buy it over there. She had twenty minutes to spare so she took a quick shower and changed into a pair of tight jeans and a billowy tunic.

Her cell phone buzzed at the thirty-minute mark. Aubrey was here. *Oh, my gosh.* This was really happening. She was doing this. She breathed in and out through her nose, and squared her shoulders. *Damn right, I'm doing this. I'm going to win my man back.*

CHAPTER TWENTY

The cab ride into Paris from Charles de Gaulle airport took over an hour, and she fought against the sleep that tugged down her eyelids. She'd caught snatches of sleep on the plane, but not much. Her mind had refused to relax enough for true sleep to come. The long drive through the rather gloomy, industrial part of the city transitioned abruptly into the stunning, picturesque heart of Paris. Her sigh was automatic and soul deep. The most romantic city in the world. She hoped some of that romance would work in her favor.

Aubrey had given her Seth's work and home address. Since it was already past eight in the evening, Tara was headed straight for his place. What if he didn't want to have anything to do with her? She wouldn't be surprised if he gave her the boot tonight. But she wouldn't let that discourage her. She planned to camp nearby and visit him every day until she wore him down. She wasn't leaving Paris until he heard her out. The problem was, she'd left in such a rush that she didn't have reservations for a room. Hopefully, not all the decent rooms were sold out.

"Is there a view of the Eiffel Tower on our way?" she asked to distract herself from her growing anxiousness.

"Non. But if we go a little around that way, you see the top of it." The driver glanced back at her. "You want to see?"

"Yes, please."

She was stalling, but the view of the Eiffel Tower might give her a dose of extra bravery. And she was right. The brightly lit tower rose into the sky—postcards and posters couldn't capture its immense presence—and even seeing just the tip of it made the fact that she was in Paris sink in.

When she'd last come to Paris, she was bold, adventurous, and fearless. But after that summer, she'd let Jason take that away from her, and she'd lived in fear since. Well, no more. Loving Seth taught her that she didn't have to curl into herself to protect her broken soul. Loving Seth meant opening up her heart so that he could help her heal. She could still be the bold, adventurous, and fearless woman she was meant to be. *No.* She already *was* that woman. And she was brave enough to come all the way across the ocean to win back the man she loved. *I can do this.*

The cab stopped and idled in front of a street filled with beautiful apartments. She didn't know her architecture, but the buildings were old and ornate. The driver got out of the car, then popped the trunk. Tara got out and met him on the sidewalk. She thanked him when he handed the small carry-on to her. For no apparent reason, she stood where he'd dropped her off and watched the cab disappear down the narrow street.

She was terrified, but she had to believe that she could convince Seth to give her another chance. She couldn't consider the alternative. For a month, she'd existed believing that she had lost him forever, and that wasn't living. Merely existing like a ghost in this vibrant, beautiful world was unthinkable. She wanted to be with him and live to the fullest.

With a determined nod, she turned to face the building. Seth was in there. After being apart for so long, being this close to him made her heart sing with joy . . . before terror knocked it aside. A single look or a word from Seth could crush her heart. But she had to remember . . . taking this risk gave her a chance at a real life. If he sends her away, then she would only be back to where she was. It couldn't hurt more than sending him away the way she had.

She looked for his name on the intercom. Even when she found it, she couldn't get herself to press it right away.

"Oh, for goose's sake." She closed her eyes and pressed the button, long and loud.

When there was no response, she peeked from one eye to make sure she hadn't pressed the wrong button. Her finger still hovered right by Seth's name. She had pressed the right one. Did he know she was out here? Was there a camera? Of course, he must've seen her through the intercom with her face scrunched and her eyes squeezed shut, and ignored it.

Her stubbornness kicked in and gave her some much-needed energy. She'd come too far to be sent away at the gate. She pressed the button again with her eyes wide open this time.

"Dammit, Seth." At least answer the intercom.

She buzzed him in three rapid successions. She wanted to hit the damn thing, but someone was coming out of the building, and she didn't want to get arrested for destruction of property.

"You come in?" asked the young woman when she opened the gate to come out.

"Really? May I?" Tara asked with her hand on her chest. She was ever so grateful. The other woman must've seen how desperate she had been to reach Seth on the intercom.

"Mais oui." She stepped out of the building and held the gate wide open for Tara to get through with her rolling bag.

"Merci. Vous êtes très gentile." Tara waved as the nice woman smiled and walked off to her destination.

He might not want her near him, but she was inside, one step closer to him. *Ha.* He lived on the sixth floor, so when she spotted what appeared to be an elevator, she walked toward it. It was the size of a small pantry and had iron railings as the door. She slid it open and got inside. She and her bag filled it to maximum capacity.

When the door didn't automatically close, she fiddled with the handle and closed it by hand. She pressed the button for the sixth floor, but it didn't light up, and nothing was happening to the elevator. Too nervous to trust the old-fashioned contraption anymore, Tara got off the teeny elevator and headed for the open stairway in the lobby.

The stairs were narrow and steep, and difficult to maneuver carrying a bag, which got heavier by the minute. By the time she reached the sixth floor, Tara was out of breath and had a sheen of sweat on her forehead. She stood at the top of the stairs taking a moment to catch her breath, so she wouldn't be a panting, sweaty mess when Seth saw her through the peephole. Maybe that was better than pale and petrified. The exertion had probably put some color in her cheeks and now might actually be the best time to knock on his door.

She dragged herself and her bag up the last few steps to reach Seth's door, and knocked.

"Seth," she called out. "It's Tara."

No answer.

"Please open the door. Just hear me out. Please." She rapped on the door again. "Are you home?"

Maybe he was out, but her paranoid mind told her that he was home on the other side of the door, silently listening to her plea. Heart steeled and cold. Wanting her to suffer. Because she deserved it.

Her knees threatened to buckle so she leaned against the door. "Aubrey says hello. Don't be mad at her for giving me your address. I'm her best friend and she probably couldn't help but take pity on me. I've been such a wreck. If I had more energy, I would've noticed how many people I was worrying. It seems I've been too *nice* lately, and it was freaking people out. I'm a little offended, but then again Little Miss Sunshine just isn't me. I think I've been trying to make up for what I did to you by helping other people."

Reason returned to her. Seth might be angry with her, but he wasn't cruel. If he was home, he would've opened the door by now. But even knowing he wasn't home didn't stop her from spilling her heart out to the freaking door. The words wouldn't stop.

"But I don't want you to worry. I'm not here to make you worry. Being here near you is making me feel alive again. And I'm terrified—really terrified—that you won't give me another chance, but knowing that I tried to win you back will help me move forward. I don't want a life without you, but I'll respect your decision. I'll continue to dream, and follow my passion. I won't be whole, but I'll be something."

She cleared her throat. It was true. She was done with existing like a ghost. Life was too precious and amazing to watch it pass by while she wallowed in a fog of grief. She was going to do everything in her power to convince Seth to give her another chance, but if it really was over, then she would go on. She wasn't going to allow anyone or anything to erase who she was. She had the power to decide who she was and to live the life she chose. Loving Seth had taught her that.

"I didn't mean it. Any of it. Especially the part when I said I could never love you. How could I never love you if I'm already in love with you? That was the biggest lie I'd ever told. But I need you to hear this. Even if I've irrevocably broken your heart and you could never trust me again, know that I love you with everything in me. I love you so much that being with you makes the world a place full of hope and promise, and I feel like I can do anything. With you by my side, I won't be afraid of losing myself again, because you bring out everything true inside me."

Closing her eyes, she soaked in the fact that she was in Paris. He was in Paris. They were so close. *Seth.*

"How did you fall in love with me when I fought so hard to stay distant? Do you . . ." Tara swallowed. Maybe it wasn't true anymore. He might not love her. He might hate her. "Seth? Do you still love me?"

"Tara?" A voice—a voice she loved and would know anywhere—said from the stairway.

She spun to face him and lost her balance, but Seth was instantly by her side to catch her from falling. They stared at each other, breathing hard. Did he know she'd been talking to the door all this time, confessing her love to it? What could he be thinking? Once she gained her balance, she stumbled back from Seth and smoothed her hair away from her face.

"Hello, Seth." She sounded so formal. Talking to the door had been much easier than talking to the real-life man. He was so tall, so handsome, and so . . . confused. She tried to rectify the matter. "Um, hi."

"What are you doing here?" he said, his eyes traveling over her as though checking to see if she were real.

"I came to see you. To talk to you." She took a step toward him. "Is it okay that I came?"

"I . . . yes . . . no . . . ," he stuttered, the furrow between his eyebrows deepening. She didn't know what to make of it. She'd never seen Seth truly flustered. She was just thankful that there was a *yes* in the middle of his muddled response. And yet she couldn't ignore the *no* either.

"Should I . . . do you want me to come back tomorrow?" *Please don't send me away. Please don't send me away.*

"What? No," he said adamantly. Abruptly picking up her bag, he unlocked and opened the door. "Please. Go on in."

She had the ridiculous image of Seth slamming the door once she walked in, and locking her in from the outside. She took a deep breath and forced her feet to move her forward and into the apartment. Her eyes widened at the modern interior, so different from the outside, and how bare the place was. Other than some boxes strewn about, the living room was empty.

She turned around to make sure that Seth had followed her inside, and jumped a little when she discovered him rather close behind her.

"Sorry," he mumbled, taking a step back. He scratched the back of his head and looked around his apartment rather despondently. Then, as though he had just discovered the fact, he said, "There is nowhere to sit."

"That's okay. We could stand."

"Do you want a drink? I have coffee and wine."

"I'll have a glass of wine. Thank you." She could use a bit of liquid courage before she poured out her soul to the man she loved.

Seth lumbered to the small, bare kitchen and opened and shut every cupboard. But other than a couple of used glasses in the sink, there were no clean wineglasses to be found. He grunted in disgust and poured the wine into two clean-looking mugs on the counter. "Sorry. I wasn't expecting a guest."

"Why not?" she asked. He lived here now. Why was he living like he was crashing at someone else's place?

His eyes rose to meet hers and flitted away. Then he shrugged in response.

She accepted the mug o' wine he offered and leaned against a wall. Seth stood by the sink, starting down at his wine. He was probably becoming irritated with the silence stretching on between them. She was the one who told him that she wanted to talk, but her mouth was glued shut with quaking nerves. She couldn't blow this. *Get it together, Tara.*

What he'd really wanted to say to her on the stairway was . . . *Yes, I still love you. More than life.* But fear clogged his throat. Why had she asked that? Did she want reassurance that he was over her, so she could go on with her life with a clear conscience?

He didn't know why she was here. Had her guilt prompted her to fly across the ocean to apologize to him? He didn't know if he was ready for her. Ready to convince her that they were meant to be together. He knew in his heart that she loved him, too, but what if she didn't love him enough to risk getting hurt again? If he failed, he didn't know if he would get another chance to fight for her.

It was agony waiting for her to speak. He wished he could just kiss her until neither of them could breathe. His memories and dreams hadn't done her justice. She was breathtaking, and he couldn't stop his eyes from traveling to her lips again and again.

Her lips at the moment were puckered adorably, blowing on the mug. Then she crinkled her nose and shook her head no as if deciding against blowing on the room-temperature wine. With a quiet, frustrated sigh, Tara chugged her wine like it was one of her brews on a hot day.

He could go on staring at her all night. God, he'd missed her so much. A part of him still thought he might be imagining all of this. But her essence, her spirit, filled his apartment with life. Hope, timid and uncertain, fluttered inside him.

"Why are you here, Tara?"

She jumped as though she'd forgotten he was there. She stole a glance at him without answering, and came up to the sink. She rinsed her cup and looked around for a towel to dry her hands. When she found none, she wiped her hands on her jeans. Her form-fitting jeans. They looked fantastic on her, hugging all her curves. He wished he was her jeans.

Without a word, Tara walked out to the living room and Seth followed. Not only because she expected him to, but because he couldn't help himself. He needed to stay in her orbit. When she reached the middle of the living room, she turned to face him. She didn't startle as much this time, but by the widening of her eyes, it was obvious he'd been following her too closely again.

But he couldn't make himself step back. They were so close, he could feel her warmth and smell the alluring scent coming off her body. She smelled fantastic. He'd so desperately missed her at times that he would've bought a bottle of her shampoo if they sold it here. He was probably being creepy, staring at her like a man who'd found an oasis after days in the desert. He should step back and give her some room, but his feet had melded to the floor. Not knowing what to do or say, he stuffed his hands into his pockets so he wouldn't accidentally make a grab for her.

Tara let out a noise that sounded like a small growl then grabbed and kissed him. He stumbled back, and she took advantage of his unsteady balance to slam his back against a wall. Somewhere in the back of his mind, he knew that they needed to talk but . . . *fuck it.* Tara was in his apartment in Paris and was devouring his mouth like a starving woman. Talking could wait. Breathing could wait.

He groaned against her mouth and took over the kiss. He couldn't hold himself back anymore, and he plundered her mouth, his tongue tangling with hers, demanding her response. And she responded with equal desperation. He spun them around and trapped her against the wall and wrapped her leg around his waist.

"Tara," he moaned, and kissed her with renewed passion. It was good—so good—to have her in his arms again. But why? Why was she here kissing him like she couldn't live without him? He needed to know. He had a right to know. "Wait."

Using every ounce of strength he had, he pulled his lips a centimeter away from hers. She growled in protest and pushed her lips against his, holding him captive with tight fists in his hair. *Okay.* He tried his best to slow things down. Now he couldn't hold back anymore. He wrapped her other leg around him and held her against him, and took his first steps toward the bedroom. Blood rushed in his ears with need. He'd been without her for too long to be able to fight this any longer.

The only one who could stop this now was Tara, but she didn't seem like she had any intention of stopping. Her legs wrapped tighter around his waist, and she kissed him until he couldn't breathe. But when he hefted her up higher in his arms and lengthened his strides, her lips finally stopped their sensual assault.

"Oh," she said quietly. Then she wiggled against his hold and said in a panicked voice, "No, wait. Stop."

Seth stopped in his tracks and put her down. His hands were

shaking so he shoved them down into his pockets again. Good. He was glad she'd stopped him. The rock-hard part of him protested loudly, but he knew in his heart that it was better this way. He needed to find out what Tara really wanted before they went any further.

"Sorry," Tara said, looking down at her toes. "Well, it's your fault, too, for looking all handsome and sad. How is a woman supposed to resist that?"

"Tara," he said with quiet warning. "Are you ready to tell me why you're here?"

"I . . . I came to apologize." Her face crumpled with regret and something inside him seemed to wither.

"I don't want your apology," he said, more sharply than he'd intended. He didn't want to assuage her guilt. He wanted to love her. But when her face turned pale, he wanted to smack himself.

"Well, you're going to get one anyway," she said, narrowing her eyes at him.

"I . . ."

"Shut up and listen." She took a deep breath. "Please. Before I lose my guts and run away."

The "run away" part shut him up good. No matter what happened, he wasn't ready to watch her go.

"I was afraid. Not that it excuses what I did to you, but I let my fear get the best of me." She slid down against the wall until she was sitting on the floor. He joined her from the opposite wall in the hallway. Their outstretched legs were lying parallel to each other. He held himself back from pressing his leg against hers. "What I told you? About my ex from college? There's more."

"I'm listening, Tara," he said in gentle reassurance. But his heart was thumping against his ribs, bruising them with its force. "Go on. I'm here."

"He wasn't just controlling. He was emotionally abusive."

A menacing sound he didn't know he was capable of making escaped his throat.

"Seth, please. Don't get angry. Just listen for now. It's all in the past and I'm finally okay with it. Don't let it hurt you. Please."

"I'm sorry. I'll try not to interrupt anymore," he said through clenched teeth, trying to control his fury. That bastard had hurt Tara. Really hurt her. He wanted to beat him to an inch of his life.

"He made me believe that I wasn't good enough. Everything I did was wanting, and he said that I didn't love him enough to do better. I kept trying to be good enough for him, but kept failing. My confidence was shattered and guilt chained my heart." She took a shuddering breath and continued, "I would hold my breath and shrink into myself when he was near so I wouldn't trigger one of his outbursts. But I stayed with him because he always convinced me that it was my fault he got angry. I think that really broke me. I didn't know who I was anymore. I was so scared."

"God, Tara. I'm so sorry." Heat prickled behind his eyes as pain slashed through him, and emotion choked his throat.

"One day, something came over me, and I fought back when he lost his temper. I didn't buy his hateful accusations. I didn't cower to his fury. The real me was still inside of me, shouting that I didn't deserve that. That I'm worth more than what he convinced me to believe. That's when I finally left him."

Seth stayed silent even as he trembled with helpless fury. He wished he could turn back time and protect her from all harm, but that wouldn't be right. She was who she was because of her past. What he needed to do was listen, and stand by her as she healed.

"The thing that tortured me most was that I'd lost myself so completely. I thought love was the destructive force that broke me. That's why I was so frightened when you told me you loved me, because I knew I loved you, too. All I could think was that I didn't want to go back to being that broken person. Or become a monster who breaks you." Her voice cracked, but she continued with renewed strength, "But now I finally understand that it was the malice and the toxicity that made me lose myself. That's the nature of abuse, not love. I won't hide in shame and fear anymore. I survived soul-destroying abuse, and that's a testament to my strength. I was so wrong to fear love. My love for you only makes me stronger, and it will never make me hurt you the way I've been hurt."

"Tara, you are amazing—smart, kind, and so strong. Never doubt that." Seth rejoiced in her admission of love, but more than anything, he was so fucking proud of her.

"Do you forgive me? For breaking your heart. For lying to you. Because it was the biggest lie I ever told. How can I not love you?" She shifted to sit beside him and hesitantly gathered his hand between her own. "I love you so much that I can't even contain it inside me. Now that I've told you . . . told you that I love you, I can finally breathe. And I don't ever want to stop saying it."

He cupped her cheek with his free hand. "There's nothing to forgive. I knew in my soul that you loved me. Like you said, you couldn't contain it. You loved me with your every glance and touch. I felt it. It was dense of me to take so long to realize that we were in love. I should've known I loved you. You filled me with joy and yearning every time I saw you, and I couldn't stop thinking about you when we were apart."

"Do you still love me?" Tara's eyes searched his as if she was looking for the very meaning of life.

"So much," he whispered. "Tara, I love you now and forever. And I'm never letting you go again."

Tara threw her arms around his neck and held on for dear life. "You won't get a chance. I might lock you in the bedroom and throw away the key."

"Ooh, kinky. I have no objections to that." His smile was tremulous, but his heart was singing.

"We don't have to . . . I'm not sure . . . can we talk first?" she said shyly into his neck.

He chuckled low in his chest, and kissed the top of her head. "Of course, baby. As long as you want. I was only teasing."

"Okay. Good. So you won't get the wrong idea if I ask to move this conversation to the bedroom? My butt cheeks are getting numb."

Seth would've loved to massage them for her, but he needed to keep himself under control. Tara was exhausted and vulnerable right now, and he didn't want to overwhelm her. Instead, he lifted her to her feet, and led her to his bedroom.

"Oh," she gasped. "Seth . . . oh."

His walls were covered with his paintings and artwork, with his recently finished work of her in the hills of Weldon placed prominently above his bed.

"You're wrong, you know." Seth wrapped his arms around her waist from behind and rested his chin on her shoulder. Her hands came to rest on his arms. "I wouldn't be giving up my dream to stay with you in Weldon. Photography isn't my dream. Art has always been my dream. I'd just lost my way for a while."

"But what about your job here?" she whispered.

"I respectfully declined the position."

"So you haven't worked a day at your new job?"

"Nope."

She broke away from his embrace and spun to face him. "Then what are you doing here in Paris?"

He pulled her into his arms because he couldn't stand to be apart from her. "I've been working on my art. I wanted to create something that will show you that this really is my dream. Once I had something worthy, I would've gone back to Weldon to convince you that we're meant to be together. But you came here first."

"And you don't think any of these are worthy?" She stared at him slack-jawed.

He shrugged. "For you, I don't know if anything ever will be."

"Then it's a good thing I came. Who knows how long I would've been waiting for you to create your masterpiece?"

"I wouldn't have lasted much longer. Staying away from you was torture."

"Seth, all of this"—she leaned back to glance at every wall—"they are all amazing. You are amazing, and I'm so glad you finally found your way back to your art."

"What would you have done if I was happily working at my new job?" He led her to his bed, and they sat side by side with their backs against the wall.

"I don't know. All I knew was that I had to tell you that I love you, and find out if you still loved me. Then, we would've worked everything else out. We might've tried the long-distance thing for a while. Then I might've taken a sabbatical from the brewery and come stay with you for a year. I don't know, but we would've found a way to be with each other."

"We'll always find a way." And because he couldn't stop himself, he leaned down to kiss her softly.

"So what's next?" she said against his lips.

"How long can you stay?" He dropped kisses along her jaw.

"I was going to stay as long as necessary to win you back," she confessed.

He found her mouth again and kissed her hard. "And now that you've won me back?"

"I don't plan on letting you out of my sight for a while," she said, her hand caressing his face. "I'll stay here with you until you're ready to go home with me."

"Good. Then there's time for me to take you on our fourth date. You haven't forgotten we have one date left, right?"

"Forgotten? No way. When you left Weldon early, I was furious. A deal is a deal."

"Yes, it is." He laughed, rubbing the tip of his nose against hers. "I still can't believe that you're really here."

"Oh, I'm here all right." This time she kissed him until he became light-headed. "Do you believe it now?"

"Yes," he said. "And you really love me?"

"With all my heart," she said without hesitation.

"I love you, Tara Park." His heart was so full of happiness, he was surprised he wasn't floating on air.

"That's what I like to hear." A single tear slid down her cheek. "Never stop telling me."

"I love you. I love you. I love you." He punctuated every *I love you* with a kiss, then let his kisses show her how much he loved her. That he was hers. Forever.

EPILOGUE

"Is it as good as you remembered?" Seth asked.

"Mmm," she moaned, her eyes fluttering closed. "It's even better."

They'd had trouble leaving Seth's apartment for a while, so their fourth date was a bit delayed. But they finally made it to Berthillon for the promised three scoops. The ice cream shop resided in an elegant multistoried stone building surrounded by rows of similar buildings. The wooden façade of the shop gave it a refined, old-fashioned air that was perfect for the exquisite ice cream they served. The narrow street in front was nearly traffic-free, adding to the feeling of being in a place out of time.

"I could watch you eat ice cream all day," he said in a low growly voice that should be illegal on public sidewalks. Even on the atmospheric, romantic sidewalks of Paris.

Tara felt her cheeks warming up, and her body softening. The man sure knew how to turn her on. But not now. They were on their date, and she wasn't going back to the apartment until they visited Sacré-Cœur.

"I actually can eat this stuff all day, and every day," she said, tickled pink by the song of French voices chatting around her. It felt wonderful to be immersed in a culture so different from hers. "But I can't have you staring at me and neglecting your work, so I'll refrain from doing so."

He chuckled and pointed at her cone. "Can I have a taste of your melon flavor?"

"Sure."

She smiled, remembering their first kiss at the park. She licked a dollop of her melon ice cream and brought Seth's mouth to meet hers. He moaned and she wasn't sure if it was because of the ice cream or the kiss.

"More later," she said. "Our ice cream is melting."

"Yes, later," he agreed. "Much more."

They made quick work of the delicious treat, walking along the idyllic streets of Île Saint-Louis, where Berthillon was nestled. The streets were quiet and peaceful in the charming neighborhood dotted with bakeries, cheese shops, and cafes. The air smelled purely of Paris, ageless and sweet. She loved experiencing Paris this way, without the throng of tourists.

But she couldn't resist walking along the iconic Seine with their fingers linked, the warm spring sunshine reflected on the water.

Seth brought their hands up and kissed her knuckles. "It feels so great to touch you without worrying about getting caught."

"I love it, too." She stood on her tippy toes and kissed him to accentuate her point. "It feels fucking glorious to be lovers in Paris."

He pulled her into his arms and spun her around. "I can be as corny as I want, and it'll still be romantic because it's Paris."

"But you are romantic," Tara confessed. "All those times I called you corny, I was actually melting into pink goo."

"Ah, so you are susceptible to my brand of romance." His grin turned cocky. "Good to know."

"I'm susceptible to you, Seth," she whispered. "I didn't know it was possible to be so much in love. It's overwhelming sometimes."

"I know. Me, too," he said, tucking a strand of hair behind her ear.

"Do you think it'll still be like this when we go home?"

"It'll be like this wherever we are." He tugged her hand and they started walking down the river again. "This isn't some Paris magic, Tara. It's our own magic. Our love."

"Corny," she teased, tears gathering at the corners of her eyes.

"Does that mean you're pink goo right now?"

"Yes, and I have hearts in my eyes."

"God, you're adorable."

"I know. And I'm all yours," she said with love glowing brilliantly in her heart. "Lucky you."

"Yes," he said, looking at her as though she was the greatest piece of art in the world. "Lucky me."

ACKNOWLEDGMENTS

The Dating Dare is my pandemic baby. At times, it was difficult to write. Who am I kidding? It was hard—really hard—to write on most days. Yet, this book has been my escape and my anchor through these incomprehensible, heartbreaking times. Tara and Seth warmed my heart, made me laugh, and moved me to tears. Writing their story gave me a purpose that helped me forge ahead. It kept me whole.

To Sarah Younger, literary agent extraordinaire. Your voice of reason and sound advice—which kept me sane through four releases and two new contracts during the pandemic—allowed me to center myself and write this book. Thank you for having my back, my friend.

To Mara Delgado Sánchez, my wonderful editor, thank you for loving my book. It made me deliriously happy to hear that I made you laugh *and* cry! Thank you for believing in me even when I couldn't and working so hard to make *The Dating Dare* shine. I'm so happy we got to work together on this book.

And to my marketing manager, DJ DeSmyter, my publicist, Mary Moates, and the rest of the incredible team at St. Martin's Griffin. Thank you so much for your support and dedication. As I so often said, you guys rock.

Thank you to Gwen Hernandez for being my friend and critique partner. Your support and candid insights helped me see this book with a clearer eye and a kinder heart. And to Christin Britton, thank you so much for holding my hand through this whole process and steadying me through the bumps and jolts. You gave me the strength to give *The Dating Dare* my everything until the very end.

To my husband and my boys. Thank you for your love and support as I wrote this book while all of us spent way more time with each other than usual. It was challenging at times, but you never lost your sense of humor. And your interest in my work always makes me so proud of myself. Your support means everything.

To Mom, Dad, and my brother, Eugene, you guys are my biggest cheerleaders. You lift me up so I can reach higher, and you're ready to catch me if I fall. Your love sustains me. I'm so lucky to have a family like you.

More than ever, we need love, hope, and laughter in our lives. I hope this book brings you, my dear readers, all that and more. And I will always strive to deserve your love and support. Thank you with all my heart.

ABOUT THE AUTHOR

Nichanh Nicole Photography

JAYCI LEE writes poignant, sexy, and laugh-out-loud romance every free second she can scavenge and is semi-retired from her fifteen-year career as a defense litigator. She loves food, wine, and traveling, and incidentally so do her characters. Jayci lives in sunny California with her tall-dark-and-handsome husband, two amazing boys with boundless energy, and a fluffy rescue whose cuteness is a major distraction.